LAUGHING WAR

Barney stood in the hot dusty breezes beside the runway watching a tragic ceremony that was part of the paratroop tradition. Standing on the runway was an army chaplain intoning mournful funeral rites. On the runway, lined up in eerie rows, were the boots of the men who had been killed at Dak To. Just the boots, nothing else.

Barney wanted something outrageous to happen. Something so outrageous that it would stun the ceremony to a halt. He wanted some mad mechanical genius to have fixed up devices that would make some of the boots twitch. Or begin to tap impatiently in the heat. Or make a pair of them walk away. He stared out into the white heat and saw the chaplain peer fearfully over the Bible in mid-vowel.

And Barney laughed to himself as he alone saw the boots turn and slowly sneak off down the runway.

"One of the best Vietnam scenes yet published."
WASHINGTON POST

LAUGHING WAR

MARTYN BURKE

PLAYBOY
PAPERBACKS

Published simultaneously in the United States and Canada by Playboy Paperbacks, New York, New York. Printed in the United States of America. Library of Congress Catalog Card Number: 81-84141. Reprinted by arrangement with Doubleday & Company. Lyrics from the song "White Rabbit" are reprinted by permission of Irving Music, Inc. Copyright © 1967 Irving Music, Inc. (BMI)

Books are available at quantity discounts for promotional and industrial use. For further information, write to Premium Sales, Playboy Paperbacks, 1633 Broadway, New York, New York 10019.

ISBN: 0-867-21068-0

First Playboy Paperbacks printing May 1982.

To A.K.
the truest New Yorker

CONTENTS

Barney

ONE

On the nights when the wind was right and the fighter planes were not taking off, the waves of laughter rolled all the way to the outer perimeter. At the perimeter, sentries peered from their tiny sandbag fortresses and listened to the distant noise. They had learned to tell who was performing at the Club simply by the type of laughter that surged across the flatness and washed over them from behind. If it was the comedy act with the ex-stripper and the short man, there was lewd whistling and hooting. If it was Sheldon the fat comedian from Brooklyn the laughter came at predictable intervals and was never loud enough to compete with even a single F-100 taking off. The fat comedian from Brooklyn was a master of pacing. He had studied Bob Hope on television for years.

If it was the young comedian named Barney there were murmuring silences and then vast roars of laughter that broke and pounded against the darkness, regathering to break again and again. The sentries could tell who was performing just by the kind of laughter. The laughter was like a comic fingerprint. On the night that Barney slipped in his first joke about the colonel, the sentries could hear the hooting until the afterburners kicked in on the F-100s. The planes were taking off for a bombing run somewhere near

Cambodia. Someone was in desperate trouble up there. The sentries could see the needles of light shooting down the runway. When the flame blossomed from the afterburners they knew it would take the count of three for the noise to reach them across the distance.

Goddam! It's like stereo, thought one of the sentries, a nineteen-year-old from the hill country of Georgia. The Air Force coming from one side and the comedians from the other. Sometimes he was grateful for the noise. It made the terrible silence of the night go away. There were nights when he had spent hours being alone and afraid in the obsidian blackness that grew more evil by its quietness. *They* were out there. He knew it. *They* had killed other sentries. The occasional bursts of gunfire from distant outposts were the only sounds he would hear until the first wedge of light appeared in the eastern sky.

But in this night, the nineteen-year-old from Georgia, did not care if there was any noise. He was providing his own. From his transistor radio jangled the sounds of another world. He eased back in his flak jacket, grinning for no reason as the Rolling Stones shouted *I Can't Get No Satisfaction* and then the Supremes urged him not to throw his love away while the Beatles told him of *Eleanor Rigby*. He was not supposed to have the radio. Nor was he supposed to be smoking this strange kind of cigarette that he had never smoked at home in the hill country. He kept grinning through his stoned stereophonic vision of the world. Blackness all around. And jet fighters from the right speaker, comedians from the left speaker and *Eleanor Rigby* keeping something in a jar that was opened and shot colors like mad butterflies across his mind. Let the bastards come now, he giggled to himself.

From inside the Club came another wave of laughter.

The sentry laughed too. He preferred sentry duty when Barney was performing. Somehow it seemed less lonely.

After Barney's last performance a week earlier everyone had expected that the colonel would have him barred from the Club. He had pushed his act to the limits and then kept going. Colonel Isaacs had sat in utter stillness at the front table as Barney demolished one of his sources of great pride. Three weeks earlier the colonel had posed beside a new metal water tower. The photo of that event found its way into *Newsweek* magazine. According to *Newsweek* the water tower was one of several examples of army officers helping the Vietnamese in nonmilitary ways.

Barney had watched it being constructed by the Americans when the Vietnamese would not do it for themselves. The Americans were angry with the local people for not putting up the damn tower themselves. And the local people couldn't understand why the Americans were putting up the tower in the first place. The only water that came from above was the rain.

Barney had stood before an audience that had tensed at the very mention of the water tower. Then he worked them. A little diversion onto safe ground with two quick one-liners about the taxis in Saigon. Then before they could stop laughing, into the water again. The laughter carried over. Like a metal hook on the face of a mountain it caught. Quickly he followed up with easy material about the water tower. The skirts on the girls who came to watch its construction. Mimicking the Bronx accent of the sergeant in charge as he explained the benefits of the water to an imaginary village elder. Anything at all. As long as it got them laughing about the water tower. The heavy stuff could come later. Now it was just important to drive that hook deeper. Otherwise it was a long bloody fall down the sheer face of the tension and the anxious stolen glances at the colonel's table. It was the way Barney liked to operate. He was always at his best when professional oblivion faced him.

After a few lines with the Bronx accent he knew that they would not turn back. The laughs were coming from all over the huge hall. But so far much of it had come on style alone. The funny accents. The different voices. The sound of planes that came from somewhere in his throat, passed into the closely cupped microphone and then exploded through the loudspeakers. It was all style. Then gradually came the content. It was the pattern he had developed in the short time he had been a comedian. First loosen them up, and then say what you're really here to say. All of it cushioned with laughter. It was always done so smoothly that no one ever caught on while it was happening. It was only afterward that people would wonder about how he had gotten them to laugh at such things.

Under the serenely cold gaze of Colonel Isaacs, Barney had launched into an imaginary dialogue among the village elders. The elders were arguing among themselves what a water tower was for. One of the elders, the oldest and the wisest, decided that it was being built by the Americans as a gesture of goodwill for the South Vietnamese army. It would give them a better place to hide once the fighting started.

A nerve was touched. And the murmurs built to a hooting that drowned out the next two lines. Every one of the soldiers in the audience hated the South Vietnamese army and every one of them had stood through hours of official speeches where bureaucrats of the two countries had praised one another's army. And in every one of those speeches there had screamed out a truth from the doziest mind of the lowest grunt: *It ain't gonna work 'cause they don't wanna fight, and we're gonna get pissed at them 'cause they're gettin' in our fuckin way!*

Isaacs said nothing amid the commotion. At his table, aides fidgeted and majors looked concerned. The concern diminished in concentric circles from his table until in the far reaches of the gloom there was nothing but laughter. This was war of a different kind and Isaacs was determined not to lose it by default. His composure was the same as it was when he came under fire. There was the same iron composure tempered by a hint of bemused impatience at the fears felt by others. It was a composure seen by the majors and the aides under the most dangerous conditions. Isaacs had made parachute jumps in areas where a commander should never go. He had personally pulled together the whimpering bloody remnants of an overrun fire base in Phouc Long and fought off a second and nearly fatal wave of attackers. And all through the times that were the most fearful for the others, Isaacs held that same cruel composure that almost mocked those in his presence. Yet back at the base, there was hardly a trace of that composure. His temper had settled across Bien Hoa like a swarm. Aides came and went, departing under a barrage of epithets or fleeing with nervous conditions. Projects were begun and canceled on whims. Computer print-outs sent from Saigon were angrily brandished like a club. Inspections were called again and again and tongue lashings were given to soldiers who had just returned shell-shocked from combat. Base camp soldiers began talking of going back out into combat. Combat soldiers began talking of returning to assassinate Isaacs. Yet none of them did when they most had the chance. For he had turned his back to them like a taunting bull's-eye in some of the worst firefights in the brigade's history. One stray bullet would never be questioned. Yet no one fired that stray bullet because without ever admitting it as a group, they were in desperate need of his terrifying composure.

The second village elder was arguing with the first and the good work of *Newsweek* was disintegrating. Maybe the water tower *was* the best place to put the South Vietnamese army. They would be high off the ground out of harm's way. They would have a good view of the battles. At least they would not be shooting at the Americans by mistake. Very wise, said the elder. Our own people are terrible at fighting. Things will be much simpler with them locked in the water tower and the communists and the Americans fighting it out. A third elder disagreed with them. That was not the reason for the big tower, he said. The big tower was to provide water for the car wash.

Car wash?

A great outburst of cheers and laughter came at the mention of the car washes. All along the short highway from the airbase to Saigon were car washes. They were mainly tin shacks with a couple of girls sitting out in front. They were really drive-in whorehouses. While a younger brother washed the vehicle the girls would be in the shack with the driver. Army trucks in that section of Vietnam were cleaner than anywhere else in the country.

Isaacs sat in an almost relaxed manner. That same bemused expression of tolerance had spread across his face and only his eyes showed anything different. For a moment Barney played directly to his table. The aides and the majors seized solid, like salt pillars of acquired righteousness. They dreaded tomorrow. But Barney had looked the enemy —silence—in the eye and kept on going. No one knew at that point what was really happening between Barney and Colonel Isaacs. No one could understand how Isaacs could be pushed so far by that one scrawny comedian who could have been easily run out of Bien Hoa, and Vietnam for that matter.

One month later Isaacs' water tower was hit by mortar

fire. One car wash was destroyed and a brigade driver nearly drowned in the middle of getting laid. He had to be sent back to the States. The mortar fire did not come from the enemies of the Free World. It came from the South Vietnamese army, the official allies of the Americans. The South Vietnamese soldiers were angry at the Americans for stealing all the prostitutes. One of the South Vietnamese officers had seen Barney's routine at the Club. The officer did not understand English very well. He returned to his base and told his commanding officer how the American soldiers had cheered the announcement about a huge new car wash that was to be built by the elders of the nearby village. A car wash with shiny beds.

The village elders later denied this vigorously. But their own army shelled the water tower just in case.

The audience was surprised when Barney's next booking was not canceled. The Club was even more crowded than usual. He was becoming something of a minor celebrity. A lot of the soldiers would show up at these performances no matter who was playing. It was a means of relieving the boredom. But on that night they were there because of more than boredom. There had been much debate as to why Barney was being allowed in again. And odds were being given not only that the colonel would show up, but that this time he would personally drill the comedian right off the stage. Isaacs did not show up. At first there was disappointment like a boxing crowd realizing that one of the fighters has skipped town. But they forgot about all that when Barney started using his own countrymen—the Canadians—as his topic for the evening. To the Canadians, it seemed as if there were ten of them and a thousand American soldiers. The Canadians were also soldiers. They had been invited as guests of the brigade. But now they were being laughed at. The Americans were laughing because

Barney had walked out onstage and begun an entire monologue about why they were in Vietnam. Not the Americans.
The Canadians. Everybody was bored with hearing why the
Americans were there. But nobody had ever thought about
the Canadians. Most people didn't even know they were
there.

Barney got the spotlight man to turn the lights around
so that the small group of Canadian soldiers sat there in a
blinding oasis of light listening to the questions that had already rung in their own ears booming out through loudspeakers. Have you ever asked yourself who these men
are? Dressed in uniforms that look like hotel porters? Why
are they in Vietnam?

They are here to keep the peace!

The peace?

It was true. At first the audience didn't believe it. There
were a few snickers. But it dawned on them that this was
the truth. Then the laughter almost deafened the Canadians.
The Americans loved it. Woody looked up from his beer.
As a captain he was the ranking officer of the Canadians.
Still in his twenties, Woody had a massive physique and
huge hands. He had often threatened to put his hands
around Barney's neck if ever he and his men became the
subjects of a comedy routine. Barney and Woody were the
closest of friends. But now Woody sat silently in the tumult
staring at his huge hands and vowing revenge.

In the middle of a blood-drenched war with every kind
of horror yet dreamed up in the name of freedom or ideol-
ogy, Woody and the other Canadians had been sent there
by people with straight faces who gave them orders to keep
the peace. Their embarrassing predicament had begun back
in the 1950s when a lot of statesmen sat down in Geneva,
Switzerland, after the French had been wiped out in their
former colony of Indo-China, which had then become

known as Vietnam. All sides agreed that no more fighting was necessary, and the statesmen in their wisdom decided to ensure that fighting would indeed not occur again. They formed a commission composed of troops from Canada, India and Poland. Troops armed only with clipboards and pens. The commission was to ensure that peace would prevail. Nobody figured out exactly how this was done. That part was left out. But anytime a bullet was fired by someone who intended to disturb this peace, the commission had to investigate the transgression and report the wrongdoer. Over the years more bullets were fired and more reports were filed. The paper work became enormous. And all over Vietnam, in dusty little towns with strange names, one Canadian, one Pole, and one Indian sat steeped in their loathing for one another. Peace-keepers hurling insults at each other through the ocher hallways of the crumbling old rented French villas. As the years dragged on, more than one officer was found slowly rocking on the edge of his cot, looking blankly out of the glassless window and muttering to himself about keeping the peace while an endless procession of Phantom jets or F-100s screamed overhead. . . . . .

. . . . . But all of this is of no interest to the nineteen-year-old sentry from the hill country of Georgia. For the Shirelles are telling him again and again to come closer for *Tonight's the Night*. He giggles to himself. Suddenly there is a motion that is not from inside his mind. It is from the blackness. Out *there!* He scrambles to put the shards of his mind back together again. But they will not come together as he had left them. Again there is the motion! He strains and whimpers, his M-16 on automatic and his eyes darting. The motion is heard—not seen—again. For it is blackness moving with blackness. The nineteen-year-old from Georgia is about to fire—but then he puts the rifle down, relieved. He laughs because he recognizes the figure emerging from the darkness. Man but ain't those Shirelles something huh? . . . . .

. . . . . In the Club Woody sat in the merciful darkness listening to a story of how the commission investigated the death of a cow. The Indian was outraged that someone should kill a cow. They were holy beasts. He demanded that this act of war be reported. So in the midst of a growing battle with mortars and jets that came from somewhere within Barney's throat, the three unarmed soldiers stood yelling at each other over the dead cow. Another clear-cut case of imperialist aggression, said the Pole.

The story was being told from the point of view of the cow, which had been unable to sleep for days because of the noise of the war. Then when it finally got to sleep it was awakened by the peace-keepers standing over it screaming at one another. The cow lay very still, pretending to be dead in order not to disappoint the shouting peace-keepers. The cow was not sure whether it should pretend to be killed by imperialism or communism. The cow had decided that it was all the same in the end. Steaks of one form or another. To be killed by the fascist imperialists meant hamburger for the masses. To be killed by the communists meant roasts for the rulers. Meat is meat, the cow decided. But the Canadian had better legs than the Pole. Both wore short pants. The cow had never seen soldiers in short pants before. The Pole had the legs of a meat-eater so the cow decided it was a capitalist.

At this point Woody decided that worse was to come. Action had to be taken. All this from his closest friend in Vietnam! And it was Barney who had even given him his nickname. Woody came from a lumber town in New Bruns-

wick and at least part of his massive size was the result of
the summers he had spent cutting down trees. At first it was
Woodchopper but then Barney shortened it to Woody. The
name had stuck. Woody had the glare of the spotlight in ferocious silence. Then in the gloom with the ocean of Yankee guffawing around him and Barney's voice booming out
of the darkness he sat getting drunk and muttering. There
were too many Yanks to take on at one time. And it would
be impossible to make it up to the stage to wring the sap out
of that ingrate. Through the last of his beers, Woody swore
murder but saw no immediate way to commit it. Yet something had to be done. The laughter was bellowing in his
ears. And like any peace-keeper Woody hated being
laughed at by other soldiers who were breaking the peace.

The cow had just gotten up and walked away in disgust,
leaving the peace-keepers yelling at each other, when
suddenly a primal scream cut through the Club.
Kaaummmmmmpaaaneeeee-attttttennnnnnnnnnshunnn!
Barney stopped in midsentence and peered out into the
darkness of the audience. The audience buzzed and snick-
ered, not sure what had happened. The spotlight man shone
his light around. There in the full illuminated glory of Her
Majesty's Forces stood Woody, up on the table amid the
beer bottles. Standing like he wore a terminally starched
uniform, Woody had his shoulders and his head thrown
back and was bellowing orders down his nose just as he had
seen the British sergeants major do in the movies. Without any planning they all acted in unison. There were
suddenly ten Canadians standing stiffly on the table.
Kaaauuuuummmmmpaaaaaaneeeeeeee-aaaaaboouuutface!
They turned in perfect unison facing the length of the table.
The tables at the back were joined together to make one
long continuous surface that stretched across the room.

With every order Woody stamped his foot so hard it split the table.

He was loving every moment of it. He had totally upstaged Barney. *Kaaaaaauuuumpaaaaneeee-march!* With arms swinging back and forth in one exaggerated arc, packed together with legs kicking out in drunken unison, the Canadians plowed down the table. Onward through the booze and the bottles they went while the band began blasting out an off-key *Colonel Bogey March.* The audience went wild. But at this point in the evening they usually went wild over almost anything. . . . . .

. . . . . And so *Colonel Bogey* races across the flatness like a tide seeking shore. It is louder than even the laughter and the strange yelling that comes from the Club and is momentarily lost in the unearthly whine of the F-100s as they return from bombing whatever it is that has to be bombed. *Colonel Bogey* washes over the lone sentries and rushes on into the darkness that lies beyond the perimeter. The darkness stretches on and on, beyond the wretches lying soaked and bloody in the swamp near Cambodia listening to metallic voices in the headset that tell them why the F-100s cannot come back until dawn, and listening to the noises in the nearby jungle that might be metal grating on metal. The darkness goes on forever. But the nineteen-year-old from Georgia can no longer hear the curling chords of Jimi Hendrix's guitar as the Armed Forces Radio brings him the Best in Rock. The nineteen-year-old from Georgia can hear none of this. A long thin knife protrudes from his chest at the place where his flak jacket should have been buckled. Thin bubbles of blood drip from his mouth. In his final act as a sentry, he has died with his eyes wide open. . . . . .

After the shambling raucous end of his act, Barney went looking for Woody. He was not too surprised to discover that the Canadians had already departed for the hotel in Saigon. Woody would probably not talk to him for days. Backstage there were still a few stragglers preparing for the last act. It was the last act that Barney particularly wanted to see. It was a group called Sunshine. Sunshine was composed of two men and three women. They sang with voices that were never meant to sing together, and they danced in an uncoordinated manner that was somehow hidden by a veneer of slickness. Barney waited in the small backstage area watching as Sunshine's leader paced back and forth. He was a man with a lined face, fashionably shaggy hair and cynical eyes that spoke of failure. He was muttering angrily because one of the women had not shown up. He was in the middle of cursing the woman's absence when the curtain suddenly went up and Sunshine went out with a barrage of smiles.

It was because of the woman that Barney had waited backstage. He had not seen her in almost a week. During her entire stay in Vietnam he had caught sight of her perhaps no more than five times. And even though she had a room on the courtyard floor not far from his room in the Catinat Hotel in Saigon, Barney—and the others—knew nothing more than her name. The guest book registration had listed *D. Martinez* in room 39. The length of the stay was *indeterminate*. People said that they had seen a suitcase being carried into her room. On it was the name Kalman. No one at the hotel had ever talked to her other than to exchange the pleasantries of the day. D. Martinez was never seen in the Catinat coffee shop, where the surly Vietnamese waiter showed his contempt for all those unable to order in French—the only civilized tongue in all this garble.

Barney had heard her called Donna by several of the

groups that she had performed with. She had first arrived with one of the unremarkable singing acts that performed for higher fees than they could get back in America. Barney had been sure that she would never survive a week in Vietnam. She would either change or flee. He had seen other girls arrive with that same bewildered innocence confronting the face of war. In those who stayed, the innocence melted and alloyed itself with a shell tempered either to withstand or to enjoy being a woman in the raunchiness of Saigon and the army camps. The first time he had noticed her was in the same backstage area at the Club. While the others fretted with costumes and instruments, she remained in the shadow almost too timid to respond to the commotion. Barney had guessed that she must have Indian or perhaps Spanish blood. Her long glistening black hair hung straight past her shoulders, framing large dark eyes that seemed to be constantly looking inward, while all around her swirled the confusion of an act that was unprepared. For a moment, Barney had wanted to go over and say something stupidly funny—anything that would help to draw her together in the moments before the show. But he was prevented by a feeling of crude clumsiness in the face of her quiet innocence.

That innocence fell from her like a chrysalis when the curtain rose. Her eyes suddenly flashed outward. With the others she danced out onto the stage, yet it was apparent there were no others in the eyes of the audience of bellowing soldiers. The spotlight man, trained in such matters, immediately picked her out and focused the beam so that it caught the outlines of her body, and the flash of her smile.

Barney stood blinded by the spotlight that shot across him, and stunned by the sensual silhouette with the spinning veil of long hair. He felt foolish for having wanted to offer help. And for feeling jealous because the yelping, wisecracking audience that had suddenly appropriated her for its own. Sex-mad imperialists, he muttered, smiling politely as a nearby military policeman turned around to look at him.

During the songs the chatter from the audience subsided. It was easy to pick out her voice from the others. It was a clear, untrained voice, the kind that made minor fortunes for girls who were folk singers in that era and would have been choir sopranos at any other time. She projected a warmth and laughter in her voice that went out to every soldier in the hushed audience and whispered that it was *he* she secretly cared about. And it went out to Barney. After the curtain fell, when cries of *More* and *Take it off* were bellowing through the hall, he waited uncertainly for a chance to talk to her. When the lights faded she seemed to withdraw once again, almost to shrink within herself. No longer was there the fiery smile. Nor the whirling body. The eyes were gazing inward. The mask of the performer had fallen away.

When Barney finally went over to her, he felt like an intruder. She smiled a polite smile of thanks when he told her he liked her performance. Then she excused herself and left. It was a week before he saw her again. This time she was with a different group. Her original group had made what money they could, become nervous about remaining in Vietnam, and left with a sufficient fund of elastic stories about the dangers of war. There were four other groups that she had appeared with. And after each one departed, Barney found himself combing the roster of names at Milligan's Talent, the booking agency on the ground floor of the Catinat. Each time, he found she had remained and felt a sense of relief. He had tried whenever possible to schedule his performances on the same night that she would be appearing. He was beginning to feel a sense of desperation.

The memories of her dark, frightened eyes clashed with the strobe images of her ferocious warmth on the stage. Barney found himself hanging around the hotel's third-floor courtyard, engaging in conversations with people he would normally never talk to. But she came and went like a shadow, and at night only the serrated glow seeping through the slits of the wooden shutter indicated that there was anyone in her room.

Barney stood outside at the back of the Club listening to Sunshine's bad version of a song called *Changes.* . . . . .

. . . . . But Barney is too caught up in thoughts of the woman who is not there tonight to notice the distant threads of light converging at the perimeter. They are jeeps arriving at the sentry post where the nineteen-year-old from Georgia stands at stiffening alert with dead eyes peering into the night as his blood cakes across his chest and around his mouth. A major arrives in one of the jeeps. Oh god, not another one, he says. We've got to get the colonel, says someone else, but the major is not sure he can be reached. They stand for a moment in silence and *Changes* rolls out to them. None of them knows or cares that *Changes* was written by an angry young singer named Phil Ochs, who at that very moment is parading in a midday antiwar rally in New York City. Placards come beating down on police horses, and the street erupts in a maelstrom of hooves, truncheons and fists. Ochs will be arrested and will be proud to be arrested in this, the continuing fight against the war. The war has come home to America and Ochs is one of the musical soldiers. Their songs are mad inspired tunes of ferocious energy. Not for them the gently hidden tears in the voice of Vera Lynn. Not for them the Nightingales Singing in Berkeley Square when Hitler was pounding London. Not for them the ready-aye-ready cadences on the Long Way to Tipperary. No, these are the mad tunes of war, the war chants that grate at the very bones of war itself. The generals with memories of Vera Lynn do not understand these new anthems but they are told that it is all very good for morale so Armed Forces Radio inducts Sgt. Pepper and sends the Lonely Hearts Club Band into the jungles. The stoned poets go off to war and behind every M-16 automatic there is a transistor radio. Everywhere there are the new anthems written by the songwarriors like Ochs. But they need the war as much as they loathe it. They are shooting stars, plummeting through the void, burning themselves out on their own war-fed energy. Ochs will survive a respectable length of time and then will be found dangling from a rope attached to the rafters of a New Jersey house. Most of the others will have already died a different death somewhere within themselves. But Jimi Hendrix, Janis Joplin and Jim Morrison are among those who will go with a velvet death fueling their veins. Somehow it is easier to endure while the war is still raging, swept along on the mad wave of a holy cause. But on the dreadful moment when that beloved far shore is finally reached, the wreckage is enormous. And the music all sounds the same.

After a long pause, the major says yes he thinks he knows where the colonel can be reached. He should be notified.

TWO

Most of Barney's comedy material came from just watching the war. He had long ago decided that Vietnam was probably more fertile comic ground than other wars had been. The worse it got, the more terrible and necessary the laughter became. And the troops were the best comedians. Nothing any comic ever dreamed of could equal the mad humor of the dimmest grunt silently contemplating the world around him.

Because of age alone, Barney had an affinity with the troops that many of the older comedians were unable to attain. He was young enough for senior officers often to mistake him for one of their own men. Until he stepped onstage, he seemed to view the world through serious eyes set in a face that still had the last vestiges of boyishness. But once onstage, he was transformed. A comic energy shot forth. His eyes would dance with shades of meaning all their own. His voice could burst through the loudspeakers as sounds that made audiences laugh. His face would become that of the character he had just created. It was all part of the comic equipment. Tools of the trade. But unlike some of the comedians who played the military bases around Vietnam, Barney had possessed the tools long before he ever performed professionally. They were part of a youthful exuberance that came to him naturally. It was an exuberance that flowed out to audiences, putting them at ease. Making an audience relax was the rare gift that all true comics possessed. It was a quality, not a technique. There was nothing that smothered laughter as quickly as a feeling of uneasiness in the audience. It was death on the boards for a comic to lose an audience to the unsettling feeling that he was straining for every laugh. Stretching his material through the wringer of gimmicks that did not work.

After the performance at the Club, Barney decided to find a ride back to Saigon. The drive from the huge airbase at Bien Hoa to Saigon was usually only an hour during the day. But at night it was different. The drive was more dangerous because of sporadic guerrilla attacks by the enemy. Reason, experience and the fervent desires of those soldiers assigned to drive to Saigon at night dictated that the road should be closed after dark. But the computers dictated otherwise. The computers had recently decided that the area around the sixty-kilometer highway was 98.47 per cent pacified. Therefore, it *must* be safe. There should be no trouble driving at any time. Nobody except the drivers who were being shot up, a few meddlesome newsmen and Barney questioned the fact that the other 1.53 per cent were making things so difficult. Barney had created an entire character out of a computer that was secretly running the war. A computer that refused to drive on the highway after dark.

At the edge of Bien Hoa, the vehicles that were heading back to Saigon left in small convoys. Barney sat in the back of a three-quarter-ton army truck while the teen-age driver waited for another vehicle to arrive. After several minutes the other vehicle could be seen driving toward them along one of the access roads that led from the runway. It was a large army truck, one of several that had been nestled under the huge Galaxy transport plane that landed an hour earlier. The plane was so big that all the trucks on the runway could have easily fitted inside. Under the pale, white glare of floodlights, supplies fresh from the United States were being unloaded from the plane onto the trucks.

Why are we waiting for this truck? Barney asked the driver. We're guarding it, was the reply. All the way to Saigon. Barney asked if the cargo was valuable. The driver laughed. Priceless, he said as the truck flashed its headlights at them. From out of nowhere a very young captain emerged carrying two M-16 rifles. He got into the passenger seat of the smaller truck. He thrust one of the rifles at Barney, whom he had never seen before. Here! he snapped. Fire if you see anything! Anything! The captain was very nervous. As the two vehicles drove slowly through the nearly deserted Vietnamese town near the airbase, it became obvious that the captain was terrified. Barney watched from the rear seat as the captain's head swiveled back and forth, fearfully searching for an enemy in the darkness.

Jesuschrist they're out there. I know they are, he muttered. Will you shut your goddam mouth, said the teen-age driver. I'm an officer you little punk! yelled the captain. You're a goddam nut is what you are! yelled the driver. Every fuckin' time you make this run you freak. And I'm sick of it. The captain's nervousness had spun into a frenzy. He was jumping around on his seat looking out for an enemy he could not see and yelling at the teen-age driver. I do not freak! he screamed. And I'll have you court-martialed. The driver slammed on the brakes sending the truck skidding sideways to a stop in front of a ramshackle collection of tin shacks by the edge of the road. You ain't gonna have anybody court-martialed cause I'm gonna dump you out here and let you walk, yelled the driver. The captain was frantic with fear. Get going! he pleaded. *They're* out there. I know it. I'm ordering you. The driver smiled and shook his head. Not till you shut up, he said. The captain told the driver that if he had been in the Russian army he would have been shot for insubordination. The driver just sat back and smiled. If this was the Russian army, you'd still be a goddam nut. You know that?

A horn sounded. The big truck in front of them had stopped farther down the road and one of the soldiers in it had gotten out to see if there was trouble with the smaller vehicle. The horn sounded again. It made the captain even more nervous. Those idiots, he muttered. They're gonna wake up every ambushing gook in town. The driver slammed his truck into gear. How did you get to be a captain instead of me? he said as they drove away.

Barney sat in the back watching the Vietnamese countryside pass by in the night. When they drove through the edges of the town, the road widened into a flat, new highway, immaculately paved and carefully graded. The highway had just been completed by a large American construction company which had built turnpikes across the United States. The tiny houses and tin shacks were set well back from the road on small plots of land. Some of the shacks were made from the metal of Schlitz beer cans. Others had Coca-Cola signs hanging from them, advertising *Number One American Food etc*. They were the dirt-floor restaurants with food and drink direct from the black market. Most of the shacks were in darkness. Occasionally the faint glow of a candle could be seen behind a shuttered window. There was an eeriness to the passing countryside. It was made more eerie by the captain. He swiveled and fidgeted in the front seat looking for the enemy.

In front of them, the larger truck seemed to be leaking bucketfuls of water from its cargo area. Every time the truck changed gears, a cascade of water would flow over and under the tailgate.

Barney was thankful for the irritable silence in the front. He decided not to ask why the water was pouring out of the truck. They drove farther until the shacks thinned out and the road was bordered by empty stretches of fields. Near a river they passed a huge American construction project. Massive bulldozers were lined up like sleeping yellow beasts behind coils of barbed wire that stretched off into the night. The bulldozers all had special metal cages around the operators' seats. The cages protected against snipers.

The two trucks raced past lonely army sentries guarding the construction project, barely visible behind tiny sandbag fortresses and fierce spotlights. Farther up the highway, the lights became more frequent. Some of the lights were colored. Others blinked on and off. They were nearing the garishness of Saigon. The sky in front of them began to reveal the glow of distant downtown lights reflecting off the low clouds. In a few kilometers the trucks would turn off the highway into the clogged mass of traffic, threading toward the center of Saigon, where Barney's hotel, the Catinat, stood as a shuttered and dingy refuge against the legions of pimps, bar girls, soldiers and thieves on motor scooters who walked Tu Do Street every night. Barney was looking forward to getting back to the Catinat.

Then it happened. The 1.53 per cent struck. Against all assurances offered up by the army computer, they were attacked. The first shots went unheard under the roar of the engines. Barney was suddenly aware of the captain screaming that *they* were out there, and the big truck in front veering madly from one side of the road to the other. The truck in front shot toward a culvert, leaning precariously to its left. Then with a crash, it spun onto its side and slid into the ditch. As their own vehicle pitched violently, Barney strug-

gled to hold on to the rifle he had been given and the driver
wrestled with the steering wheel. A loud flapping sound
came from the tires that had been shot out.

They too ended up in the ditch. The captain yelled and
fired. The teen-age driver got out and yelled at the captain
to shut up. Two soldiers from the larger truck crawled out
from their overturned truck. They had suffered only minor
cuts. The teen-age driver sat down on an embankment and
watched the captain blasting away into the night. They've
gone you idiot, he said. By the time you've been hit on this
road they've already cleared out. The captain would not listen to him. He was frantic with fear. He yelled to Barney to
open fire. Barney just looked down at his gun.

Barney noticed something that was moving at his feet.
He was standing in a growing pool of water. The water was
pouring from the overturned truck. Whatever it was that
was moving at his feet was small but shiny. It reflected the
light as it crawled.

Do something! screamed the captain. They're going to
kill us! Barney disappeared around to the side of the truck
from where the water was flowing. Soon he could be heard
chortling to himself. Then he laughed out loud. Suddenly
from the side of the truck something hard and shiny was
thrown through the air toward the other side of the road.
Then another shiny object was thrown. Barney could be
heard laughing still louder. His laughter punctuated the
bursts of the captain's rifle fire. The driver was bored with
watching the captain and went to see what Barney was
doing. Soon he too was laughing and yelling things like
Launch one! and *Fire two!* More projectiles flew over to
where the attack had come from.

The captain backed around to the side of the truck, still
blasting away. Fire goddammit! he yelled. Barney stood

knee-deep in water. I don't know how to, he yelled back. Well what the hell are you doing? shouted the captain.

I'm throwing lobsters, answered Barney. The captain stopped firing for a moment and looked around wide-eyed. Lobsters? he said. Lobsters, said Barney. The captain waded into the water and picked up one of the live lobsters that were pouring out from the overturned truck. The captain was almost speechless with fury. You idiot! he screamed, those are for the banquet tomorrow in Saigon! And you're throwing them away.

They make good weapons, said Barney. They might grab one of the enemy by the toe. Very difficult to aim properly with a lobster hanging from your toe. The driver began imitating the enemy firing with lobsters on their toes. The captain was on the verge of a fit of screaming or crying. Or both. Do you think I was risking my life just so you could throw these lobsters away? he asked frantically.

I wouldn't risk my life for *any* lobster, said Barney. These came all the way from Maine, yelled the captain. Specially flown in all goddam twelve thousand miles for the banquet. And I'm in charge of it.

Fuck the banquet, said Barney. *They* are trying to kill us. Remember?

That's exactly what I've been telling you, said the captain. And we've got all the goddam technology in the world to stop them from killing us. And you're using lobsters! Lobsters are better, said Barney. I know how to use them.

God gave you a gun, shouted the captain. Now use it! Barney shrugged. I've told you, I don't know how.

Why not? said the captain. Because I'm a comedian, said Barney. The teen-age driver interrupted his lobster pitching. So what? he asked. Everybody over here is.

Suddenly from the other side of the road came a short,

sharp cry. It was a human cry of sudden pain. Goddam, muttered the driver, maybe we're onto something here.

When the rescue trucks arrived, there were no enemy guerrillas to be seen. It was determined by footprints that there had been three or perhaps four of them who had ambushed the two trucks. At least one of them was barefoot.

THREE

It was a big night for the hotel porter. Bob Hope was on the army television station again. Tonight, no matter who complained of cockroaches, no matter which beggars banged on the protective tin doors, no matter which toilet overflowed, Bob Hope would have his faithful audience in the small dingy lobby of the Catinat Hotel.

It was at such times that the war became a nuisance. From the distance, a clatter of the howitzers drifted in as muffled thuds that occasionally forced him to turn up the sound. Sometimes helicopters would drop their eerie green flares into the nearby night skies and that too would disturb the porter as he watched the great American comedian. Usually the flares were dropped when there were guerrilla attacks from the enemy. One noise compounded another.

The porter was Vietnamese. He spoke no English but spent most of his days watching American television through glassy eyes. His expression never changed. Every program from comedy to murder mystery was received with the same dozy expression. Only Bob Hope received a different reception. For Bob Hope there was an occasional impassive grunt of approval.

Barney had arrived back at the Catinat just after the Bob Hope show had started. He wanted nothing else than to lie on the lumpy bed in his third-floor room and fall asleep. But the chance to watch the porter watching Bob Hope was something he never missed unless he was working at one of the clubs. Barney was sure there was a comedy routine somewhere in the porter.

A wedge of light suddenly shone into the long dingy corridor. The corridor was the Catinat's excuse for a hotel lobby. It stretched the full length of the building. At the far end it opened onto the night life of Tu Do Street, which seethed just beyond the heavy metal gates that kept out the thieves and beggars. The light came from an office near the far end of the corridor. Milligan's Talent Agency—*Supplier of the Finest in Armed Forces Entertainment*—was once again host to one of Saigon's longest-running poker games. Milligan's voice, cursing over a lousy hand, echoed down the corridor. Other voices told him to shut up and deal.

Into the wedge of light stepped Sheldon. He formed a short, pudgy silhouette. Christ! he muttered. It's Bob Hope! Sheldon ran down the hallway and stood wheezing and sweating in front of the television. Sheldon was from Brooklyn. He never wavered in his conviction that all the best comedians came from Brooklyn. Sheldon was a small man who sweated a lot. Always mopping his bald head and fussing with the bow tie he refused to give up, Sheldon was worse than Milligan for lectures. Of all the comedians in the Club, he received the least enthusiastic response from the audience. After the death of vaudeville he had spent too long in burlesque telling jokes from the side of his mouth. The burlesque circuit had dulled whatever small sensitivities he once had for his audiences. He had long ago decided that whether they laughed a lot or not at all had nothing to do with him or his jokes. It had to do with how many hicks there were in the audience, how horny they were, and how much tits 'n' ass the previous act had flashed. Sheldon played Vietnam like it was another burlesque house. And when the soldiers failed to laugh as much as they did for other acts, it was simply because the house was papered with hicks. Yet he was forever walking up to the younger performers and telling them what they were doing wrong.

Sheldon's wheezing drew a cold glance from the porter. It went unnoticed. Years of playing third-rate clubs filled with drunks had enabled him to shut out the reactions of those around him. His flat laughter echoed around the small lobby. God what timing! he shouted after the first punch line. Did you see that? he yelled after the joke about how badly the stock market was doing. He got away with a money joke. Money jokes ain't easy kid. Remember you heard it from me.

Sheldon loved watching the big-time comedians on television. It allowed him to talk back to them, to criticize just enough to feel that he was one of the group. The next joke was about the way men were beginning to wear their hair as long as women. The laughter was only moderate and Sheldon was like a trainer in the corner of a boxing ring. Urging his man to pick up the timing. Feint into what looked like the old mother-in-law joke but pull it out with a beauty about Hollywood and the huge crowd scenes in the movie *Cleopatra* being simply a film of Elizabeth Taylor's personal wardrobe attendants. Sheldon roared. His boy was doing fine. God what an artist!

But then Sheldon suddenly stopped laughing and noticed the Vietnamese porter. The porter remained glassy-eyed and without expression. The lack of reaction began to offend Sheldon. Hey kid, where did you get the statue, he asked. Sheldon laughed uproariously at the next two jokes just to see if the porter would even twitch. Nothing. Hey, you been left out in the cold too long? yelled Sheldon indignantly. No one sat there like a stone when Bob Hope was

on! Sheldon waved his hand in front of the porter's eyes.
The man slowly raised his eyes to Sheldon, who asked No
likee No funnee? The porter looked at Sheldon for a moment with the same bored expression that he had granted
Bob Hope. Jesus Christ these people are locked in neutral
yelled Sheldon, who could stand it no longer. No wonder
they're losing the war!

Sheldon was halfway down the corridor when he
stopped and shouted to Barney. And kid I tellya something
as a favor. You understand? This place ain't good for you.
It's gonna make you weird. At this stage in your career you
can't afford to play just to weirdos, slants and hicks. You
need good normal audiences. Believe me, I know comedians. Go play Kleinman's in Buffalo. It would be better for
you. I don't want to play Kleinman's said Barney. Look
what it does to people who played it.

What do you mean look what it does? I played Kleinman's. That's what I mean said Barney. It was bad for your
development. You needed a few hicks.

Christ kid I ache for you. You just don't understand comedians. Sheldon disappeared inside Milligan's office. His
voice could be heard through the glass door yelling about
zaftig kids who got a couple of jokes together and became
comics. Never make it at Hanson's. He'd be a lamb to the
lions at Hanson's. Barney stood outside the door listening to
talk of Hanson's and then suddenly flung it open and roared
in an unnatural voice *Shelly ya steal all the way from the
Olympia to Loew's. If jokes were jewels they would put you
in jail*. And then slammed the door leaving Sheldon, Milligan and the other poker players staring after him. Barney
was already in the chaos of Tu Do Street when Sheldon
caught up with him asking How do you know about Hanson's? Barney just grinned and then did another booming
imitation of Sam Senior in the days when he hung around

Hanson's. Good god yelled Barney in a voice that cut through the neon furor of Hondas, beggars and whores swirling around them—*I hear an echo! No it's not an echo. It's Sheldon. Shelly my boy it's not that I mind you stealing my jokes. As a matter of fact I took up a collection for you. Old jokes for poor Shelly. He needs 'em. I passed the hat Shelly. But it came back empty!*

Sheldon stood staring at Barney in the middle of Tu Do Street while their faces changed color as the signs on the bars flashed on and off. He was hearing the mad cries from Sam Senior, the cries that had terrified him over a decade ago at Hanson's in New York. It was the same crackling voice. Or almost the same. But it came from this pisher who couldn't possibly remember Hanson's. Sheldon retreated back through the crowds.

The few times that old Sam Senior had allowed Barney to accompany him to Hanson's were among the clearest memories of his childhood. Sam Senior had come into Barney's life when he was eight years old. Barney's mother had married Sam Junior and among the many changes in his life was this dignified old man who suddenly became his grandfather. Sam Senior had eyes that silently took in everything. He could stand looking solemnly around like an undertaker at a plague and then quietly begin making Barney laugh.

When Barney was twelve he was allowed to take the train from their home in Montreal down to New York where Sam Senior lived when he wasn't on the road. Sam Senior lived in a tiny room in the old Edison Hotel. It was dingy and cramped and Barney could not understand that this was Sam Senior's home. At first Barney kept asking where his real home was. Sam Senior just smiled. Nor could he understand that the contents of the old suitcase were the sum total of Sam Senior's possessions. His new grandfather had always seemed so elegant. Barney had imagined him with a big house and maybe a servant or two. Just like the house he himself had lived in ever since his mother married Sam Junior. But the room with the faded curtains, peeling paint and a view overlooking the wall of the adjacent building was all that Sam Senior had for a home. It was also all that a dozen other comedians had for a home. The Edison was the last refuge for those who had not gotten fabulously rich in the profession of making people laugh.

But it was a refuge at night only. During the daytime it was too depressing. So most of the comedians gathered at Hanson's, the drugstore with the lunch counter in the back. Hanson's was on Broadway opposite the Taft Hotel. Right next door was the building where the booking agents for the resorts in the Catskills had their offices. Hanson's was one of the few places where an unemployed comedian could sit over one cup of coffee for most of the morning and trade wisecracks with those of his own profession. Sam Senior used the hours he spent in Hanson's almost as a laboratory for new routines. He would hone his latest jokes on the abrasive wits of his peers. They were the best and the toughest audience a comedian could ask for. And when he was not developing new routines he would go there to help the others with the benefit of his own criticisms.

Barney loved it. For a week he was a part of a strange little fraternity, one that sheltered its members from the indignities of the outside world. On a good day the booths would be filled with grown men laughing and slinging jokes at one another. It was a change from the way he saw them in the Edison. Barney was proud of being known as Sam Senior's grandson. Sam Senior enjoyed respect from the others. And Barney observed that his face did not seem so lined when he was in their presence.

Barney began dividing the comedians into types. There were the droll straight men who could sneak out the deadliest of one-liners that caught everyone by surprise with delayed-reaction laughter. There were the smooth young polished comedians, who seldom got on with the intense social critics. And the impressionists were always rattling off impressions of Humphrey Bogart till the back booths seemed like a set from *Casablanca*. And there were the storytellers. Sam Senior was a storyteller. He could take the thread of an idea and weave it into a tale that would have Barney laughing with the others. Reading a review of a play gave Sam Senior the idea for a story about the theater critic who always fell sound asleep during plays—until an angry playwright wrote a part for a sleeping critic into the opening-night performance. And riding the subway gave him the quixotic tales of the people who always read the newspapers of the passengers next to them.

Some comedians seemed pleased to have Barney there. A tall thin comedian with a drawl began trying out his material on Barney. When the new joke about the police paddy wagon colliding with a cement truck—police are now looking for a dozen hardened criminals—made Barney laugh, the tall thin comedian went away ecstatic, convinced his bad spell was over. Most of the comedians were polite to Barney because he was with Sam Senior. But some were cold, almost fearful. They were the ones steeped in a kind of dread. The ones who could not stand to be too close to any kind of audience. Rejection was stamped on their faces. But on a good day these same faces could hold off the ravages of dread with a mask of laughter. The masks could be worn for hours. Until exhaustion set in and the dread returned. The Edison Hotel was filled with dread.

Todlachen said Sam Senior one day when they sat together in a booth too close to the jukebox. It means laugh till it kills you. It's a German word. Oi, God too has a sense of irony. One day at Hanson's Barney saw his new grandfather become angry. Sam Senior's eyes turned to coal when a chubby young comedian named Sheldon walked in. He had just come from a successful three weeks on the road. In those days Sheldon was just beginning to lose his hair. He was sure he was going to be the next Bob Hope. He slapped a lot of the other comedians on the back. *Goniff!* roared Sam Senior at Sheldon. You steal jokes all the way from the Olympia to Loew's. If jokes were jewels they would put you in jail. Sheldon tried to look indignant but began to sweat. What are you talking about? he huffed. Ten days earlier Sam Senior had returned from the Olympia in Miami, humiliated. He had gone down there with his best new jokes. Jokes he had lovingly honed at Hanson's. And in the loneliness of his room at the Edison. But on his opening night at the Olympia there was something wrong. After the first few minutes of his routine he was aware of talking in the audience. His best jokes were not getting the laughs they should have gotten. After the show the manager rushed up to him and told him he was a fraud. Sam Senior had never been called a fraud before. He stood as erect as he could in his only good suit and inquired as to the nature of the fraud. With much profanity the manager told him he was using the same jokes that had been told by last week's comedian. A damn promising young comic named Sheldon.

The only other person who sparked anger in Sam Senior was his own son. Sam Senior loved his son. But over the years the love had become anger and then filtered into an eroding bitterness. He covered his feelings with jokes. When he was in the presence of his son, people thought Sam Senior was nothing more than a nice funny old man. Only Barney seemed to realize how much Sam Junior had destroyed Sam Senior. The first time they met was at the wedding reception in Montreal. They had been placed at a table off to one side. They both watched in silence while Sam Junior made toasts to Barney's mother and other people made toasts to both of them. The reception was held in a private club. There were two orchestras, real French champagne and a lot of Cadillacs parked outside. The reception was being paid for by Sam Junior, who seemed to be very rich. A lot of the single women at the reception called Barney's mother a *shiksa* and said things about her that were not what they said when she was present. It was different from what he had known in the quiet section of Montreal where he had lived. Most of the families in his old neighborhood were English or Irish.

Sam Junior's friends were different too. There was a closed, almost angry quality to many of them. They all seemed to have a lot of money. Their money was used to smooth over rough edges. Most were clothed in fine silk suits. When Sam Junior was surrounded by his friends at the reception Barney had been surprised to hear the silent old man beside him suddenly begin to tell jokes. He told jokes about everything in sight. About the six-foot wedding cake. About the dancers in the middle of the floor who could hear both orchestras at once. And the men who were getting drunk in their expensive suits. Barney and Sam stayed at their table talking for the whole evening. Sometimes other men would come over and tell Sam Senior how long it was since they had seen him and how did he like living in New York away from old friends in Montreal. But most of the others ignored them. Both Barney and Sam Senior were content to be ignored at the reception.

Sam Senior hated coming back to Montreal. He hated it because he had to come to terms with the fact that Sam Junior had become a criminal. He was a part of what the newspapers of the country later called the Jewish Mafia. Sam Junior was one of a few men who had carved up the city for gambling. As sidelines Sam Junior dabbled in stock frauds and prostitution. Sam Junior's main problem was with the real Mafia—the Italian Mafia. The problems went all the way back to Lucky Luciano, the most famous Mafia leader of them all. Years earlier, Lucky Luciano had decided to streamline the Mafia of his adoptive country, the United States. Streamlining meant killing. First he invited the top Mafia boss to dinner at a Coney Island restaurant. The top Mafia boss and Luciano were old friends. They talked and joked and played cards. Then Luciano said he had to go to the washroom. While he was in the washroom four men filled his old friend with bullets. Luciano then streamlined even more. In two days forty Mafiosi in New York were gunned down. When the killing had stopped Luciano had organized the Mafia like any good business. His true genius lay in organizing. He set up twenty-four Mafia families across the country. They were to be under the control of the Commission composed of the nine most powerful bosses from the twenty-four families.

The real power lay in New York. It had five families. Luciano decided to give one of the five families to a man of criminal wisdom far beyond his years. He was Joe Bonanno. At twenty-six he was the youngest leader of the Mafia. His territory was vast for it extended all the way up into Canada where he ran Montreal as a criminal branch plant. Montreal soon became one of the most important Mafia cities in North America. It was a depot for heroin from Europe and for Mafiosi from Italy. Both were then smuggled into America. Joe Bonanno did not want to lose his branch plant to the Jewish gangs, who were also powerful. But there were riches for both groups so Joe Bonanno decided to take a diplomatic approach. He sent his number two man up to Montreal as ambassador. His number two man even looked something like an ambassador. His name was Carmine Galante. He was bald, wore glasses, and was studious in appearance. Carmine Galante was also a ruthless killer, one of the most feared men in the Mafia. His temper was such that other stone killers—men with cauterized emotions—could actually know fear when Carmine Galante's eyes turned cold. As an ambassador for Joe Bonanno, Carmine Galante was extremely effective. During the two years he lived in Montreal he imposed a truce and brought the Mafia and the Jewish groups together. Almost everyone in the underworld was as content as people in the underworld could be. Everyone but Sam Junior. He was a man who always wanted more of everything.

Sam Junior was charming. He had an easy manner, warmer than those with whom he associated. Women were attracted to the vulnerability they thought they saw beneath the self-confidence. And the men he dealt with were inspired by the self-confidence without a hint of vulnerability. Barney moved into Sam Junior's house on the day after the honeymoon. The house was huge and very modern. The house had been built especially for Sam Junior by a contractor who owed him a fortune in gambling debts. But Sam Junior always wanted more. Just after the house was built he informed the contractor that a swimming pool and a tennis court were to be constructed. The contractor went red in the face and began yelling in broken English. One of Sam Junior's men hit the contractor with a lead pipe and told him the swimming pool and tennis court were the interest on the loan. The contractor burst into tears. During the work on the tennis court he went bankrupt and fled Montreal. Barney's room overlooked the pool. Like everything else in his new stepfather's house it was luxury unlike anything he had ever known. Everywhere there was a plush broadloomed silence of wealth. It was never too hot and never too cold. His clothes were picked up after him. And there were no more drunks walking past his window late at night. Barney began to hate it. He missed his old neighborhood and the school where he had played marbles in the cinder-swept courtyard. He was sent to the best private school. To show her faltering sense of independence, his mother had insisted that it be a Catholic private school. Maintaining his heritage was important. Wearing a blue blazer and gray flannel trousers Barney sat in a class under the cold ascetic eyes of Brother Louis, who demanded obedience, silence and high marks. Barney was going crazy with all the silence. It was all around him. So he began telling jokes. At home he told Sam Junior that he wanted a bar mitzvah but he wanted it to be held in the Catholic cathedral. When he said the same thing in class, Brother Louis boxed his ears until he could hear a ringing noise. You *schnorer* he yelled at Brother Louis, who then instituted his own private Inquisition. He caned Barney's hands until they began to swell and then assigned him large sections of the New Testament to be memorized. Two days later Brother Louis announced to the class that a recitation was about to be given. He strolled down the aisle and tapped his wooden pointer on Barney's desk. Barney looked up into the milk-white face with the little veins that stood out whenever Brother Louis felt threatened. The little veins were very visible. Barney was slow in standing up. Brother Louis whipped the pointer across Barney's already stinging hands. At that moment Barney declared war on Brother Louis. He got only as far as

> The Lord is my *tumler*
> I shall not *darf*
> He maketh me to *kvell*
> in green pastures

when Brother Louis began swinging the pointer like a demented swordsman. Barney ran all over the room with Brother Louis in hot pursuit. When Brother Louis caught up with him Barney yelled that he was a Jew-baiter. This is a place of the Holy Mother yelled Brother Louis as he thrashed Barney. And you'll remember you're as Catholic as the Pope in spite of your evil mouth. Not on my *tushie* yelled Barney covering his rear end with his hands.

During that school year Barney was expelled twice, his mother began drinking and Sam Junior spent increasingly fewer hours at home. When he was at home he was always polite to Barney in the way that one is polite to guests. Sometimes he would absentmindedly tell Barney that he would buy him a car when he was old enough. Sam Junior and Barney's mother began to fight. She was spending most of her nights in the house wondering what Sam Junior was doing. After each of the fights Sam Junior would give her more money to spend and tell her not to interfere in his business.

In early April, Sam Junior was shot as he returned home late at night. Barney was lying in bed when he heard a noise that sounded like a twig breaking. The noise was repeated several times. Then there was a yell and banging at the door and screams from his mother. He raced to the front door where his mother knelt smelling of whiskey and sobbing over Sam Junior, who was still conscious. It was only from his legs that blood seeped through the silk suit onto the concrete steps. His breathing came in loud choking bursts and he was trying to say something about his briefcase when he passed out. The police arrived soon after and then the ambulances. Most of the neighborhood stayed up all night talking in small groups and waiting impatiently to tell their side of the story to the police.

Sam Junior had been shot seven times in the legs. His left leg was never expected to be the same. On the third day after the shooting he developed an infection that became so severe he was given only a slight chance of surviving. In

New York, Sam Senior heard the news and went immediately to number 1650 Broadway where the booking agents were. I'll take Montreal he told the booking agent, an old man who sat in a dreary office surrounded by photographs of people he had forgotten. The booking agent was surprised because Sam Senior had always said he would play blackface to the Ku Klux Klan in Alabama before he would play Montreal. Sam Senior went to Montreal just to be near Sam Junior. When Barney met him at the train station there was already a kind of defeat hanging about him. At the hospital Sam Senior stood beside his son in silence. Sam Junior lay with tubes protruding from his body and a cast on one leg. He flickered in and out of consciousness. Sam Senior took his son's hand and held it until Sam Junior opened his eyes and stared up at his father. For several minutes they looked at each other. Then Sam Junior faded back into a heavy rasping sleep and Sam Senior left the room with tears streaming down his face.

There were those at Hanson's who ranked Montreal somewhere near Peoria. Sam Senior had sworn he would never play the burlesque house up there because it was professionally degrading. Almost no one in a burlesque audience ever cared for jokes. They were there simply to see as much jiggling female flesh as the local laws allowed. Comics were simply an annoying interruption. The best that most of the comedians hoped for in burlesque was an eye-level knothole in a dressing room located next to the strippers' dressing room. Hanson's was filled with stories of many happy offstage hours spent with comic faces pressed flat against walls in decrepit buildings across America. But in the really bad places in Montreal not even a good knothole was enough. The problem was the audiences, who were no worse than the normal repressed burlesque audience except for the fact that they could not understand one single joke even if they wanted to. The entire audience spoke nothing but French. It was like playing to a brick wall. A noisy brick wall. More than once it had been announced in Hanson's that even those *maziks* who went to the Catskills were like a congregation by comparison.

Sam Senior stood up in front of his French-speaking audience and told jokes as if the laughter was rolling over him in waves. He played into the face of the irritated buzz from the darkness with perfect timing. An inner laugh track was warding off that world beyond the footlights. After the second matinee Sam Senior would hurry to the hospital and sit with Sam Junior, who lingered in a half life for days. He would tell stories of how Sam Junior had been such a good student and what it was like in the old days when Nessa and he would take their son to the lakes north of the city. Sam Junior would wheeze in and out of consciousness until Sam Senior had to hurry off to the next show.

On Sam Senior's third day in Montreal, Barney managed to sneak into the theater by telling the doorman that his mother was one of the acts. Backstage he tried to look as if he knew where he was going. One of the strippers came up to him and ran her finger through his hair. She asked him in a teasing voice if he was one of the new acts. Barney went red in the face. He had never seen a woman wearing so little clothing. From the wings he watched Sam Senior tell his jokes into the buzzing darkness, introduce a marvelous little lady whom he was sure they would all find captivating, and then stride off the stage with a triumphant smile and a wave. The moment he was offstage Sam Senior seemed to sag into defeat, his features collapsing like wax from a candle. When Barney opened his dressing-room door Sam Senior was sitting on the broken chair staring at the floor. When he looked up at Barney his face showed no surprise, no emotion. Finally Barney broke the silence.

Todlachen! he said defiantly and Sam Senior at first looked irritated. But then he suddenly stood up and wrapped his arms around Barney. *Todlachen!* he roared back. We're laughing and it's killing us. He began to shake and for a moment Barney was sure he was weeping instead of laughing.

Until the next show they sat in the tiny dressing room. For Barney it became a time of magic. Sam Senior talked and laughed and remembered the best of his days. Playing the Palace. Matching wits with Jack Benny. Meeting Charlie Chaplin. And the old days of burlesque—the real burlesque—oi they were such fun. Not all this flesh and grunt for the mouth breathers with their hats on their laps. In those days it was different. The comedians were the heroes of the neighborhood. Burlesque was a family thing then. And all the poor people and the immigrants would go to hear the comics mock the people who were putting them down. The corrupt judges. The meanest of the bosses. They were all our targets and oi such fun it was. What an audience. Sensational. They were a dozen languages out there but nobody needed an interpreter when we had the judge yelling *Not guilty* at a pretty pair of legs and beating the immigrant over the head with a slapstick. Sensational he said softly and Barney wanted to yell for joy at the old man's happiness.

Later in the week Sam Junior's name was on the front page of every paper. He was charged with corrupting judges and policemen whom he had paid not to interfere with his gambling operations. The charges were based on documents found in the briefcase Sam Junior had dropped on the night he was shot. For three days after his son's name was in the papers Sam Senior would stride out onto the stage with a triumphant smile and tell his best jokes into the rustling void. On the fourth day when he did not show up for the first matinee they sent someone to his hotel room. Sam Senior was found dead of a heart attack.

Barney was twelve years old and was proud that he had not cried since he was eight. For two days he sat in his room overlooking the swimming pool and cried. The funeral was very large and formal. Sam Junior wanted it that way, almost as a show of defiance. Let them arrest him. And let the respectable people who owed him fortunes dare not to show up. From his wheelchair Sam Junior was steeping in hatreds. He appeared gray and stooped, lashing out with his eyes and wanting to get even. For the funeral, Barney's mother had to be pumped full of black coffee. She wore a veil that covered her eyes and the smell of the whiskey. Barney sat in the angry silence of the large limousine determined to do things his way. After he had stopped crying he decided that Sam Senior should be honored for what he had truly been. And no one else seemed to be honoring Sam Senior. *Todlachen.* At the cemetery after the last of the long line of cars had been parked Barney stood fearfully at the head of the coffin, his heart pounding into his breast. In a quavering voice he blurted out Did you hear about the drunk who put a dime in the parking meter and when the dial went up to sixty he said my god I've lost a hundred pounds. There was a stunned silence from the hundreds of mourners. Just like it had been in the burlesque house. Same silence. Same jokes. Sam Junior was furious. His eyes flashed threats and he hissed between his teeth a barely heard warning. Ha! cried Barney, I'd know you anywhere. You heckled me twenty years ago. I always remember a man's suit. A murmur rose from the crowd and Barney stared into the embarrassed looks that darted at him across the suspended coffin of Sam Senior. He felt a sense of exhilaration for Sam Senior—whom he had loved more than anyone else in his world—was having his jokes told over his own coffin to all these people who did not know how to act. Barney hoped that Sam Senior was watching. And laughing. Did you hear about the drunk in New York—Enough! screamed Sam Junior—who got lost in the subway and gets back to the street where he meets his friend. The friend asks Where were you? The drunk says Man I was in some guy's basement. Has he got a set of trains! . . . . .

. . . . . and someone just out of sight snickers while someone else laughs. It is a laugh that ignites a trail of emotional powder which explodes in jokes that cannot be silenced even as Sam Junior grapples with his wheelchair yelling at Barney to shut up. Have you no respect? No decency? he screams across the coffin. *Decency?* The word echoes across a continent for at that very moment as Sam Senior is being buried Tommy and Jimmy Dorsey the famous bandleaders are wondering if perhaps they have made a terrible mistake. Is it all within the bounds of common decency they wonder as they watch the rehearsal for their Saturday night television show. The young singer with the long hair and sideburns is unlike anyone they have ever seen before. Offstage he is not too bad. He is polite, says Sir, and talks in a shy drawl. But once he begins singing—it is another matter entirely. And decency is definitely involved for the kid is up there clutching the microphone and doing things with his body that make him look like the Puritans' incarnation of the devil. Like a crazy man overdosing on memories of whorehouses. Loins pumping into the air. Hips swiveling. Tommy and Jimmy Dorsey do not know what to make of it. There was nothing like it in their best days of the Big Bands. And Lord knows they were accused of enough by the pious. But *this!*—this is different. This writhing orgasmic bundle of libido who has turned the studio into a fortress besieged by armies of females who have sensed true north on the sexual magnet. And so Elvis Presley goes on the air and thrusts his loins into the living rooms of America and the raunchy pounding of his music is matched beat for beat by the thundering pulpits frantically issuing calls for a return to decency. But it is too late for Elvis has claimed the decade for himself. The 1950s are his and *Heartbreak Hotel* becomes the emotional address for millions of young women who long just to touch Him. And a generation of teen-age boys grow their hair long, slick it back with hair oil and hope their sideburns are like His. Elvis is everywhere.

But all this changes. . . . . .

FOUR

. . . . . in the next decade which does not belong to Elvis. And on the Armed Forces Vietnam Network Sgt. Pepper is blowing sweet smoke through the 50,000-watt clear-channel airwaves. Saying no end of strange things that the generals do not quite understand. But the stoned warriors cradling their M-16 automatics in the jungles and the rice paddies recognize sedition and subversion when they hear it and grin through the fog of another just fine day. Fine because they are still alive. Jungle-rotted or desert-dried but alive. And overloaded with music that seeps out to them in the most distant fire base. Music that says fuck this particular war in a way that the generals cannot decipher. And neither can Elvis. It is all too much for him and he retreats to his mansion in Memphis burrowing deep into a musical and emotional exile. For outside the gates is America and America is going berserk. Screaming, rioting and growing hair all over the place. Not the carefully greased-back pompadour that Elvis had created upon a million heads. But unruly crinkly defiant yards of the stuff, looking wired with too much juice from the current of madness. . . . It looks practically . . . *indecent!* Elvis seizes upon the problem. With these subversive crazies running around making music and love at the same time nothing is safe. None of the old ways are revered. Not the good old days of a little innocent loin-thrusting on the Dorsey show. And so Elvis sits out the sixties in his lonely fortress of decency. Honoring the flag, paying taxes and riding in endless lonely circles on his motorcycle around the grounds of the mansion. The days and nights of isolation blur into one another and whatever money can buy to make the time go away is promptly bought. Jukeboxes, cars, companions, televisions, bodyguards. They are all bought and waved in front of Elvis, whose eyes are glazing over from too many pills that make the time go away. And the once taut body is coating with fat. It is food that also makes the time go away. Elvis is trapped in this terrible decade and he wants it all to go away. But it does not and his mother dies leaving him ruined by grief for it was his mother whom he worshiped even more than his beautiful young bride . . . who tires of the isolation and falls in love with the karate instructor hired by Elvis to help make the time go away. The despair and isolation grows deeper within the walls of the mansion . . . until one day the indecency of it all penetrates even the pill-shrouded boredom. Elvis sits up in front of a television set that has just relayed the latest news of the war on the streets of the nation against the war of Vietnam. Vietnam? He decides to do his duty and sets off on a foray into the enemy territory out there beyond the gates of the mansion. With bodyguards as point men Elvis sets off for Washington and another fortress, the Federal Bureau of Investigation. There he is ushered past acres of deskbound feds whose orders are to wear short hair and white shirts. These orders are from the man whom Elvis has come to meet. It is one legend meeting another for J. Edgar Hoover in his own way has as much claim to history as Elvis. Hoover was on the front pages before Elvis was born, chasing the most famous crooks of the nation, and showing up in time for the photographs. For all those years he has held the same position, and as Director of the FBI he has become so entrenched in his power that he now runs the massive police organization as a personal fiefdom. Hoover greets Elvis with a smile that is mellower than it would have been in the days of the Dorsey show. For Elvis is one of *them* now. In fact Hoover is positively beaming. It is the smile of power. It is the smile masking the dirty little pieces of knowledge that have preserved this power for all these years. The day-to-day knowledge of John F. Kennedy's latest lay. And Eisenhower's wartime mistress. And which senator is shacking up with his nontyping secretaries. And which congressman is doing the same with young boys. And the sex life of Martin Luther King—which is useful for sending President Johnson off for a gleeful hour of reading and gloating laughter. Hoover has perhaps the truest understanding of what is needed to keep power. It is simply the secret knowledge of the discrepancy between private conduct and public image. It is a discrepancy fueled by either greed or lust. And here standing in front of Hoover, shaking hands and calling him Sir with a soft Southern drawl is one of the national catalysts of lust: the sexual idol of America a decade later, standing in this, the office whose massive power is preserved by the knowledge of the sex lives of those who might attack that power.

But neither Hoover nor Elvis is given to reflecting upon such public ironies, for the private lives of both do not, at the moment, lend themselves to such thought. Hoover is living as he has lived for decades, a prissy male spinster who spends every night dining with Clive his longtime friend and confidant. Clive is also single and is a neighbor. Because of the affection Hoover has for him, Clive has risen up to be the number three man in the FBI. But for some reason this discrepancy between public image and private conduct has never been noted by Hoover's many enemies.

Elvis gets down to the reason for the visit. Sir, he says in his soft voice, I love my country and the flag and I want to stop those who are tearing America to pieces. The subversives. The kind you see on television. The longhairs with no sense of decency. I want to be a special agent, Elvis declares solemnly. I will work with the FBI at my own expense to get information that will help you fight these people who are against us being in Vietnam. Sir, I want to help fight the commies.

Fight the commies! The very phrase rings Pavlovian bells within the temple of all that Hoover holds dear. Hoover has hated commies more than the Mafia, more than John Dillinger, and more than some Presidents. He has driven his men furiously to find spies and subversives and if none were to be found during the lean periods then they could damn well be created. And now in these the final days of his career, after all his efforts America should be a desert for communists and subversives. But instead he feels like a gardener after a spring rain. The damn things are popping up all over. Sprouting. Blooming. Flourishing. America has gone to subversive seed and Hoover cannot understand it. But for the moment all that is forgotten. Hoover's bulldog features beam as he finds a kindred spirit in this most difficult of decades. And even though he will go with his instincts and not use Elvis as his most conspicuous secret agent, the gesture warms him. There is hope for the future . . . but the future is short for both will be dead before the end of another decade. Elvis will be enshrined by weeping millions as America's version of a saint and Hoover's memory will be kicked into the swamp of petty tyrants. . . . . .

. . . . . but Sgt. Pepper, as the army disc jockey calls himself, comes steaming through those 50,000 clear-chan-

nel watts and is seized by a fit of nostalgia that very afternoon. It is time to clear the airwaves of all the stoned, head
music and get back to basics. Just this once. He plays
Heartbreak Hotel and Elvis reaches out into the marshes of
the delta in the south where army riverboats are firing at
whatever moves. And up, five hundred miles up, in I Corps,
where Marines, stripped to the waist in the heat, are stack-
ing their dead for the helicopters that will soon land on the
cratered, blasted hills. And to Tan Son Nhut airport in
Saigon, where Barney arrives in Vietnam.

Barney walks through the dusty chaos of what once was
a small colonial airport. It is now fifteen years since he sat
in at Hanson's with Sam Senior. Barney is now almost a
head taller than old Sam Senior ever was. The roundness of
his face has melted away. But the look of the boy is still
preserved in the face of the man. His dark hair is still cut
short. And his eyes are still capable of thoughts of their
own, like those of the boy who silently watched the comedians in the other booths.

It is five years since Barney had become a comedian.
More precisely it is five years since someone paid him for
doing what he would have done anyway. A maker of laughter, as Sam Senior had once said to him with a wink. Make
laughter where it does not exist. Go where there is least to
laugh about Sam Senior had told him. And then after that
make sure you get rich, he had grinned looking around his
tiny hotel room.

In the Saigon airport, there is no one to meet Barney as
the booking agent in New York had said there would be:
Don't worry kid, the man had said. We send over dozens
just like you. You're gonna be looked after. Just like you
were playing Vegas. But the airport is a tangle of noise and
orders from loudspeakers. Hercules troop transport planes
lumber down the runway with the low drone of their propel-
lers.

Troop companies are either moving out or waiting in the heat while sergeants with clipboards yell more orders. Barney waits in the heat and the noise until someone tells him to get on the bus with the wire mesh across all the windows and he rides into Saigon. The drive becomes a kaleidoscope of peasant colors and army green. Roaring jeeps and plodding oxen. A dusty inferno of humanity without stillness. American soldiers looking bored and nervous at the same time, standing in tiny sandbag fortresses in front of army buildings. Acres of filthy houses made from old beer cans. Beggars, cripples, whores, all chanting their litany into the din of the clogged streets.

And nowhere is there a hotel with a spare room. Not the Caravelle. Nor the Majestic, nor the Continental. And finally he comes to the Catinat on Tu Do Street. Milligan's, the talent agency, is supposed to be here but it is late and everything is closed. There is one room he is told when he finally gets in past the sliding steel doors. In the dark room on the third floor Barney falls exhausted onto the bed wondering why he ever left the safety of the syndicated television and the little clubs in the Village. He does not wonder for long because something begins to itch and he catapults from the bed. When the light is found he discovers that the bed is crawling with its own form of life. And so . . . . .

. . . . . Barney groped through the darkness, past the little green lizards on the walls and down the stairs to the coffee shop, which he expected to be closed. To his surprise it was open. Inside was a sullen Vietnamese waiter who wanted to go home and a hulking young man who was providing the bulwark against any semblance of early closing. The young man sat in a chair methodically ordering one whiskey after another. He seemed to be angry at something. Barney was also angry but he was not sure what he was angry about. He sat at the far end of the coffee shop and also ordered whiskeys. Neither man spoke except to order whiskeys. Barney was soon aware of a certain belligerence in the way the other man was drinking. It was becoming almost a duel. Barney and Woody would later laugh over their first meeting but at the time of the fourth drink each thoroughly disliked the other. Barney had noticed that Woody was wearing a military uniform, the lower half of which consisted of short trousers and knee socks. Barney looked at Woody's legs and began to snicker. Woody looked at his own legs and then back at Barney. Woody was always defensive about his abbreviated uniform. Somehow he didn't feel like a true soldier wearing them. Barney's snicker had turned to laughter which then got totally out of control. Barney began laughing so hard that tears streamed down his cheeks. It was a finger-pointing, thigh-slapping hoot that had him almost on the floor. Are you a Boy Scout? he managed to ask. I, sir, said Woody rising up to his full height of alcoholic indignation, am a member of Her Majesty's Armed Forces. The *Canadian* Armed Forces. I, sir, am a peace-keeper!

A peace-keeper? Barney blubbered through his tears. Here? Yes said Woody archly. A peace-keeper! Woody's eyes took on a murderous squint that more than once had foretold brawls. But this time he was not going to yield to such urges. Not against this hooting little creep. Woody grimly ordered another whiskey and sat back to write his findings of the day on the official form in his clipboard. The hooting subsided. You must excuse me, Barney said wiping away the tears. You really must. For a while the scratching of the pen seemed to rasp through the coffee shop.

How is the peace going? asked Barney on the verge of convulsing again. With an angry little smile Woody replied that the peace was coming along nicely. He ordered more whiskeys and continued writing. What are you doing? asked Barney. Writing a report said Woody through clenched teeth. A report on the peace.

You have the easiest job in the war, said Barney. Woody drew up in quiet wrath. The memory of his endless day asking stupid questions in the dusty heat of the Vietnamese summer was too fresh in his mind. I beg your pardon he said dropping his clipboard.

Anyone can do that job, said Barney blithely. Woody stared at him for what seemed like a very long time. Woody's knuckles were turning white around the edge of the chair.

I see, said Woody. And just how would you go about this? Barney replied that it was all very simple. You lie.

Lie?

Lie? asked Woody. Of course said Barney. If you're writing about a peace that doesn't exist you're lying anyway. So go all the way. Woody sat in the chair rooted by indignation and too many whiskeys. There was the impression that Barney's words were having great difficulty filtering through to any last bastions of thoughtfulness. Finally Woody picked up the clipboard and slowly held it out in front of him. You do it, he said menacingly.

An angry bridge of silence existed between them. Then Barney's solemn dark features were pushed away by a needling smile. He reached out and accepted the clipboard. The Vietnamese waiter raised his eyes to the ceiling, looked at his watch and then began yelling at them in French. Barney yelled back at him. Le whiskey monsieur. Et au revoir.

By the time the waiter left in disgust, Barney was writing a report on a Vietcong attack using a dead water buffalo stuffed with dynamite. Then he made up a new psychological warfare technique being tried near the Ho Chi Minh Trail. Spotter planes were dropping photographs of naked couples in various stages of lovemaking. The intent was to increase the level of libidinous tension in the lonely enemy soldiers. Such increased tension would inevitably lead to lower morale. According to the report the leaflets were dropped in the wrong location. They were dropped on an American Special Forces outpost. The soldiers there had not seen civilization in months. The report noted that the outpost was easily overrun by the enemy the following day.

But that's a crock of shit, said Woody clinging to the neck of the bottle. It's all lies.

So? Nobody believes anything in this war anyway. If everybody thinks everyone else is lying, the lies become truth. Before too many more whiskeys, Woody had decided that he was as good a liar as anyone else.

By dawn they had joyously sent the 1st Marines looting and pillaging halfway to Vung Tau; caused the 1st Infantry to engage in a race riot that was hushed up and hinted at a kickback scandal in the running of the USO Clubs for American servicemen. There were seventeen major violations, a handful of scandals and several documented atrocities on both sides.

By dawn they had also destroyed the glass door of the coffee shop when Woody walked through it. Neither had realized the waiter had locked them in. They had also been arrested for staging cyclo races up and down the deserted Nguyen Hue Street. Barney was in the process of pulling his cyclo across the finish line when the American military police jeep cut him off. A gallant loser, Woody interjected on his new friend's behalf by filling out another cease-fire Violation Report on the spot. The report alleged that the MPs had violated the commission's freedom of movement. The report claimed that Barney was the senior political adviser to the Canadian delegation. The American MPs read the Violation Report while Woody hummed some unknown national anthem and Barney quietly and contritely recited the opening lines from The Quality of Mercy. Finally the Americans gave them coffee and drove them back to the Catinat.

The next day the report was accidently turned in by one of Woody's men. Two days later on the Saigon golf course where the American senior officers played against the Canadian senior peace-keepers the report was discussed. It was discussed while the Canadians illegally passed the Americans secret information from their men stationed behind enemy lines. The shame of the USO Club kickback scandal was noted between a chip and a putt. After the golf game, the Americans looked at each other and asked: What kickback scandal? They assigned someone to look into the matter. No one wanted to look bad by not being up to date. It was inadvertently discovered that a master sergeant was running a nationwide racket in USO kickbacks. It grew into a huge scandal.

A week later, Brigadier Mosby, the senior Canadian peace-keeper, dryly congratulated Woody on the improved quality of his peace-keeping reports.

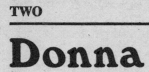

TWO

Donna

FIVE

On the night after Barney told his peace-keeper jokes to the American soldiers, he awoke to find the door to his room being chopped down by someone with an ax.

There had been nothing in the preceding hours to indicate that his door would be chopped down. The Catinat had seemed quiet enough. The third-floor courtyard outside his room had shown no signs of violence or insurrection. But in the instant that the first cold wedge of steel crashed through the door, the thought shot through Barney's mind that he had really seen nothing of his surroundings for the entire day. He had been too preoccupied. He had blocked out all that was unnecessary to his quest.

Barney had spent the entire day trying to meet the woman in room 39. But D. Martinez had avoided him. She avoided most people. She had become the Garbo of the Catinat, coming and going at times when few people saw her, keeping to herself, and somehow existing in a world that no one seemed to share. But sometime before dawn on the previous morning, Barney had been awakened by voices in the courtyard. From his window he had seen a man in an army uniform walking slowly, aimlessly, among the ferns and potted palm trees. Then a light had glowed behind the curtain in room 39. Another man had emerged from the room, a man who moved with quick, certain motions. In the darkness, both men were unrecognizable. After they left, the light in room 39 remained on until dawn.

All morning, Barney sat in the sun watching the Vietnamese hotel maids bustling around the courtyard. They made up every room except number 39, where the curtains remained closed until noon, when Barney went downstairs to Milligan's.

It took half an hour for Milligan to finish cursing the old French phone system and give Barney next week's dates of his performances at Bien Hoa airbase. Milligan's office was always the same chaos of glossy photographs, raised voices, cigar smoke and file folders misplaced under mountains of paper. When Barney returned to the third floor the door to room 39 was open and the curtains were open. Inside, a cleaning maid was flapping sheets across the bed.

Barney waited all afternoon. She did not return. After sunset, he left for Cholon, the Chinese section of Saigon, where for one night he had second billing in a dilapidated officers' club. The club was only half filled. Barney had played there twice before and each time had vowed he would never return. The empty tables. The stiffness of the audience. The echoing marble walls of what had once been a huge lobby in a bad hotel. When the U. S. Army took over the hotel for officers' quarters, the lobby became the club. Paper streamers and balloons officially marked the transformation.

When he got back to the Catinat, he entered through the Tu Do Street entrance, walking down the dark narrow hallway, past the Milligan Talent office to the hotel reception counter. There was no one around and the tiny, cluttered reception area was illuminated only by the neon bar lights on Tu Do Street. Barney stood for a moment expecting someone to appear. Then he pounded the palm of his hand on the counter. The noise echoed throughout the hallway and then there was silence. Again he pounded. Several seconds later the wall behind the counter seemed to part with a long slow creak. It was a door that had been built into the wall. It opened slowly to reveal the old Vietnamese porter sitting on the edge of a cot. He peered up at Barney with a serene expression and eyes that seemed to be looking at some distant truth. I want to see the registration book, said Barney. The old man seemed not even to know that Barney was there. He looked away and rubbed slowly at the stringy traces of a beard that dangled from his chin. Guest book, said Barney. Still no response. *Cahier du registration* he blurted out, hoping his schoolboy French had survived the years. The old man nodded slowly. For several seconds he simply nodded. Then he pointed to a shelf above the counter. On the shelf, Barney found the registration book. First he turned to the new arrivals of the past three days. There were only two, a construction man from Louisiana and a journalist from Australia. Neither of them had been given room 39. Then he spun back through the pages until he came to D. Martinez. To his relief there was still a blank space for *Date of Departure*. As he put the book back on the shelf, a loud grating came from the end of the corridor. Another watchman had slammed down the heavy metal door that guarded the portal at night. It was midnight. Curfew time. When the metal door came down, it guillotined the neon lights of Tu Do Street and Barney had to grope his way past the little green lizards on the walls, up to the third floor. There was no light coming from room 39. Barney went into his room and fell asleep until the ax crashed through his door.

Long after curfew the light remained on in Woody's ninth-floor room at the Catinat Hotel. A small group of Canadians were drinking and defending the honor of the country against the Americans and against the traitor Barney. His demise was plotted in progressively less coherent plans. Miller, a lieutenant from Saskatoon, wanted to ask the brigadier to cancel Barney's visa. Too easy, said someone else. Put lice in his bed. That can be cured said Dr. Joyal, the medic from Quebec. Try the clap. Of course the clap! They all sat in boozy contemplation, paying the suggestion its proper respect. The clap was not to be wished on anyone, said Miller finally, not even a traitor like Barney. They solemnly agreed, each remembering stories of American soldiers decaying and drooling in special camps for the syphilitics. What about photographing him in bed with one of the Tu Do Street hookers, asked a young lieutenant from a proper family. He would just ask for enlargements of the print, said Woody. They nodded in agreement. The traitor knew no shame.

They sat in gloomy silence waiting for the beer to run out or inspiration to come. But the perfect revenge was not forthcoming and their thoughts were the litany of soldiers without weapons. At last Woody teetered to his feet. We have been wrong he said. We should not be angry with Barney for letting the Americans know that we are in this war to keep the peace. We should feel sorry for him. He cannot see the true nobility of our situation. After all, what is more noble than soldiers who do not need guns? Soldiers without weapons, looking into the teeth of war? Where in all the annals of war is there a parallel? We are unique gentlemen!

They were nearly all drunk on Canadian beer flown over at great expense to help keep them out of the Saigon bars. But even though they were nearly all drunk Woody somehow made sense. The young lieutenant from the proper family had never felt noble before. He liked the feeling.

If the Americans laugh said Woody, then we should pity them. They have not seen the light. They—with all those weapons, loaded down so heavily they sink into the earth and waddle like grenade-carrying ducks. They with their M-16s and their Phantoms and their aircraft carriers. It is easy for them to be soldiers inside their metal cocoon.

But gentlemen, announced Woody after a solemn pause caused by a momentary lack of anything to say, we who stand naked before this armored onslaught—*we* are the true warriors! He raised his beer bottle in a toast. One by one the other weaponless Canadians stood up to drink to the fact that they were the only true warriors. Then they drank to the Queen, the brigadier—whom they all disliked—Lyndon Johnson, and Ho Chi Minh. They even drank to Colonel Wzcninski, the head of the Polish commission. They disliked him even more than their own brigadier. The Poles were on the fourth floor of the hotel. There had been many nights when subtle warfare flared between the peacekeepers on the ninth floor and the peace-keepers on the fourth floor.

They departed in a spirit of goodwill and harmony. The spirit prevailed until each returned to his own room. Then came the feeling that while being noble was all right, it would still be better to have the odd M-16 kicking around. And perhaps a howitzer or two. At least it would stop the Americans from laughing.

In his room, Woody lay on the bed muttering hatred at the cockroaches. Every night when the lights were turned off, he could hear them clicking across the tiled floors near the bathroom. He had developed his own form of warfare against the cockroaches. He would silently pick up one of his combat boots in his right hand and hold it behind him in preparation for throwing. With his left hand he would switch on the light beside the bed while throwing the boot in the same moment. The effect of the light on the cockroaches was like a starting gate opening in front of a racehorse. From a standing start, they shot across the tiles and dove for the cracks in the wall without breaking stride. Usually it was a photo finish between the boot and the cockroach. But on this evening, the boot went sailing into the bathroom. Woody sank back onto the bed and lay there looking up at the high ceiling. One thought rang through his mind again and again: Barney was a traitor. Action must be taken.

Woody descended to the third floor and then stopped to make a survey of the terrain. The third floor was unlike any other floor in the Catinat Hotel. The other floors were of conventional hotel arrangement with a hallway in the middle and rooms on either side. But the third floor had neither elevator nor hallway. It was instead an open-air courtyard that jutted out beside the main structure of the hotel. The doors to the rooms faced into the courtyard. In the center of the courtyard were small trees and flowers. Were it not for the noise in the daytime, the effect would have been one of tropical tranquillity. The noise came from beyond the high walls at either end of the courtyard. Beyond the north wall was Nguyen Hue Street, a broad boulevard that bore the unmistakable stamp of Saigon's French heritage. Until they cut the trees down in the name of some unknown dictum of war, the street evoked images of Paris. On the south side of the courtyard was Tu Do Street, overflowing with its gaudy bars, beggars and pimps. At fifteen minutes to every midnight the night air of the courtyard exploded with the roar of the Tu Do motor scooters. The bar girls were being driven home by boy friends who had spent the evening clustered around their Hondas, coldly watching the Americans in the bars. The scooters fought their nightly race with the

curfew and then suddenly Tu Do Street was empty except
for the military police and the tiny orphans who slept in
doorways on the stone steps.

Woody sat on a bench in the courtyard holding the fire
ax. The last of the scooters had long ago departed. Now
there was only the soft thumping noise that came from artillery somewhere to the west of the city. Flares hung in the
sky illuminating the western half of the night with a strange
and gradually fading glow. The silence of the courtyard was
broken by voices. Woody strained to hear the direction
from which they came. Once there was a throttled little cry
that he recognized. It was Lawson, the free-lance newspaperman. Lawson was a big, red-faced man with glassy yet
fierce eyes. He drank too much and his drinking was getting
worse because the *Herald Tribune* was about to fold in New
York. The *Herald Tribune* was his last thread of journalistic
respectability. Lawson often cried out in his sleep. It was
always names of women that spluttered out in a sobbing cry.
Once someone had kidded him about his nocturnal cries
and he had broken down in a fury of purple-faced denial.
He had spent the next two days drunk.

But there were other voices than Lawson's. Woody
looked around and could see nothing but the dark, shuttered windows of the rooms. The voices continued. Woody
listened for a moment and then let the ax head slip a few
inches to the tiled floor of the courtyard. It fell with a sharp
metallic clink. The voices stopped instantly.

When the ax first came through the door, Barney dimly decided it was all a bad dream, like the kind
that Lawson in room 34 was always having. From the
depths of sleep he was awakened by a splintering sound that
seemed very near. Terrifyingly near. He sat upright in bed

and watched in horror as a jagged crack of light from the night flares suddenly became a gaping hole. The hole had burst in the middle of his door with an explosion of splinters and what he thought was the glint of an ax. Then a hand groped through the hole in the door and pawed at the inside door handle. It was a huge hand. Ever since he had arrived in Vietnam, Barney had asked himself what he would do if he was confronted with death. Like everyone else there, he always expected that death would only confront other people. It might peek around a corner occasionally, but never really confront him. But the hand coming through the hole in the door was, in Barney's terrified eyes, the hand of death. He knew that any moment the door would swing open and one of the hordes overrunning the hotel would blast away with an AK-47. There was nothing he could do. He had no arms weapons. The situation had all the odds of facing a firing squad. The image of a firing squad lingered and he thought of the blindfolds that covered the eyes of the condemned. At least they would not see their own last moments. With that thought in mind, Barney threw himself back on the bed and pulled the sheet up over his head.

He waited for the end, wondering how much gunfire one would actually hear. Instead of gunfire, he heard the Canadian national anthem. It was being drunkenly sung as something like another bedsheet was flung over him.

Woody? Is that you Woody? There was no answer. Barney pulled the sheet down from his face and tried to talk but a piece of cloth was shoved into his mouth. All he could do was grunt. His arms were tied to his side, strapped against a strangely silky material that seemed to cover him from head to toe. Then he was lifted out of the bed and carried into the courtyard. Woody was now belching out the national anthem with great and sodden patriotism. Lights flickered on and off in the surrounding rooms and several doors opened just wide enough to let sleepy mutterings be heard. Only Snider, the United Press photographer, came out into the courtyard. He stood there in his underwear, a cadaverous frame lit deathly pale by the light of the flares. He was both sleepy and furious. What the hell's going on? he wanted to know. Woody's reply was too muffled and drunken to mean anything. Woody was laboring in rapid clumsy motions as he tied Barney to the courtyard flagpole. Look man, said Snider angrily, I gotta be in Danang today. You know what that means? It means catching a goddam 4 A.M. car over at JUSPAO. And I don't appreciate all this shit, man. There are people who gotta sleep you know.

Snider received a solemn apology that meant nothing to him. He looked down at Barney whose eyes were making Help Me motions. Barney was now tied to the flagpole, and wrapped in the Polish flag. . . . . .

. . . . . So Snider the photographer angrily turns back to get what sleep he can. He is determined not to let these idiots spoil his chances for a shot at a LIFE cover. For UPI in New York has told him that LIFE magazine is looking for color shots on the Marines up in I Corps. A cover on LIFE. It is the nirvana of Snider's existence. He has joked that he would kill for LIFE. And there are those through the length of Vietnam who think he might. For Snider is known in every Corps as the FOLI man—First Off, Last In the helicopter. He has jumped from the gunships into fire fights that troops would not unload in. All for *that* shot. *That* picture to match Capa's shot of the Spanish Civil War soldier at the micro-instant of his death by gunfire. Snider has stalked that shot with ice for emotions. And in so doing, he has stalked death. Every soldier on the helicopters, every grunt on patrol, is simply a potential accumulation of developed granules on a piece of paper that will be awarded prizes for showing what war was *really* like. Some of the soldiers have sensed this, and the presence of this lean ghost with metallic eyes has spooked them. But Snider concerns himself with nothing more than the right lens. Fear is to be photographed, not felt. So Snider goes back to bed, knowing that the day will be long. There will be the walk through the curfew-emptied streets to the lone black Ford. The Ford's Air Force chauffeur will drive the few sleepy passengers out to Tan Son Nhut Airport. At the airbase, Snider will wait for hours and watch the darkness burned away by the sun. Always there is the waiting in crowded, barren little rooms. And then the hours in the air, strapped sideways onto the webbed seats in the C-130s whose noise leaves his head vibrating. Snider knows it will be a long day. But anything is worth the cover of LIFE. . . . But . . . . .

. . . . . Not so! LIFE is dead! says the world-famous English professor to the class who have come to pay homage. For they dare not question Marshall McLuhan, who dismisses challenges with a raise of eyebrows and a vicar's stare. McLuhan teaches, or, perhaps more accurately, enunciates wisdom, from the old converted mansion on Queen's Park in Toronto. And from the mansion, his words go out around the world and are inscribed as writ all during the period of the Vietnam War. Advertising agencies will humbly submit to his opinions in their New York boardrooms. While not understanding what he says they will pronounce it genius. The Medium is the Message, says McLuhan and heads nod. The enunciation of wisdom is a serious business, conducted with the distance of Merlin. For the recipes to these potions of thought can never be too closely examined. Only the potion itself is to be viewed. And because it bubbles then so be it—Wisdom! In the converted Queen's Park mansion the class will sit—literally—at his feet on the floor. He spreads his magic about him: Radio is Hot. Television is Cool. Print is Through. War is Hot. Spread the word!

Print is Through? No one has told Snider as he prepares to risk his life for yet another shot. For the cover of LIFE. Yet the old sage of Queen's Park may have something here. Not necessarily what the potion says, but something that is causing the editors of LIFE magazine to convene in the publisher's office for a late afternoon meeting. As Snider checks his lenses, the editors in New York are told what they all know: that LIFE is dying. Money is being pumped in to keep LIFE alive, but these are transfusions that cannot last forever. And nor do they. LIFE magazine, the American institution, dies in its middle age. It will later be brought back but it will never be the same. The legends of LIFE will be gone. It is the war that provides the final blow. Snider's covers may be fine but they are from last week. And in the age of the 2:20 min. report on what happened this morning (via satellite) LIFE has become optional. So the war kills it and the sage of Queen's Park will sprinkle the holy water of his potion at the gravesite, and heads will nod at the wisdom of it all. Then McLuhan will return home and pass the evening reading, for television is something that he considers an abomination in the home.

But Snider knows of none of this, nor does he care. He locks his door carefully and steps over the splinters of Barney's door, paying no heed to the grunting pleas from the figure wrapped in the Polish flag. Goddam fool Canadians, he mutters as he sets out for the 4 A.M. car to the airport.

Barney watched Snider leave and then settled back to wait for morning. His arms were tied so closely at his sides that all he could do was slump against the flagpole and hope for other, more sympathetic early risers. He had no way of knowing how much time had passed when he was first aware of another presence. He had lapsed into a light sleep that was ended by a faint whisper coming from somewhere on the other side of the courtyard. It was still dark. All he could make out was the outline of two men standing behind the courtyard shrubs. The men were consulting a piece of paper, illuminated by a tiny flashlight. For several minutes they whispered and shone the flashlight at numbers on nearby doors. One of the men stepped out from the shadows and Barney recognized him. It was an officer, a major he thought, whom he had seen at Colonel Isaacs' table in the Club. It was the same major who had made sure he was noticed shaking his head in disgust at Barney's performance. Barney pushed himself back against the flagpole, straining to peer over the shrubs. The major waved the other man away. Then he walked toward a door, shone the light on the number, and rapped softly. It was number 39! Barney shot against the ropes that held him to the flagpole. The doorway was partially hidden by the shrubs. Even pushing against the flagpole, he still could not see above the shrubs. Again there was a soft knock on the door and this time it was followed several seconds later by a soft response. Barney recognized the voice. It was her! There was a whispered conversation on either side of the door and then silence. Barney was suddenly aware that the second man was standing not far from him. The man loomed as a shadow and then hunched over into the light. It was Bannon, the colonel's driver. Bannon peered at Barney somberly without any indication that he thought it strange for a man to be tied up in the Polish flag in the middle of the night. Bannon had never been seen to smile. Until he had been badly shot up, the other troops had complained about how he acted on patrol. Twice he had tried to cut off the ears of prisoners. When prevented the second time, he had thrown a tantrum that made so much noise he was virtually assured of a discharge on psychological grounds. But before that could happen, his

tantrum attracted other attention. While his squad was trying to calm him down, they were ambushed by an enemy
patrol. Only Bannon and three privates survived. All were
seriously wounded, and none of the privates told what had
happened for fear that Bannon might come after them. But
Bannon was appointed the colonel's driver as a reward for
his brush with death. He was the perfect driver. Silent,
never wasting the colonel's time with small talk. A loner
who did not babble personal secrets to the troops. The colonel was immensely pleased to have found someone like
Bannon.

Bannon leaned over, his face not far from Barney's. He
studied Barney without expression. It was as if Barney was
an object under clinical investigation. Barney's eyes followed Bannon and tried to communicate with him. He
wanted Bannon at least to take the gag out of his mouth.
But Bannon just peered at him from only a few inches
away. Then he whispered. My brother's a funnyman, he
said. Barney's eyes darted in confusion. He's a funnyman
too, repeated Bannon. Nightclubs. It's hard to be funny. I
know that. Bannon's stare went right through Barney, who
suddenly felt very cold. But I'm on your side, whispered
Bannon. From his combat jacket he took out a small dark
object and held it in front of Barney's face. With a smooth
little zipping sound a gleaming blade appeared from the object and Barney suddenly remembered hearing the story
about the ears of a prisoner. Everything will be okay, whispered Bannon across the other side of the blade. We'll make
'em laugh.

The snap of a chain lock suddenly caught their attention. Bannon hurriedly put the knife away and retreated
back into the shadow with the same slumped and woeful
posture that made him appear the eternal servant. Voices
came from in front of number 39, and a man stepped out of
the room. Barney recognized the man. It was Isaacs. There

was a low angry conversation and phrases could be caught. The major was hurriedly explaining something. Another one, he said. Another what? Another murder. You *did* say to let you know. I know, I know goddammit. But how do you know it was not just another Vietcong attack with a knife? Who else knows?

Isaacs was pacing angrily in a tight little arc. He was dressed in civilian clothes. He returned to the room and emerged again wearing a jacket. As he left with the other two men, the door remained open for a moment. In the doorway, in the fading light of the flares, was Donna. She remained there after they had departed, staring after them with the same haunted expression that Barney had seen in those backstage moments. The door closed. Barney strained against the ropes, and cursed Woody, Isaacs, the war and D. Martinez or Donna or whoever she was.

In the first light they stood in a small grouping out near the perimeter where the body of the latest murdered sentry had been found. Isaac's car approached, driving off the road, its headlights bouncing through the lifting darkness. It was the portable radio that attracted his anger. The colonel switched the radio on. In the final gasps of the batteries, the radio blared out strange words that none of them understood. *Feed your head* intones the song, called *White Rabbit,* and the words throb like a war cry across the flat dusty plain where soldiers riding in the back of jeeps pass around a toke while the officers in the front sit with their eyes facing the army of their past. *Feed your head* says the song again and again from a thousand newly bought radios all over the base. It is a war fought with the latest theories of Leisure Time, so the PXs on the base go through stereos and radios like artillery shells. And the strange words and music that none of the generals understand, are pumped relentlessly through the new radios. *Feed your head?* a Vice-President of the United States will ask in a speech that he is soon to make. He repeats the other lyrics. They are evil he says and suddenly the White Rabbit blinks in the glare of the national headlines. But Spiro Agnew is soon to have other problems. By the time he resigns because of corruption charges, the White Rabbit has died like those of his stoned masters who did not survive to buy business suits or join strange religions.

What the hell was he doing with a portable radio on sentry duty? Isaacs looked up but there was no one who would answer. He reached out to pick up the radio but was stopped momentarily by an objection from a sergeant. Sir, said the sergeant nervously, what about having the radio checked for fingerprints first? The sergeant was a clerk in the brigade office who had been brought along to take notes. Isaacs reached out and picked up the radio. To hell with the fingerprints, he said. That would bring the military police in. And official investigations. This is not a murder gentlemen. This is a Killed In Action. Is that clear? The major and the sergeant nodded. The sergeant decided to drop the matter of the footprints. While the colonel flipped the radio dial, the sergeant wandered around looking at the ground. Most of the footprints had already been obliterated. The sergeant was aware that he was being watched. He looked up and saw Bannon, the colonel's driver. There was something funny about the footprints he whispered to Bannon. What's so funny? Bannon asked, looking down at the blur of footprints. The sergeant bent over and scraped the ground with his finger. I thought one of them looked like a woman's footprint, he said.

A woman? Bannon squinted and blinked at the ground. You know something mac, he said finally, smiling through his stained teeth. You're a nut.

SIX

Barney woke up because someone was yelling at him. When the voice thrust aside the curtain of his sleep, he squinted into the wagging finger of the angry man in the bathrobe. The man in the bathrobe was yelling at Barney in a language that he did not understand. At first, Barney understood very little. Until the sleep cleared away from his mind, he had trouble remembering how he came to be tied to a flagpole, wrapped in a Polish flag and gagged. Only then did he realize that the man in the bathrobe was one of the Polish peace-keepers. The Polish peace-keeper had a broad Slavic face and thinning hair combed straight back. His face was becoming red as he continued his tirade, pointing at the flag in which Barney was wrapped. Barney began yelling back at him but only muffled grunts emerged through the gag in his mouth. He was furious with the Polish peace-keeper for not untying him. Barney didn't care if his own angry tirade was muffled by the gag. He couldn't understand a word that the Polish peace-keeper was saying, so their insults would be on equal ground. Barney soon became as red-faced as the Pole.

Other Polish peace-keepers arrived on the third-floor courtyard. Most of them were in uniform and staring with disapproval at Barney. Then a sharp little command from the other side of the courtyard caused the angry Polish peace-keeper to fall silent and the others to open their ranks. Two men walked toward them. Barney recognized one of them. It was Brigadier Mosby, the head of the Canadian peace-keeping group. Barney instantly decided that he would rather not see Mosby's impeccably pompous face at that particular moment. Mosby was one of a dying breed, and more than once Barney had wished him a swift end. He was the kind of Canadian officer who had probably wept more than once because he had not been born in England. Everything about Mosby was more British than the British. The Empire lived on in the colonies.

Mosby peered down at Barney with imperious eyes as the other man spoke in broken English. Barney realized that he was being made the subject of an international incident. Mosby listened with diplomatic concern while the other man, whom Barney realized was the Polish colonel, accused the Canadians of defiling the Polish flag. Finally Mosby interrupted and said My dear sir, you are forgetting one thing. He is not one of *ours*. Barney began yelling through the mouth gag, telling Mosby not to be such a phony bastard and that it was because of one of *ours* that he was sitting there throttled in the flag. But no words came out. There were only the garbled sounds that were lost in the cloth that covered his mouth. Other people began arriving in the courtyard to watch the heads of the two peace-keeping teams maneuver one another into untenable positions. The Pole demanded that Mosby's soldiers unwrap the man in their flag, and then return the flag to the fourth floor. Mosby said that such a thing would be quite impossible. It would be an admission of guilt. And that was clearly out of the question. Barney looked up as the two peace-keepers fought over who was responsible for him. In the background, a strange motion suddenly caught his attention. He looked over and saw Woody and all of the Canadian soldiers who had been at the Club on the previous night. They were all grinning and Woody was pretending to be milking a cow. His mouth formed a silent word.

Moo, said Woody with a smile.

The cow and the peace-keepers. Barney began yelling at Woody, telling him how the Americans would fall on the floor laughing at them after his next act at the Club. But again the words were swallowed up in the cloth around his mouth. So he began mooing. It was a loud bellowing moo, and it was the one sound that came out with no distortion. The courtyard resounded with moos. Mosby's sense of decorum was offended by the noise. He turned and walked crisply from the courtyard ordering his men to do the same. As he left, Woody could not resist giving Barney one more teat-pulling motion for good measure. But halfway through his farewell gesture, he realized that Mosby had turned and fixed him with his most withering stare.

Moo said Barney with a smile.

Refusing to have to retrieve their own flag, the Poles were piped out of the courtyard by Barney's mooing. Angry glances and insults were hurled back at him. Suddenly the courtyard was empty except for the old Vietnamese chambermaid, who had seen too many strange things from the foreigners to think that this was anything unusual. Barney stopped mooing, happy that at least he had driven the peace-keepers away. There was silence in the courtyard. Then there was a staccato tapping sound. Lawson. Barney jiggled and twisted until he could barely see the open door of Lawson's room. Lawson always kept his door open when he wrote his newspaper articles. The tapping of the typewriter came in rapid bursts followed by long thoughtful silences. Lawson sat at the desk biting his lip and jiggling his foot as he wrung out the words. He was a large man, made larger by the correspondent's suit he had bought at one of the tailors on Tu Do Street. A correspondent's suit had become almost a uniform for newsmen in Vietnam. With the extra-large pockets, loops and pen-holding slots, the correspondent's suits with the Saigon label were one measure of status in the news profession. They were generally good for at least one or two wearings back at the home office. But in Vietnam, they were usually visible in inverse proportion to the number of bullets being fired in any given area. Lawson's correspondent's suit was not merely worn as an entree into the bar on the top floor of the Caravelle Hotel, where most of the other newsmen drank. It had the stains and tiny patches to show its initiation by fire. For Lawson had never shirked from opportunities to let his readers know firsthand the combat situation in Vietnam. *His* readers. He loved the words. He repeated it often to himself. Too often in the interval between some big news story and the typing of an article. It was in these intervals that he would sometimes go on alcoholic binges that would wipe days from his calendar. He would finally come to and discover that his latest news happened not this morning, but three days ago. One by one the opportunities to work for one of the bigger news outfits in Vietnam closed to him. And the *Herald Tribune* kept sending encouraging notes denying the rumors that the paper would fold. But the notes were somehow a little too encouraging. And their payments were becoming more erratic. It had become difficult to survive with dignity. And when he decided to save a few piasters by doing his own laundry, Lawson had provided for the demise of his correspondent's suit. He washed it in water so hot that the suit shrank. Now it strained against his large belly, bulging like flaws on an inner tube. To buy a new one was impossible. He was barely surviving by eating the terrible spaghetti in the Catinat coffee shop. It was the cheapest item on the menu. Every night he ordered it in French, speaking with enough of a casual air that the haughty Vietnamese waiter would not realize that he could afford nothing else. Yet always there was the hope of the big story, the event of significance that he alone would discover, sending his by-line across the newspapers of the world. The big story. It had become a vision for him. A hope that sustained him through all the lonely meals of bad spaghetti.

While Barney tried to attract his attention, Lawson fidgeted and juggled on his chair, tugging at his beard. The beard was short, like that of a British naval officer. It had recently become flecked with gray strands, and it made his face seem even rounder than it was, framing an expanse of whiteness mottled by tiny red veins like lines on a road map. Barney yelled again, with the same muffled effect. Lawson peered over at him with his sad watery eyes and then went back to tugging at his beard and fidgeting. Again Barney yelled.

Coming, coming, said Lawson without looking up from his typewriter. He tugged at his beard, fidgeted, and then made a sprinter's dash, pounding madly on the keys until he completed his article. With a flourish, he pulled the paper from the typewriter and then walked into the sunlight, blinking and stretching. He finally lumbered over to Barney with a wheezy little laugh. When Barney began muttering at him, Lawson decided to leave the mouth gag on until last. The first few knots came away easily but the others had been tied with all of Woody's drunken strength. Lawson began breathing harder in little gasps of stale alcohol. While he was wrestling with one of the knots, the door to room 30 opened just enough to reveal half of a large expressionless face peering at them through thick glasses. Barney saw the door open and knew that it was Mr. Thomas once again waiting for his chance to talk to Lawson. Mr. Thomas was the preacher from Kansas who rented room 30 on an annual basis even though he spent most of his time at his small mission up near Pleiku in the highlands. Mr. Thomas was always trying to get Lawson to write an article about his missionary work. He had decided that publicity was the only way he could get the extra donations he needed for the mission. The other missions in the area had received newspaper coverage. But then they were already large and wealthy to begin with, most of them being Baptist or some other equally established denomination. At first he had wanted to expand his mission, telling himself that it was God's will that he, the unheralded preacher from the small church in Kansas, should have the largest flock in all the Orient. As the war became more savage, the other missions moved in and expanded around him. His mission was in danger of extinction. The local people no longer came, and the buildings were falling into ruin. He had begun to offer prayers that asked for a sign, anything that pointed the way in which to do His will.

The sign did come. It came in the form of Lawson, reeking of drink and trying to get into the wrong room. In his drunken state, Lawson had mistaken Mr. Thomas's room for his own. That meeting had begun an unchanging dialogue. Mr. Thomas had offered silent prayers of thankfulness when he discovered that the boozy hulk trying to break down his door was a newspaperman. For a paper in New York. No less. The occupational permutations of being merely a free-lancer did not trouble Mr. Thomas, who knew nothing of the news business. He was sure that Lawson was simply the messenger who would take His word to the people. And if messengers came in drunken shambling forms, then so be it. There were times when He worked in strange ways. Lawson had been immediately pulled into room 30, and pushed into a chair, where he was barraged with desperate tales of the good work being done by the small mission near Pleiku. Tales—he was told—that would make wonderful newspaper stories. Through the veil of his drunkenness, Lawson made an editorial decision that the tales were lousy copy. He got up to leave, explaining that he needed a drink. Mr. Thomas pushed him back into the chair and refused to let him leave. Normally Mr. Thomas was a silent, pious man who spent his life frowning upon the weaknesses of the flesh. Second only to fornication among these weaknesses was alcohol. It was the devil's very blood. But this was different, he told himself, for Satan had disguised this messenger, who would take his plight to the multitudes in the form of a drunkard. Mr. Thomas would not be fooled by Satan.

Lawson was aware only of the fact that his host had bustled from the room, knocked on a nearby door and then breathlessly reappeared with a bottle of scotch. Excellent scotch. Lawson revised his editorial decision immediately. All night the scotch was bestowed, not poured. And only once when Lawson referred to it as holy water was the evening with his newfound friend in jeopardy. Lawson left at dawn, vowing banner headlines. He awoke with no recollection of Pleiku or anything else. When pressed about the progress of the article, he informed Mr. Thomas that his editors had requested more information. However he was presently too busy on other, more pressing articles to obtain that information. The other, more pressing articles were suddenly forgotten when another bottle of scotch appeared through the open door of Mr. Thomas's room. Mr. Thomas had gone out to buy it on the black market from a street vendor. The thought of searching out alcohol had sent him into a fit of prayerful remorse. But he told himself that Satan must be met on his own ground. When Lawson awoke the next morning he remembered much more of the conversation. This was not due to a lesser amount of drinking or to divine guidance. It was due to the watered-down scotch that the black-market vendors had sold Mr. Thomas. The black-market vendors had removed nearly half of the original scotch with a hypodermic needle that had pierced the bottle top and the cork, sucking out the scotch without leaving a trace. Water was then added by the same hypodermic needle. The scotch that was sucked out was then sold to the cheap bars, where it was also watered down. On the following morning, Lawson had remembered much more than the conversation. He remembered one searing revelation of his own. Lawson's revelation was that here, in this very room, was the source of free booze for the rest of his days!

Mr. Thomas was on the verge of despair as he peered out at Lawson untying Barney. After nearly six months and countless bottles of scotch, the Lord's article had still not been written. He had tried approaching other newsmen as they came through the battle areas near his mission. But none of them was interested. Mr. Thomas had begun to feel like a salesman for God, existing on commission alone in a barren sales area. More sources of donations were becoming a matter of survival and his only hope was this fat, beery man who cried out women's names during the night.

Barney watched Mr. Thomas approach and settled back to watch the familiar dialogue. Lawson was unable to untie the one key knot so Mr. Thomas offered his assistance explaining that he just happened to be passing. Barney talked into his mouth gag. None of his words could be understood. How is our article doing said Barney in his mind. How is the article coming along asked Mr. Thomas.

Fine, thought Barney. I sent the draft of it off to New York but my editors asked for more information. Lawson's brow furrowed as he wrestled with another knot. I thought the last draft was nearly there, he said. But New York wants clarification on certain points.

Clarification? On what? asked Mr. Thomas. Lawson managed to loosen the knot. I'll have to look for it, he said. It's in my room. Unless it's been thrown out.

Goodness gracious, laughed Barney into his mouth gag. I had no idea it was half past kingdom come. I'm late, I'm late for a very important date. Lawson muttered something about his watch being slow these days. Have you got the time, he asked. Nearly nine o'clock, said Mr. Thomas. Lawson's eyes widened. Nine? So late? My god I'm late. Have to meet Zorthian over at JUSPAO. Not every day one gets a personal briefing from Zorthian you know, he said dusting himself off. Mr. Thomas nodded in desperate agreement as he was left struggling with the one knot that would not come undone. Lawson headed for the stairs, walking slow enough to allow Mr. Thomas the time to catch up. When the last knot came loose.

Barney was left to unwind the ropes and the flag and remove the gag from his mouth. He returned the flag to the Poles on the fourth floor. It was accepted in silence and Barney felt no compulsion to intrude upon that silence. Later in the morning he decided it was time for a talk with Milligan. Milligan must know more than he had let on about D. Martinez. Halfway down the stairs he stopped and wondered why he was going to talk to Milligan when D. Martinez had a room on the same floor that he did. He returned to the courtyard and walked softly up to room 39. When he was very close he stopped. The faintest sound of her voice came through the door. The melody of a song— Barney thought it was *Scarborough Fair*—could be heard. It came a few lines at a time as if she were rehearsing. He waited almost afraid to breathe. Then he knocked on the door and immediately regretted that he had knocked so timidly. The singing stopped. Who is it, she called out. Barney hesitated, afraid that she would not open the door. Again she asked who was there.

It's the colonel's driver ma'am, he said in his thickest Texas drawl.

The door opened immediately. Barney was not sure if it was fear or anger that came to her eyes. Before she could slam the door, he leaned against it with his shoulder. I'm sorry, but I didn't think you'd open the door if I said it was the third act from last Tuesday's show calling to pay his respects. There was no response. The same frightened innocence that he had seen backstage now confronted him. Your name is Donna isn't it? he asked awkwardly. She nodded. I was hoping that perhaps I could talk to you for a little while. I mean, we're neighbors. Barney tried to smile but felt even more ridiculous. Please go away, she said.

Who were the men in here last night? The question hit her with a jolt. Barney was suddenly possessed by that same fear that she might go to pieces in front of him. There were no men, she replied. There were, said Barney, the two who came during curfew. Then he paused, watching her eyes flash inward, and then look up at him waiting for what was to come next. They were the ones who came to get Isaacs, he said. Something seemed to give way, as if her breath had momentarily left her body. Finally, without looking up, she asked him to come into her room.

Inside the room, he waited for her to talk. She sat on the edge of the bed, her eyes darting from him to the floor. Barney looked around the room. In the shuttered gloom there were the trappings of the profession. A guitar case lay in one corner. A makeup kit and dance costumes were on the desk. A small metal trunk lay nearby, laden with sheet music, clothes and a few records. On the inside of the open lid of the trunk were several photographs. The largest photograph was a portrait of a young man. Next to it was a photograph of the same man with slightly longer hair holding a microphone and singing before a huge outdoor audience. Behind him, looking much younger, almost like a teen-ager, was the woman who now sat on the bed opposite him. She too was holding a microphone and singing. There were other photographs. One was of Donna clowning with another singing group. The name on the drum said *Jefferson Airplane*.

The photographs were pinned onto the faded red velvet that lined the inside of the small trunk. Built into the velvet lid were five slender scabbards. In two of the scabbards were long glistening knives, the kind used by old-time vaudeville knife throwers. The other three were empty. The lid of the trunk suddenly slammed shut. He had not seen her hand reach out toward the lid. He found himself staring into the ferocious dark eyes of the performer that resided within this woman. No longer were there the timid doelike glances darting out at him. I didn't know you were a knife thrower too, he said. She told him the knives came with the trunk. It was a trunk that had been passed down in her family. Her dark hair had fallen around her eyes only to be swept away with a flick of her head. Images of the sensuous silhouette with long hair flailing like a veil passed for a moment through Barney's memory. For your own sake, she said, you must never mention that you saw Isaacs here. Barney chuckled. For *my* sake? She responded with a quiet ferocity that he had never seen in her. Yes. For your sake.

Why did the other men come and call for him, he asked. A major and a brigade chauffeur don't come into Saigon halfway through curfew just to offer the colonel a ride home. She said nothing for just long enough to tell him that she would lie. I don't know, she said. Barney walked across the room. You know this would make a great subject for the next show. I mean it's way better than the water tower. Barney was talking in a rapid angry voice but something inside him was saying Don't be a fool; don't say it; if you hurt her now it's over. The colonel and the lady, he said throwing his arms open. And then he stopped. She had looked away, no longer possessed of the flashing eyes. There was a long silence. I don't know what it's all about, she said finally. All I know is that there are a lot of murders happening.

Murders? Barney was taken by surprise. You mean snipers. Or enemy attacks. No, she said. I mean murders.

She told him all that she knew. That Isaacs had told her a dozen or more people had been killed on the base and they were sure it was not the enemy. Only a few people knew about it, she said, and now he was one of them. It was information that she had sworn to keep secret. Then why are you telling me? Barney asked. Because you need to know what kind of game you're playing in. They will do anything to keep all this quiet. And you wouldn't even be a battle statistic, she said. Then she told him that she had to rehearse for the performance tomorrow night. It was as polite a way of asking him to leave as she was capable of. The fuse of a dozen unasked questions burned out as Barney tried to leave her as anything but the interrogator he had been. He apologized for intruding.

He thought she smiled for a moment. Except onstage, he had never seen her smile. When Barney left the room he went over to one of the benches in the courtyard. He spent almost an hour listening to the faint chorus of *Scarborough Fair* that occasionally was obliterated by the tonal chatter of the Vietnamese cleaning ladies. He wanted to go up to her door and tell her that the reason he was asking all those questions was simply to keep himself from doing something ridiculous like saying that he was in love with her. That was all. It was that simple. But shouts of *Take it off!* and *More!*

ricocheted from his memory, for he was just a part of her audience, paying homage to the whirling silhouette that had remained on a stage during their entire talk. The homage had turned to anger whenever he allowed himself to picture her lying there in that room with Isaacs. Why Isaacs? It was a petal picked by an iron fist. He felt a bitterness which he realized he had no right to feel.

Downstairs, in Milligan's Talent Agency, Barney inquired, as discreetly as was possible with Milligan, what was known about the woman in room 39. Immediately he realized it was a mistake. Milligan had a way of turning discreet talk into a broadcast. He answered Barney in a voice that echoed down the hall. Look son, you don't worry about the women. Just shape up your act, huh? I've seen too many of you studs come in with a fast laugh and then burn up in a month by fucking your way through the chorus line. Milligan got louder as he continued. He always talked louder when he talked to people who depended on him for employment. These days he was almost always talking loudly. As one of the most important talent outfits in Saigon many of the army club bookings passed through his office. The war had saved Milligan. Alimony payments and gambling debts had forced him to close his fading New York office. He had arrived in Saigon early enough to establish contacts on the army bases and put money in the right hands. Now for the first time since television began he was a success. His only regret was that he was not younger. Listen to me, he would tell all those who would listen. I know what I'm talking about. Success and youth are what this life is all about. It means you can screw all night with some classy dame and then order champagne in the morning. I know. Listen to me.

Barney did not want to endure another of Milligan's lectures. But before he could extricate himself from the office, his problem was compounded by the arrival of Shel-

don, who stood mopping his brow. Howya doin' son? he
greeted Barney. You're here to steal some of my jokes I can
tell. He gave Milligan a big wink and straightened his bow
tie. You tell him, yelled Milligan. You been around. This
kid here is chasing after skirt again. Room 39. The wingy
one. Christ, said Sheldon with professional concern. Do
yourself a favor kid. Go out and get some of that Tu Do
tail. Do anything but don't go bananas over something like
that. I seen it happen a dozen times. A kid with future starts
pokin' something from the same show and pretty soon it's a
wrap for one of them. Don't mess with dames in the business. They'll get ya so you won't be able to tell the dirt
chute from the manhole. Get something stable I tell ya. So
you can concentrate on your timing. That's what this business is all about kid. Look at Hope. Look at Jack Benny.
Timing I tell ya.

Sheldon stood between Barney and the door. His voice
carried down the main corridor. Barney had visions of
Woody lurking just around the door silently laughing to
himself. But Sheldon was only in his warm-up. And something else, he said jabbing a finger at Barney. Ya better quit
insulting the army brass. Lay off those colonel jokes. Milligan took his feet down from the desk and seized upon the
issue. See kid. I been telling you. Other people are noticing
it. And if the colonel comes to me with the finger, you're
out. I ain't risking all I built up here so you can pop off at
the brass. Yeah, said Sheldon, whatsa matter with you? It's
like standing up and saying the theater owner is a baboon.
Ya never insult the paycheck. I dunno what's with you
young guys. Insults. Smartass routines. If you wanna insult
someone try the sergeants. Or the cooks. You know, food
jokes are always great in the Army.

Colonel jokes are better, said Barney. Milligan began to
look worried. Kid you don't understand. *You* don't under-

stand, interrupted Barney. The audience here is different. Maybe you haven't realized that, he said to Sheldon. I realize that someone's paying the shot for you to get up onstage, said Sheldon indignantly. The least you can do is show some respect. If ya wanna insult someone insult the enemy, the goddam gooks.

And what'll that get you? asked Barney. A lot of yawns. They don't give a damn about insulting the enemy. And how the hell do you make food jokes when those dumb bastards get fresh lobster and drink cold beer out in the field before they get shot up? They don't give a damn about food jokes or enemy jokes. But they love it when you take a shot at the brass. It's a different war gentlemen. This ain't Hitler versus the rest of us you know.

Milligan looked at him sourly. What's your problem with the colonel?

He's stealing my audience, said Barney with a sly look. He's what? asked Milligan. He's stealing my audience, repeated Barney. He's sending them out to get their asses shot off. We'd be playing to an empty house if he got his way.

Milligan was not sure if the remark was to be taken seriously. He decided it was. He jumped to his feet and pounded the table. Well goddammit that's his job, he yelled. Your job is to make 'em laugh and his job is to get their asses blown off while they're still laughing. And I don't want any act that I book to start telling the brass how to run the goddam war. Understand?

Sheldon and Milligan exchanged withering glances. I dunno kid, said Sheldon. Bob Hope would never do what you're doing.

. . . . . Bob Hope?

Isaacs

SEVEN

. . . . . *Ladies and gentlemen: Bob Hope!*
. . . Christ I don't believe it, says Snider the photographer,
sitting back in the big comfortable chair and watching the
Bob Hope show on the television set. Snider has not made it
to Danang. After waiting nearly all day at the airport, he
finally took off in a C-130 jammed with grunts being flown
to the highlands for their turn as front-line fodder. The
plane lumbers into the air and an hour later the hydraulic
system lets go with a roar. Some think it is ground fire and a
flash of terror goes through the grunts. Snider is ready with
the 12-millimeter lens at .95. Just in case. The plane lurches
across the sky and makes an emergency landing at Nha
Trang on the coast. Prayers are muttered as the plane
touches down but they are said too early. The airstrip is
under mortar attack. Snider wonders if this will be *the* shot.
His cameras are ready. He watches the faces and sees the
sweat and the strain as the sound of shells comes nearer. He
sees terror, and terror is marketable. Terror makes the best
photographs. Then suddenly there is blackness. Absolute
blackness as the tiny lights on the ceiling go out. Yelling
breaks loose along the length of the plane until the copilot
at the front shines a flashlight and demands silence. He tells
them that the electrical system has failed. It is being fixed he

says. Well open the fucking doors says a voice in the blackness. We can't snaps the copilot. The hydraulic system has failed. Remember? And then the flashlight is gone and suddenly Snider feels what he has never felt before. He feels fear! Sitting there in darkness listening to the muttering of soldiers about to crack, he begins to wonder if the shells aren't coming too close. Hail Marys are murmured in the inferno of stale humid air and Snider listens closely to the words. He is afraid because for the first time he can see nothing. He can photograph nothing. The blackness is total and it renders him helpless. Never before has he been helpless. Always there has been a candle or shell flash. Always there was the magic wand of his camera that waved away all fear. Fear was what went to the magnet of the other men's faces. But now he can see none of this and he realizes he is imprisoned in a metal tube sitting atop thousands of gallons of fuel that with just one shell could make all the light he would ever see. He is terrified. And he will never recover from that terror. Not even after he begins talking to the man next to him and discovers he is talking to Angeloff from LIFE magazine. And not even after Angeloff invites him to stay at the LIFE villa for the night. There in the walled security and the gleam of the teak floors, they dine in a way that Snider is not used to dining. They talk of the other correspondents who live in the villa and of their experiences in the war. And then on the tiny television set that someone has left for safekeeping they tune in to Bob Hope. And for a moment Snider forgets all about his terror and sits blankly in front of the image of the famous American comedian who soon will be coming to Vietnam. He wonders if there would be a LIFE cover in it. He decides there would not be. For Bob Hope has entertained the troops since Hitler was around, so at best it would be a feature story. Snider begins to lose interest. . . . . .

. . . . . But Sheldon is chewing harder on his cigar and pounding the side of the old television set in the lobby of the Catinat whenever the image flickers. Christ what timing, he mutters to himself. At first he is worried that Bob Hope is already in Vietnam and that this is his show for the troops. But then Sheldon realizes that this is just another rerun of one of Bob's old shows. He is not scheduled to arrive for a month at least. Sheldon has waited for years to meet Hope. The timing of that man. Incredible. He kicks the set again as the image flickers . . . but it is not the television set that is at fault. There is a storm to the north of Saigon and the storm makes Bob Hope flicker all across the nation. For Bob Hope is at this moment simply a large band of magnetic videotape that is whirling through an electrical playback head at seventeen thousand feet in the night sky. The videotape is being played in an old Super Constellation aircraft that has been specially outfitted to bring television to the war. Every night the plane circles high above the jungles and swamps. Again and again it flies the same elliptical pattern over the darkened midsection of the country. If blood flows in the swamps at sea level, there is nothing but the best in family entertainment at seventeen thousand feet, pushed out of hundreds of thousands of watts . . . . .

. . . . . into the unnoticed flickering television set at the Bon Accueil Bar just off Tu Do Street where Lawson has taken off his new elephant-skin shoes and is polishing them on the thighs of the latest bar girl he has decided to marry. Lawson is in his finest form, drunk on the scotch of Christian public relations, roaring at Mr. Thomas that it is a miracle! And a miracle it is for Mr. Thomas had begun his mendicant's search for the *Herald Tribune* article by saying that there was only enough money to buy one drink. And now bottles later, Lawson is roaring that it is a miracle equaled only by Christ feeding the multitudes with five loaves and three fishes. From one little drink: a river of scotch! yells Lawson slipping and falling against his latest fiancee who keeps saying You number one. Number one. Mr. Thomas is near tears at what he has wrought. He can no longer control Lawson and he begins to pray in the midst of the tumult. The Vietnamese bar girls will not leave him alone for they see that he is paying for the watered whiskey of the bearded drunken man. They sit beside him, putting their hands on his lap, saying Same-same. He removes their hands and tearfully begins to tell them of Christ. But they do not understand and begin to curse him with epithets they have learned from the troops. Lawson roars out his latest headline—*Gooks and Baptists Overrun Mission!*—into the bosom of his betrothed who giggles as Mr. Thomas tries to get up but something within him gives way. He sits on the floor, unnoticed, reeking of the spilled scotch and sobbing like a baby. . . . . .

. . . . . But not all of the scene is visible to the distinguished gentleman standing in the darkness of a doorway behind the bar. The man decides not to enter. It would not be proper to be seen there on this evening. He is the part owner of the bar. But his name can never be attached to anything commercial. This bar and the one outside the Bien Hoa airbase are officially in the names of his Vietnamese partners. Not a hint of scandal can be attached to the name of Brigadier J. A. Mosby, Upper Canada College; Royal Military College; Dispatches; D.S.O. It is simply an investment like any other. He had purchased his share in the venture from a Canadian colonel whose tour of duty ended a year ago. It was, said the colonel, the sort of investment that would ensure a retirement of decent means. Much better than the pittance paid by the Army. The remark had struck a chord in Mosby. He had always wondered how a man could afford to live like a true officer once retired. The colonel had been proven correct. It is indeed a wise investment. . . . . .

. . . . . and across the dusty plain outside Bien Hoa toasts in honor of the brigadier are called out from the bouncing old car loaded with beer. Woody and Barney are off to take care of the war's business. Woody is in a particularly strange mood because once again he has told his friends and fellow officers that it is time to piss on the altar of peace.

He has been ordered to compile reports on the violation of the peace.

Peace? They have set out to make Peace where there is none because until Barney unlocked the secret, Violation Report duty had been an arduous and humiliating experience for the Canadian officer assigned to it. In earlier days when a form of peace existed in Vietnam there was meaning and purpose in reporting the cease-fire violations. But once the war began in earnest, it became a useless exercise carried on for the sake of form alone. By the time Woody arrived in Vietnam, the original form of reporting violations had been discarded. However, Brigadier Mosby occasionally decided to reactivate the Violation Report. He found it to be an effective form of discipline much like a teacher who makes errant pupils fill a blackboard with useless phrases.

But Barney thought he detected another justification. Mosby was almost unnaturally interested in cease-fire violations around Bien Hoa, where the 173rd Airborne was based. Bien Hoa was only an hour's drive from Saigon. Mosby studied reports of this area with fanatical interest.

Every detail from minor stupidities to major atrocities was minutely examined. Mosby's obsession with the area began to make sense to Barney when he heard rumors of a Canadian officer owning property in Bien Hoa. A lot of property. Bars. Brothels. Which was all there was to own in Bien Hoa. Barney began to believe the rumors when he heard that Mosby flew into a rage whenever the commander of the 173rd Airborne, Colonel Isaacs, declared Bien Hoa off limits to his men. Mosby would stride around his office playing with his mustache and muttering Stupid ass! while his distinguished face grew florid. Without the soldiers of the 173rd, there were no customers for the bars and brothels and in Mosby's mind this had come to be the worst offense of all. He was sure that Isaacs was doing it on purpose. Out of spite. But he would show Isaacs. He would dispatch Woody with orders to find violations of the peace. At Bien Hoa, Woody would stand in the deafening roar of the jet fighter planes and walk through the black smoke or mortar attacks asking if anyone knew of any violations of the peace. And then get roaring drunk.

Mosby would send a copy of the Violation Report to Isaacs, intending it to be a stern warning. A rap on the knuckles if you will sir. But Isaacs seemed to enjoy it all. The last Violation Report had been returned to Mosby with additional peace violations written across it in Isaacs' own handwriting. There was also a notation saying that further violations could be learned by contacting the brigade press-relations office. Mosby had walked around his office muttering to himself for an entire afternoon.

It was Barney who perfected the Violation Report system. With Woody, he set up the Yankee Spy network. It was a handpicked team of some of the best liars in the American Army. No lie was too great and no gossip was too petty for the Yankee Spies. They were capable of inventing any story or twisting any truth.

Barney had suggested that it was only fair for the Americans to have a chance to report their own cease-fire violations. In a land of no peace, the least the peace-keepers could do was let the violators lie about their own violations. Otherwise the truth would be told and not believed. Woody had pondered the swamp of his friend's logic.

Barney contacted some of the soldiers he knew at the base. The soldiers had been ecstatic at the thought of sitting around and telling lies. They soon decided that they were engaged in the opposite of espionage. Instead of ferreting out already secret details of the war, they were making up the details, declaring them secret, and then proclaiming them to the world. Barney told them it was a good old-fashioned American way of spying.

So they called themselves the Yankee Spies. Barney was the spymaster. Like all spies, they had their price. Three cases of Canadian beer per Violation Report. The Canadian beer was the only real beer in Vietnam. All the American beer in Vietnam had a reduced alcoholic content. To keep the troops sober. Canadian beer was the delicacy of the war with a 5 per cent alcohol content. For the sake of the extra percentage, the Yankee Spies created lies and shaded the truth in a manner that put the official army briefings to shame.

With three cases of Molson beer from Canada loaded into the old black Citroën, Woody and Barney drove out to Bien Hoa. It had been arranged that they were to meet the Yankee Spies at the base.

As Barney and Woody approached the trailer they could hear the music and fits of laughter. The trailer was parked behind a group of wooden buildings, not far from the tents where the soldiers slept. On the side of the trailer were the words Yankee Spies. For several minutes they listened to the hooting and watched the trailer shake. Then after one sustained outburst, Barney banged his fist on the door. The door swung open and Barney shouted into the cloud of cigar smoke. Okay you idiots, what are you doing laughing at your own jokes? A dozen voices shot greetings from the trailer. But suddenly a hand reached out and grabbed his shoulder and the laughter died. Barney looked up and found himself staring into the cold blue eyes of a man he had not seen in the trailer before. The infamous Sergeant Lover, Barney said with surprise. Sergeant Lover was the oldest sergeant in the brigade. He had fought in the Second World War when most of the Yankee Spies were not even born. He was known as a tough, almost suicidal fighter and a wild companion for a tour of the bars and brothels. Long ago, the younger soldiers had stopped calling him by his real name which was Jones. In the middle of one particularly lecherous evening he became Sergeant Lover. The name had stuck ever since.

The other Yankee Spies began shouting their assurances to Barney. Sergeant Lover's okay man, said LeRoy a black member of the Yankee Spies. He's the biggest liar of us all. He's been doing it for years. The others laughed until Woody slung the first case of Canadian beer into the trailer. Amid the scramble for the beer, LeRoy kept yelling that they did indeed have some fine violations. Violations like you would not believe.

The Yankee Spies began to settle back and drink the beer as LeRoy explained the serious business of lying.

The thing to remember in all this lying and truth telling, said LeRoy, is that things are so fucked up in this war that no one knows what's gospel and what's bullshit. And that's where the terrible Yankee Spies have been doing some innovating in this here violation business.

We, proclaimed LeRoy with a flourish, are gonna tell
the truth! *Whoooooooeeee* yelled LeRoy. The call was his
trademark. *Whoooooooeeeee!*

There was more hooting, especially from the eighteen-
year-old with the two bullet scars on his stomach. The beer
was having more effect on him. *The truth!* he yelled with
tears of laughter coming to his eyes. The others began
laughing at him. The eighteen-year-old with the two bullet
scars could not stop laughing. You see, said LeRoy finally
prevailing, the idea really came from the terrible Sergeant
Lover over here. He got inspired during one of his whorehouse car washes. And somewhere between the car wash
and the penicillin the terrible lying Sergeant Lover decides
to rifle the files of the press officers.

Hell, drawled Sergeant Lover, I didn't rifle anything. I
just went to those forlorn idiots who serve as public relations men for the brass. I just asked to look at all their press
releases for the last few months. Said the boys would like to
know good news. To cheer us all up. Hell, I came away
with what must have been four pine trees' worth of paper.
He motioned to a large pile of paper. When he talked the
others fell silent. Not once was there the need to raise his
quietly drawling voice in order to prevail. Barney watched
him closely, wondering why he had joined the Yankee
Spies. He was an unlikely member. In the faint light, the
creases on his face seemed even deeper. Across one cheek
was a smooth horizontal scar, about two inches long. One
rumor said it was a bayonet scar from Germany. Another
rumor said a woman knifed him in Korea. Once when
asked about it, he had just grinned and said it was a
bayonet-carrying Korean woman in Germany.

And soooo! said LeRoy his eyes dancing, what we are
going to do is choose the best of these press releases. Most
of what they say is made up or written in such a way as to

make the generals look like geniuses. Now when it gets into the Violation Report it will come back to the same generals, who will automatically deny it all as being lies.

Where everything is true everything is lies.

The Yankee Spies had taken note of the press release from the computer people in Saigon, who proudly announced that the surrounding area was now 99.9 per cent pacified. Their press release came out at the same time as the one from the Airborne. It announced the biggest military action in all Vietnam. Right in the same area.

One after the other the absurdities came rolling out. Some of them were passed over. Others became the genesis of Barney's future comedy routines. In the Yankee Spy sessions he often sat back and listened with professional interest. It was like being at a rewrite session among mad gag writers. And there was a glorious sense of absurdity to it all. Everything made sense, yet nothing made sense. Everything was tales of life and death, yet nothing seemed important there in the beer-drenched laughter of the Yankee Spy trailer. The only aim was enough laughter to drown out the noise of the war. For it was a time where all the proper words were marched out—Victory, Honor, Truth—but they had been used to fit so many different meanings, for so many different purposes, that in the end they had no meaning at all.

LeRoy was telling the story about the scout dogs. In one of the press releases it was announced that scout dogs were now being used to track down the enemy. No further mention of the scout dogs was made in any later press releases. LeRoy and Sergeant Lover had inquired and learned of the celebration at Long Thanh. One night after a long day of sniffing out the enemy, the dogs and their masters stopped at the friendly village of Long Thanh. The dogs were locked in a local farmer's animal pen. They were unusually quiet that night, not even barking during the celebration held by the villagers. The next morning, the soldiers discovered the reason the dogs had not barked. The dogs had been the cause of the celebration. The dogs had been cooked and turned into stew. The village was immediately declared an enemy area. The company commander radioed a message back to base. Operation terminated, said the message. The enemy has eaten our scouts.

EIGHT

Long after the others had left, Barney remained. The show at the Club was to begin just after sunset and Donna was scheduled to perform. To pass the time he sat in a parked jeep and watched the curious spectacle of Isaacs' baseball practice. Apart from winning battles, Isaacs' only other public passion was his baseball team. In every one of his commands, he had made a successful baseball team a matter of personal priority. This team was different from all others he had coached. It was made up entirely of Vietnamese boys between the ages of nine and thirteen. It was Isaacs' contention that if baseball could be exported to places like Cuba and Japan, it could also be grafted onto Vietnam. And he wanted to be the man to do it. Over the months, he had spent much of his free time training his team. It had not been easy. There were the problems of even finding boys who could be induced to play this game that seemed so alien to the Vietnamese. But when the parents of the first few boys were rewarded with jobs at the base, he soon had an abundance of human raw material to choose from. For weeks, silent staring Vietnamese could be seen outside the gates of the base thrusting forth the hands of equally silent children. Whenever a jeep appeared carrying anyone who looked important, the child would be yanked forward. On some days there were crowds of parents and children milling around the gate. It was later found that some of the children did not even belong to the adults who had been thrusting them toward any American who came from the base. The word had spread in the town that jobs were awarded in exchange for sending children off to engage in what seemed like a silly but harmless pastime. Every Vietnamese suddenly became a talent scout and every boy was snatched from the streets.

The training had been difficult. More than once, the soldiers who had been pressed into subordinate coaching positions had wondered how Isaacs could show such patience on the baseball field and so little patience off it. It took months of careful effort simply to overcome the language barrier and to get the boys not to burst into fits of laughter when they were expected to hit the ball. But with careful repetition Isaacs had shown them the endless details of playing baseball: the holding of the bat; the way to kneel when fielding a ball; the throwing of a curve ball. After a year, even his most vehement detractors would admit that something resembling a baseball team was taking shape. The other coaches had recently noticed he was beginning to pressure the boys to perform more than ever before. What none of them knew was the extent of Isaacs' plans for the team. He had quietly been maneuvering through channels for the team to show up at the American embassy for the Vietnamese New Year celebration. The idea had met with great favor in the embassy. Happy children's faces were always good for photographs. And the joyous alloy of the two cultures could receive no better recommendation than a children's baseball team. At first Isaacs had been acutely aware of the publicity values. But then he gradually began to resent the intrusion of outside requests upon his team. Before anything else, it was *his* creation. He took great satisfaction in watching his team begin to function and in comparing its performance with its original ineptitude. And as he began to view it as an extension of himself, he slowly and almost gently began to impose his own will to win upon the boys. The boys were unaware of when determination replaced joy. But they knew their attitude toward the game had changed. Isaacs had learned their names and kept a file on their performance and their background. He listened patiently to pidgin English explanations of personal problems and took care that the parent-employees understood the importance of what their sons were doing. Every evening was practice time and after the first month no one was allowed to be late. Isaacs himself was the only one ever to miss the practices and then it was only because of the more pressing problems of the war.

In the final weeks before Tet, the Vietnamese New Year, the words Kanh to Minh to Tan constantly rang out across the baseball field. Again and again Isaacs hit the ball to Kanh, the tenacious little infielder whose baseball glove seemed to dwarf him. Kanh was the tiniest member of the team. Yet there was a will in the boy that Isaacs immediately recognized. Every ball hit to him was a personal challenge and even if he had to throw himself in front of the ball, it was not going to get past him. He would seize the ball and drill it to Minh, the big chubby second baseman who was capable of bursting into tears when Isaacs lectured him. Minh was the most emotional member of the team. Tan, over on first base, was the coolest. He was tall for his age, towering over tiny Kanh. There was speculation that somewhere in his ancestry there was one of the French soldiers who had occupied the country when it was known as Indo-China. Tan had impressed Isaacs with his sure control of almost every situation. When the time came to choose a captain from among the fifteen boys, he had decided that Tan's name should be favored.

On the flat plain beside the airstrip, the baseball team became a collection of racing silhouettes against the cloudless twilight. The sky had turned from pale blue to scarlet, and the cut-out figures formed a strange dance group moving to the cadence of their own tonal chatter and the curt orders from Isaacs. *Kanh to Minh to Tan!* Barney had watched them from the distant jeep until the faint curl of cigarette smoke caused him to turn and confront Sergeant Lover. He was standing with one foot up on the jeep, peering out from under a combat helmet that somehow made him appear more menacing. Barney wondered how he could have arrived so quietly. Sergeant Lover did not look at Barney. He continued staring at the baseball team and it was not until Barney had turned his back on him that he spoke.

He's a dangerous man right now, said Sergeant Lover with his soft drawl. I thought you and Isaacs were friends, said Barney. Sergeant Lover replied quietly that yes, that was certainly true. He and Isaacs did go back a long way. A long way.

Then what are you doing joining up with all of our foolishness? The Yankee Spies? Barney's questions were almost taunts but the cold eyes under the edge of the helmet never left the baseball field. I'm a beer drinker, drawled Sergeant Lover. For a while only the chatter of the players was heard.

I ain't exactly joining up, he continued. Don't you ever go making that mistake. Because that bastard and I were saving each other's hides before some of these runny-nosed soldiers around here were born. But it's different now. I've been around him long enough to know what's coming up. And pretty soon he's gonna go out and do something that'll get a lot of us killed. I know it. And I don't want to end up as rat food on the side of some hill just 'cause he's feeling his age.

Barney looked for the edge of a grin which would tell him that it was not meant to be taken seriously. That this man with the fearful reputation as a fighter without nerves was only making a joke. But there was just the cold blue eyes and the flinty voice. You gotta remember, said Sergeant Lover, that I was a sergeant in Korea when he was just a greenhorn lieutenant. Well now he's a colonel and I'm still out carving new assholes. But you know something? Up till a little while ago, we could both pitch off all that damn braid and stripes and go out on some fearful sessions. God I tell you! What we did to the whorehouses from here to Thailand and back. We had us some times he and I. 'Cause like I said, we do go back a ways. He saved my ass in Korea and I saved his enough to keep him from getting cashiered right out of the Army. He was forever having to fight his way out of screw-ups that he should never have got into. There was always some colonel yelling at him for trying to push too far ahead or else not retreating when he was ordered. They yelled first and then gave him medals afterward. But it was all a joke to him. One time we were frozen into some forlorn little shithole village on the way to the Yalu. It was so cold that anything with oil in it froze. Guns. Trucks. Everything. And this one night we burned every piece of furniture we could find just to stay alive. For the whole goddam night we stayed awake 'cause we were scared of having to be chipped out of the bunker in the morning. And all night we talked and shadow-boxed just to keep from going into the ether. All he could talk about was how the colonel and generals had got the rotten luck of the draw. With a crummy little war like Korea. He kept on saying that you only get one good shot at a war when you're in command. Everything else is when you're either too young or retired. If you get a chance at taking El Alamein, or Iwo Jima or Normandy, you're lucky. You have a chance with history. But who gives a shit about the poor idiot who takes Pusan? Who's going to remember? He was standing there— a greenhorn lieutenant with his breath coming out in clouds and freezing all across his face. Who's going to remember? He said it again and again.

And I never heard anything more about all that until nearly a year ago. I was in his office and we got to talking about some stupid little village down toward Vung Tau. He started to explain all the tactical support he had lined up and how he was sending in the sappers, and the way that two companies were going to swing around to form part of a pincer. On and on he went, almost like he was talking to himself. Until finally I looked at him, and said shit, who's gonna remember all this effort in a year's time? I was just kidding but I swear to god he went purple. He started yelling at me that I was an asshole and that I didn't know anything about history. I tell you, he was about to put his fist through the wall. Never talked to him since. And that stupid little village down toward Vung Tau was finally taken but there was nothing left of his big pincer. Those two companies had to be scraped off the ground and put in a pail.

They were wiped out.

That was when I started thinking back to that night in Korea. Because suddenly *he* was now the poor bastard with some crummy little war on his hands. A war that people are gonna forget. No matter how many goddam press officers he's got trailing after him. There ain't no one who'll know one stupid little village from another and none of his battles are gonna get into the textbooks. But he's going scratchy trying to give the world a war to remember.

He turned to Barney for the first time. Have you seen the casualty lists for this goddam brigade? he demanded. Barney shook his head. Well look at them! If you can find them. . . . . .

. . . . . he says walking into the darkness as the laughter comes. It drifts across the flatness of the base in weak little bursts. For Sheldon is having another night of playing to hicks. Sweating in the heat of the spotlight, he tells them all what a great audience they are. But christ why do I get all the hicks? he wonders. One final mother-in-law joke and then kisses are blown as he bustles offstage. Hicks, he mutters. The same kind as you find in the strip shows back home.

In the audience is the sergeant from Isaacs' office, who gets up and leaves. He has work to do. But even if the sergeant did not have to arrange for the late-night briefing in Isaacs' office he would not stay for he has been bored by the jokes. They remind the sergeant too much of the kind he used to hear at the strip shows with the traveling carnivals. They were all hick comedians in those shows. With corny jokes. The sergeant from Isaacs' office hurries around the side of the building. In his arms are the sheets of paper that have been disgorged from the computer. It is the statistics on these sheets of paper that, in the late-night briefing, will be the cause of bitter arguments between Isaacs and the advisers from Saigon.

A bulbous little figure emerges from a backstage door as the sergeant hurries past. It is the fat comedian, wheezing and sweating in the cool air. Christ, says the comedian with his Brooklyn accent, ain't nothin' funny anymore? The sergeant from Isaacs' office does not reply. He hurries off into the darkness, for he is late and Isaacs will be furious. But suddenly the sergeant stops, for someone has called out to him. The voice if there was one comes in the blare of the second-rate band playing in the Club.

But Sheldon still wheezes in the cool air and wonders what the hell has happened to humor. Right into the crapper. That's what happened to it. He turns back toward the wooden stage door that is marked with graffiti and carved initials. On the door someone has scrawled something that makes him stop.

Pull the President's pants down! says the writing on the door.

Jesus! mutters Sheldon. What kind of joke is that?

. . . . .

. . . . . But somewhere back in America a man with steel-wool hair, dancing eyes and a nasal voice has told them all it is the best joke in the land. The man is Abbie Hoffman, who for a few years is famous across America. It is Hoffman's belief that the war can be laughed to an end. So the idea of the dropped presidential pants is hatched in Abbie Hoffman's mind.

But of course there are those (like Sheldon) who are infuriated by such an idea. Such talk is nonsense. Pull the President's pants down? Stupid. Outrageous!

Exactly! says Abbie Hoffman and across the land the word goes out. Outrage! The more outrageous the better and suddenly America turns into a seething theater of outrage. The streets become a stage and the pranks against the war spread blood and laughter. And no one is a better comic than Hoffman, who climbs the sacred steps of the New York Stock Exchange and throws dollar bills from the visitors' gallery. There in the temple, with thousands, millions, billions, being ticked off like beads of moving lights on a huge rosary board, the stockbrokers suddenly look up into their own particular heaven. For there it is!—money!

Floating down from above. As the floor of the Stock Exchange explodes with grappling bodies lunging after dollar bills a mad cackle breaks out from the visitors' gallery.

Outrage! intones the board of governors. The gallery is immediately enclosed in unbreakable glass to prevent the dread spectacle of brokers clawing one another for dollar bills. But what price outrage? Would the glass wall be erected if it were thousand-dollar bills being thrown? Bond coupons? Bank drafts? No one on the board ponders the cut-off point because they know that at a mere one dollar, the lunging bodies definitely constitute an outrage.

But the glass wall still does not silence the cackle that echoes throughout the marble hall and out across the land. It is the new trumpet of Jericho and one entire generation begins to cackle. The fortress of all that is sacred to the waging of the war is shaken by the mad roar of cackling. Words tremble in the foundation of their meaning. Duty. Honor. Sacrifice. And later, after the street riots of the Chicago Democratic convention, Abbie Hoffman will be charged with conspiracy. Conspiracy? Of course it is a conspiracy, he will cackle, showing up for his trial wearing judge's robes.

But for the moment it is the presidential pants that concern him. History might have been changed by a few dropped drawers here and there, he muses, asking out loud what would happen if Hitler's pants had suddenly fallen down in the Nuremberg Rally. Just imagine! Right there in the drum-driven, war-dripping, goose-stepping vortex of that vast spectacle! Through the miracle of gravity, with a thousand floodlights upon him, Adolf Hitler is instantly reduced from a demigod to a funny little man grappling with his pants. Duck-walking across the vast stage, frantically searching for refuge, clawing at the wayward breeches that have slipped all the way down to the jackboots. Yelling at the ashen, horror-struck Goebbels to do something. But nothing can be done. For no propaganda can rebuild the Fuehrer's image now that his white little bum is bobbing before the masses. Goebbels' wife begins to snicker and he punches her but it is too late for other snickers have begun. They build to a laughter from a million throats that echoes into Abbie Hoffman's mind as he ponders the image with glee. For who would have followed Hitler into war after laughing at him for having no pants?

And who would follow Lyndon Johnson, President and Commander in Chief, into war after having laughed at him for having no pants? So, determined to stop the Vietnam War by pulling down the presidential pants, Abbie Hoffman trundles off across the land with stolen airline tickets. The deed itself is unnecessary. For it is the era of the Movies and a million mental projectors click on, projecting an image of Lyndon Baines Johnson reviewing the troops as his pants fall down. At campuses and antiwar rallies the image takes hold. The audiences begin to laugh and the laughter becomes a cackle that follows Abbie Hoffman to the other side of America—to San Francisco, where the troops depart for Vietnam and where the sweet scent of revolution fills the Pacific air.

It is here in San Francisco that the antiwar rallies are the most creative and bittersweet of all. Standing to one side of a makeshift stage, Abbie Hoffman waits his turn to go on and once again project his gleeful outrage in psychedelic widescreen into the minds of the vast, stoned audience. On the stage is a woman with dark hair who sings a hypnotic song called *White Rabbit*. The woman is Grace Slick, a friend of Abbie Hoffman's, and her song is just becoming famous. *Feed your head!* The pounding cadence weaves into the multitude of stoned minds drawing them together and then keeps going. The *White Rabbit* goes out past the fringes of the huge crowd, to the helmeted, truncheon-carrying riot police who are made more ferocious by the sunglassed blackness where their eyes should be.

Not far from the riot police is a small group of middle-aged men. They are army officers on leave from Vietnam. The officers stand rooted in a stunned anger at what they see before them. One of the officers is Isaacs. The truth laid out before him is worse, far worse, than what he had imagined. For this is his first time in America in two years. He wonders where they came from in such a short time—these acres of grubby, stoned, rebellious hoboes. And where did the crew-cut, junior-prom convertible-polishers go to? They have vanished without a trace. And Isaacs feels that part of him has vanished too. Is this what we are fighting for? he asks. This weasely collection of commies, faggots and professors? Men looking like women? And women acting like men? Bitterness wells up inside Isaacs and he decides that he prefers the enemy at his front to the enemy behind him.

The pounding music finishes and on the stage a man with electric hair appears. He seems to be some sort of comedian. It is Abbie Hoffman, exhorting the multitudes with anarchistic wisecracks that sound to Isaacs like treason. Laughter breaks loose, acres of it, and Isaacs realizes that they are laughing at him. For Hoffman is making treasonous jokes about the Army and about the war. Isaacs can stand it no longer because the laughter is chipping away at his chances for the textbooks. Could Patton have become famous if the war in Europe had been reduced to a joke? Could Lord Nelson have sunk the French fleet with a shipload of dope-smoking long-haired freaks hanging blissfully from the mainsail? Isaacs begins to yell. Angry taunts break loose from his throat and he wades into the edges of the crowd cursing into the laughter. As his fellow officers pull him back, Isaacs shakes his fist at the distant figure on the stage. Later, over a silently bitter round of drinks, Isaacs will regret losing his temper. The next time it will be different, he vows.

The memory of the comedian mocking him on the distant stage stretches across Isaacs' mind like a welt. . . . . .

. . . . . but now, on this night in Bien Hoa with the meeting already started, Isaacs can think only of the goddam print-out sheets that should be here but are not. He hates these meetings with the computer-ridden military bureaucrats from Saigon. And the music from the Club reminds him that Donna is about to go onstage. Isaacs roars at one of the nervous aides, ordering him to go out and find the sergeant with the print-out sheets. The aide hurries out, pausing at the door to ask Bannon, the chauffeur, if he has seen the sergeant. Bannon is slouched down in the driver's seat of the colonel's car. Why would I see him? mutters Bannon without even looking up. The aide curses at Bannon, calling him a stupid hillbilly, and rushes into the darkness. The aide does not have to go far. For there in the soft breeze between the barracks is a fluttering white concertina of computer paper. The aide follows this trail of whiteness and then something he sees makes him run toward the shadows.

It is the sergeant. He lies sprawled facedown. From somewhere blood is flowing across the computer print-out sheets. The aide yells to the sergeant but there is no answer. Turning him over, the aide sees a hideous patch of redness bubbling from the sergeant's chest and throat. The aide draws back in horror and yells for help. But his shouting is swallowed up in the music and the cheers from the Club. No one hears his frantic cries because the girl with the long black hair has once again stepped onto the stage.

NINE

Shortly before the sergeant was found dead Barney arrived at the Club while Sheldon was still muttering to himself about the hicks. He mopped his face and hurried to keep up with Barney. Christ kid, I tell ya it's a forced march in there with those hicks, he wheezed. Sharpen up your timing kid. You're gonna need it. Timing. That's what makes 'em laugh. But it's strictly pearls thrown to swine in there with those goddam hicks. Even Bob Hope would be in trouble with those hicks. Barney paid no attention to Sheldon and left him wheezing at the doorway.

The darkness of the backstage area was broken by a torrent of racing figures as Sunshine prepared to go on. The leader of the group was pacing angrily, his white shoes like dots in the darkness. Where is that crazy broad? His voice cut through the strangled melody being played by the out-of-tune band on the other side of the curtain.

In a sliver of light at the far end of the backstage, Donna appeared. Look honey, yelled Sunshine's leader, I don't care how much of a star you are in this dump, I don't want to have to go looking for you again when it's time to go on. Understand? She nodded with the same expression of silent fright that Barney had seen before. Barney felt suddenly protective. He wanted to go over to the man and shake him loose from the hairpiece he was now fussing with. When Barney reached the other side of the backstage area she was not there. He searched through the darkness, coming to a door that had been left slightly open. Beyond it was the distant runway. The jet fighters were hurtling through the last wedge of twilight, the red flames of their afterburners pushing up into the dark of the sky. Someone, somewhere was in trouble. In some distant jungle someone would be praying, screaming for the fighters. On the runway other planes waited to take off, their lights blinking malevolently in the blackness. From somewhere not far away came the soft deadly *whoomph* of mortar fire. Barney walked through the grass to a wire fence. There was no one in sight. From the Club the sound of the slightly out-of-tune band could be heard when the fighter planes were not taking off. Barney stood beside the fence surrounded by the music and the roar of the planes.

The one sound washed over the other until a different noise suddenly cut through the music. It was a human cry of some sort. A sharp jagged cry. It came from somewhere beyond the building and was immediately smothered by the roar of another jet. And then there was nothing. Even the band had stopped playing. The human cry was not repeated. He started to return to the Club but suddenly stopped. Someone was there in front of him in the darkness.

What do you want from me? It was Donna. The directness of her question caught Barney off guard and he could manage only a reply telling her that he was a comedian. That it was his duty to make people laugh. And that she seemed to be in need of laughter. It was an answer he wished he had not given. She looked away and finally uttered just one word. Perhaps, she said.

The sound of the fighter planes rolled in like waves muffling all other sounds. So neither of them heard the rustling of the long grass made by the figure that had crept close to the fence and was now watching them.

I don't think you should go onstage tonight, she said. Barney did not understand. He replied that it was not his turn tonight. It was only Sheldon who was scheduled to perform. But why? What was wrong in going on tonight? The words seemed to fail her for a moment. It's because of the colonel, she said finally. He's going to destroy you. Barney began to laugh but she stopped him simply by drawing closer into the light. You don't understand, she said. But I know. I've listened to him talk about it. Have you ever wondered why he hasn't had you thrown out of here? Or why he sits quietly at his table while you make all those jokes about what is happening here? He's just building you up. To destroy you. He has ever since you first came here.

Barney wanted to seize her in his arms and say all the passionate things he remembered from his days at the Saturday matinees when he was a kid. All the glorious clichés used by the heroes to tell the heroines how much they were in love. But she stopped him when she reached out to touch his arm. Please, she said. She suddenly pressed against him lightly kissing his cheek and for an instant all the sound and breath left him. The world was shut out. Barney heard neither the distant roar of the fighter planes nor the fanfare from the Club as her lips brushed across his face. . . . . .

. . . . . nor does he see the figure creeping through the long grass on the other side of the fence. It is Bannon. An involuntary little whimper escapes Bannon as he peers in cold wide-eyed fascination at the embracing couple before him. And when they kiss for that one instant he scampers closer, as close as he can get to the fence. The noise of his movements is swallowed by the fanfare that blares from the Club. In the darkness Bannon clings to the wire mesh like a mad caged primate, his lips moving silently as he realizes that the woman is the same one who has so often sat in the back seat of his car. The fanfare comes again. It blasts out like an angry warning and suddenly the woman pushes away and hurries toward the Club, her hair streaming after her in shades of glistening blackness. From inside the Club comes a man's voice yelling, Where is that goddam broad? And Bannon stands wordlessly behind the comedian wondering what the colonel's reaction would be if he knew. Bannon smiles through stained teeth at the thought of it. . . . . .

. . . . . But the colonel is already angry. He has sent his aide off to find the sergeant with the computer print-outs. Neither of them has returned. Secretly he is not displeased that the computer print-outs have not returned. They are merely more statistical meat for the baying hounds from Saigon. Tonight there are three officers from MACV— Military Assistance Command Vietnam. A colonel and two majors. All three arouse suspicion in Isaacs. They speak in modulated voices and lawyers' sentences. They have none of the rough edges of battle about them. Around the cool light of the conference table they never argue. Instead they take positions. One will move in to spell off another with reserves of military rhetoric, buttressed if need be by the writ of computer print-outs. It is all that Isaacs loathes. Desk soldiers manning verbal cannons. Playing war and spewing theories. He hopes the computer print-outs never arrive for he has just stunned them into silence. He has just leaned across the conference table and told them that he intends to keep Xuan Loc.

Keep Xuan Loc?

The reserves of military rhetoric wallow for a moment. Heresy has been uttered. Isaacs knows that within all three of them there is the urge to stand up and yell at him telling him what an idiot he is for wanting to hold on to some worthless chunk of jungle. Outdated! Stupid! He sees the thoughts curl from their minds only to lie silently on the table beneath tautly drumming fingers. Isaacs knows that the theories of this war—the *Modern* theories—dictate that holding on to a piece of ground is simply not done. It is charging the Gatling gun with the horse cavalry. It is the muzzle-loader of strategies.

But Isaacs has decided. The men from MACV shoot glances at each other feeling naked without their computer print-outs. A paper artillery without shells. One of the majors begins to enunciate the finer points of counterinsurgency strategy but Isaacs has heard it all before from other majors speaking for other colonels who were speaking for other generals who were told what to do by men with clean fingernails and a grasp of history. The major recites the latest in logic, which, it is said, will make history. But Isaacs has long ago decided that it is history which makes logic. He is tired of the lectures from these men who will one day return to America to work in clean offices. He stands up and says Gentlemen: War is simply an extension of the real-estate business. So I'm keeping Xuan Loc. And good-bye.

The major becomes red and flustered, scampering to the higher ground of statistical analysis, but Isaacs is fed up with the modulated voices and he bellows at them to get out. He no longer cares that they will go back to Saigon and report to the generals. For Isaacs has his own vision of history. A vision that has congealed in the drying blood of the morning after slaughters at a dozen forsaken jungle outposts that he has fought for and then been ordered to abandon. All because of the new strategy. The new logic. But in Isaacs' vision the entire civilization is being abandoned, outpost by outpost. And while the appendages shrivel and fall away these men from the computers desperately adjust their mirrors to reflect only health and beauty. But everywhere Isaacs looks the gravediggers are marching, piped in by the tunes of fair play and morality. Isaacs hears the music but it sounds to him like a rehearsal for a cottonfield musical— slaves' music! The spirituals of the conquered. And Isaacs will have none of it. For he has long ago decided that it is indeed simply a matter of real estate on a grand scale and it is only in the pauses of history, the moments between the cataclysms, that the tunes of morality may be permitted as diversions until they are lost in the roar of the guns.

So he will keep Xuan Loc. It will be an outpost of the civilization that will not be politely abandoned as the blood is drying and the medals are being allocated. And to hell with it all, he snaps as the aide comes rushing through the door jabbering something about the sergeant with the computer print-outs being murdered.

Isaacs hurries out into the night, into the noise from the Club as Donna flashes across the stage in whirling sequins that dance on the memories and fantasies of the men beyond the footlights. But the sergeant hears none of this for by the time Isaacs gets to him much of his blood has drained across the computer pages and the last moments of life are ebbing. As the men from Saigon look on, Isaacs turns the sergeant over and the major who had enunciated the finer points of counterinsurgency strategy automatically vomits. He has never seen a wound before and the wide pulpy crescent of a slashed throat is not one to begin with. The poor bastard, says Isaacs again and again until the men from Saigon are surprised at the shattering effect caused by the loss of one soldier. What must it be like for him after one of the slaughters that the brigade has endured? But they do not understand; it is not the fact of death but the history of death that has suddenly consumed Isaacs' thoughts. The computer print-out is unfolding, and for a moment it looks to him like a paper banner wafting in the breeze. Isaacs stares at it thinking of other wars—of Waterloo, of Borodino —when the banner of an army was infused with powers so mystical that men would die before allowing it to fall to earth in battle. The banner was the cross, the cannon and the flag. There was no honor greater than the honor of dying for the banner. But this poor bastard, mutters Isaacs to himself—oozing all over a long fluttering piece of paper imprinted with false numbers.

TEN

The best public relations minds on the base were immediately put to work trying to decide who killed the sergeant. This time the murder could not be covered up. There were too many eyes that had seen the bloody computer print-out sheets. And it had taken too long to get the body dumped into the cooler at Admissions and Disposition. Already there was talk on the base. And if this murder was compared with the knifings of the sentries, conclusions could be drawn. Either the base was too easily infiltrated by the enemy or there was a crazy on the loose. Both conclusions were offensive to Isaacs' sense of control.

And so the major, several aides and as many of the press liaison officers as could be found sober spent the entire night deciding who should be blamed for the murder. After an hour they were all fed up with the task. The suggestions grew even more bizarre. Blame it on his Vietnamese girl friend. He doesn't have one. Then blame it on his Vietnamese boy friend. Who gives a shit? Blame it on the computer; say it had a nervous breakdown with all the garbage those guys from Saigon were feeding into it. Blame it on Karl Marx. He started it all. Try Hegel. Who gives a shit? What about suicide? Yeah sure, he gave himself a paper cut on the throat with the print-out. Kiss my ass willya. What about the Lone Gook? Or . . .

The Lone Gook! . . .

They all looked around with the exhausted joy of revelation. It was perfect. They congratulated each other. Euphoria cut through the exhaustion as the best public relations minds on the base rejoiced. Who else indeed but the Lone Gook? By dawn it was official and the Lone Gook was named as the murderer.

The Lone Gook would have no way of knowing that he was now officially a murderer. The Lone Gook was the little old man from some nearby village who sat at the end of the runway and tried to shoot down the planes as they were taking off. In all the years of the war he had hit nothing with his rusted old single-shot rifles. His lonely assaults always followed the same pattern. He would emerge from the tall grass at the end of the runway, dressed in what looked like ragged pajamas and wearing the conical straw hat of a peasant. With a stooped, slow walk and with one leg that seemed to be stiffer than the other, the Lone Gook would circle like a dog about to lie down, finally settling in the bushes just beyond the barbed wire. Pretending to be a guerrilla he would sit patiently until the jet fighter planes began screaming down the runway toward him, hurtling into the air over his head. The Lone Gook would wait until the third or fourth plane and then thrust himself above the bushes aiming the rifle in a moving arc directly over his head. Sometimes the force of the arc would send him teetering backward, landing him on his back as the rifle blasted into the sky. At other times his withered reflexes would simply be too slow to follow the flash of the plane. After every wasted shot, the old man would stare into the sky with a look of infinite sadness. Then he would trudge back into the elephant grass, not to be seen again for another two or three weeks.

The Lone Gook had been carrying out his one-bullet guerrilla attacks long before any of the present American troops had arrived at Bien Hoa. In the early days of the war he had been regarded as a threat. But after his third or fourth attack, he acquired both his nickname and a status not unlike that of a mascot. Occasionally the pilots would fly extra low over his head, leaving him flattened by the roar. Once a helicopter pilot dropped him a food parcel when he showed up at Christmas. The Lone Gook fired off his bullet at the helicopter, picked up the parcel, waved to his benefactor and then trudged back into the elephant grass.

When it was announced that the Lone Gook was now suspected of the murders, most of the troops on the base reacted with surprise. When Barney heard the news he went into his room at the Catinat and spent the day writing down jokes and pacing across the floor practicing lines. And skimming through the old notebook that was Sam Senior's only legacy. The notebook was covered with the scrawl of one-liners, anecdotes, funny stories and phone numbers that would no longer be answered by the names written next to them. And across the top of the pages were instructions that Sam Senior had written to himself. Find out what's bothering them, said the scrawl. Make it funny instead! Remember burlesque! All afternoon Barney walked back and forth with the voice of Sam Senior playing in his mind. He talked to Sam Senior through the notebook. From the pages came the gruff voice and the tumult at Hanson's with a dozen comic voices battering each other and carving up the jokes about the Lone Gook.

That night Barney stepped onto the stage and demolished all that had been accomplished by the best public relations minds on the base. Can you imagine the joy? he asked into the spotlight, his voice carrying through the loudspeakers across the hundreds of troops. Can you just imagine the joy of that poor little old man when he got home this morning and was told by his wife that he'd finally made it! After all these years of being blown off his feet by planes. Imagine what he felt like knowing that someone believed he could actually hit something! He phoned the colonel's office twice today just to thank him! The laughter took hold and began to ripple across the hall as the image of the Lone Gook flashed from the lines. A spindly little man in ragged pajamas. The men from press relations looked over at the major, who sat angrily wondering where Isaacs was and why he allowed all this. Think of it, said Barney. Here we have our murderer: this teensy little old man who can barely make it to the edge of the runway. Carrying his one bullet that it takes him two weeks to make.

Barney never actually saw Isaacs. He sensed him. Standing in the shadows of the doorway beside the stage. A presence more intense than all the silhouetted audience. Barney was moving into his stories, working to keep a momentum going. And trying not to notice the presence in the doorway. A one-liner about press relations requesting the Lone Gook to dress a little more fiercely. The ragged pajamas no longer fitted the image. From the audience came the first of the hecklers. Barney had been waiting for it. And had known where it would come from. One of the press relations men was lumbering drunkenly onto a table. Unpatriotic bastard! he was yelling. Arms were reaching into the light propping up the heckler. But other hands were reaching out trying to pull the man back down. The major was muttering orders that went unheard in the din and the audience took on a life of its own. Lines were drawn out there in the darkness and as the shouting broke loose Sam Senior

whispered with a chuckle that it was just like the resorts in
the Catskills. Oi such *ploshers* you have out there. No time
for tact now. Zing 'em. You asshole! yelled the man on the
table. You can tell that this man is in army public relations,
can't you, Barney shot back. The laughter took hold and
the hoots and the jeering from the thousand or more soldiers who still felt the dirt of their last battle. Who had
never quite figured out why they were fighting. Who had
never quite figured why they could not tell their enemies
from their allies. Barney waited for the moment. Have you
ever wondered why we get such bad press back home? he
asked. Fuck you! yelled the press relations man, florid and
teetering into the light. Help him out, retorted Barney. He's
run out of words. The whistling rose around the press relations man. *Number one!* yelled Barney and from an ocean
of figures in the darkness shot back a language never used
in the press releases. *Zap the dipshit! Same-same. Never
happen sir!* . . . . . Burlesque, whispers Sam Senior
. . . . . and Barney's one-liners flashed across the millions
of watts of clear channel, instantly decoded by war-wizened
minds. Minds that were trying to put the war on bulk erase.
Music. Dope. Booze. But the terrible images never left and
friends holding entrails always came through in color while
the sound track played the press releases that told of winning the hearts and minds, and pacification quotas, and
whatever else was dutifully written by the overweight, middle-aged men or the young zealots with dead eyes and clean
shirts. The truth. *No lie G.I.!* And now here was one of
them drawn out of cover. Exposed on all flanks. Fragged in
a verbal fire fight. The press relations man bellowed into the
cheering and was pulled down from the table by friends.
Whistles and hooting swelled through the hall and the
major began yelling orders to the man from press relations
who could hear nothing but the uproar and goddam voice

from the stage asking the pilots to drop the Lone Gook eyeglasses as they flew over him. The noise from the audience was still rolling in at Barney and little pockets of angry words or laughter could be heard as he shifted out of the one-liners and into the stories. Have you heard that the Lone Gook went to the colonel and asked to become an American citizen? When he went back to his village and told them what he was doing, they were stunned. Why do you want to do that? they asked. So I can commit suicide. Now his villagers were really horrified. Why do you want to commit suicide? they asked. The old man said sadly, It's the only way I can kill an American.

Number one. Number one. The cries echoed through the hall and the major wondered again at troops that could even laugh at jokes about killing their own people and why the colonel ever allowed this idiot up on the stage. They were much better off with the fat comedian who sweated a lot. But from the doorway beside the stage Isaacs watched the performance and was able to find one positive element in the proceedings. A weakness had been exposed. Isaacs believed in the process of natural selection. If press relations were such idiots as to set themselves up for this, then let them be cut down. The war of the clerks. With laughter following him he walked out of the club thinking of that terrible afternoon years ago in San Francisco.

A few days later the Lone Gook experienced one of the high points of his life. He shot down his first plane. Nobody was more surprised than the Lone Gook. It did not matter in the least that it was not really a plane. It was a helicopter piloted by a twenty-year-old on whose helmet was the painted inscription Pray for War. Ever since Pray for War had been in his first gang fight back home in

Brooklyn he had always been in favor of the underdog. He himself usually was the underdog. After hearing Barney's call for an airlift of eyeglasses, Pray for War decided that 20/20 vision was the least that could be done for this forlorn little ancient who was accused of such awesome crimes. On the following day he was returning from Dak To when he saw the old man sitting like a myopic duck hunter beside the end of the runway. Pray for War knew this was his chance for charity. He maneuvered his helicopter over the old man, dropped the three pairs of eyeglasses he had brought, and watched. The old man hobbled over to see what had been dropped. He stared at the glasses for a moment and then began chirping indignation into the skies. He shook his bony fist at the helicopter. Pray for War thought the old man was waving at him. Put the glasses on, gookie, he yelled. The old man jiggled up and down making angry screeching noises that were lost in the roar of the helicopter. Pray for War waved down at him. Still jiggling and chirping, the Lone Gook closed his eyes, pointed the gun somewhere into the air above his head and pulled the trigger. To his amazement there was a sudden metallic belching above him. The helicopter seemed like a fat green bird that was having a nervous breakdown in mid-flight. It lurched and shuddered, farting flame from unlikely places. The Lone Gook looked up with pride. In the helicopter Pray for War was screaming to the crew members and wrestling with controls that would not respond. The floor spun under him. Gears blew up. The horizon dipped. The helicopter spun downward into the tall grass with a roar. Men jumped from it yelling curses. Pray for War had never been shot down before. He leaped from his helicopter ducking its slicing blades and screaming at the Lone Gook. Pray for War grabbed an M-16 from a grunt whose eyes were blank. He ran over to the edge of the runway and sprayed bullets. The

Lone Gook was not there. Pray for War ran into the tall grass. Frag me willya four eyes, he yelled blasting the tall grass with the M-16.

All week Pray for War talked about how ungrateful the Lone Gook was. He flew back and forth to Dak To every day. The battle in the arc around Dak To was becoming savage. On some days Pray for War had difficulty even landing his helicopter. The enemy fire was intense. Entire companies were cut off. Hilltops became mass graveyards. Corpses piled up and reinforcements could not be flown in. A battalion was ambushed from the rear and its men were picked off in bunches during the two days they were trapped. Pray for War flew like a maniac. He went where others would not, flying low through valleys under a cross fire. Or dropping through the mortars onto a hilltop screaming orders to frantic men who bellowed desperate blessings through the typhoon of dirt around the helicopter. Ammo in. Corpses out. All week it was death and noise. And pills that shot him into perfect pitch. Other helicopter pilots hesitated or muttered prayers and were blown out of the skies in awesome explosions that convulsed into a series of fireballs before the wreckage fell to the ground. Pray for War saw it all in super-Technicolor played back at varying speeds and didn't give a damn. All he thought of was the Lone Gook. No one had ever shot him down before. On the fourth day of the Dak To battle he saw the old man sitting beside the runway. Pray for War was returning from Dak To flying what was as much a morgue as it was a helicopter. He circled around the Lone Gook and then turned the controls over to his copilot. He clamored back through the bodies and took control of the .50-caliber machine gun mounted on the side. He shouted orders to the copilot, who flew closer to the Lone Gook. Just like the last time. Pray for War waited. The old man looked up and Pray for War screamed at him. Shoot *me* down willya you dumb dinky-dao, he yelled. The machine gun chattered above the roar of the helicopter. The earth around the old man erupted in tiny geysers. The old man just looked up at Pray for War. Then he shook his fist. Pray for War began yelling and firing at the same time. The old man was flung into the air by the force of the bullets.

There were those on the base who maintained that Pray for War was always slightly crazy. Others said that what he did was a result of all the pills and the endless days of strung-out skidding over treetops. Dodging ground fire in his few hours of sleep. Pray for War landed his helicopter in a forbidden area next to the press relations office. He kicked open the door. The rotor-driven winds howled into the office lashing papers and dirt into the faces of the press relations men. The man closest to the door was knocked off his chair. The others clung to desks and shielded their eyes, yelling at the apparition in the doorway. But their voices were sucked away in the roar. Pray for War stood in the wind-whipped inferno holding the body of the Lone Gook. He walked over to the desk of one of the young officers and draped the body across it. Pray for War yelled at the press relations men but only fragments of words could be heard. His eyes were glued circles. He turned and walked out through the wind and took off in his helicopter. The silence in the press relations office seemed as loud as the roar of the helicopter. In the shambles of the office the men stared at one another and at the body of the old man. He seemed tiny, far too small to have committed the murders they had attributed to him. There were patches of blood across the desk and one of the press relations men began bellowing for someone to get the body out of the office. There was a desperate quality to the man's voice.

Within hours the Lone Gook was buried and Pray for

War had flown straight into a mortar shell that blew his helicopter to pieces. The young officer in press relations spent all afternoon scrubbing his desk and insisted he could see the spots of blood when no one else could. The next day he continued to scrub and finally demanded a new desk. He was still scrubbing when another officer came in with news of the latest murder. A lieutenant had been found dead beside his tent. It was quickly agreed that officially it was impossible for the lieutenant to be dead. The official murderer had been dumped lifeless across a desk in that very office. No further murders were officially possible. Who gives a shit? asked the agitated senior press officer when he returned from a meeting with Isaacs about Dak To. When we're up to our ass in bodies who cares about murder?

ELEVEN

That night Barney gave one of his best performances. He told jokes about the Lone Gook and about the latest murder. They were jokes that sprang from anger and guilt. I should have taken him the eyeglasses myself!—and in the middle of a story about the press relations men frantically searching for a new murderer he stopped and demanded a better response from his audience. His audience consisted solely of Woody.

The performance was being held in Barney's room at the Catinat and Woody was getting drunk. The more he drank the more he heckled Barney. Something told Woody it was good for both of them. Sheldon's mother-in-law jokes are better, he yelled at Barney, who shot back with a monologue about the peace-keepers and the press relations men arguing about the latest murder. The peace-keepers were insisting that the Lone Gook was officially still alive because officially there was no war in which he could be killed. Therefore his latest murder was indeed possible. The press relations men were indignantly asserting that the Lone Gook's latest murder was impossible. Any asshole could see that there was a war going on.

Woody made an obscene noise and through the open door came Lawson's angry voice demanding silence. The sound of his typewriter echoed off the courtyard walls in sharp little bursts. Now try two fingers, Woody yelled. The reply was another burst from the typewriter. Barney subsided onto the tiled floor and sat listening to the noises of the Saigon night that swelled from Tu Do Street just beyond the courtyard walls. The roar of the motor-scooter legions and the woven cries of the whores and beggars and radios. And the stillness of the courtyard itself. Light came from only a few rooms. Donna's room was in darkness. Mr. Thomas was back at his mission in Pleiku. Snider was away somewhere photographing the war. Barney sat staring into the courtyard, wondering again how much he was responsible for sending the helicopter pilot off on his crazed hunt for the little old man at the end of the runway. One death among thousands. Somehow the thousands had a way of becoming just terrible numbers on a page. But the one was always even more terrible. He had seen it on the faces of the soldiers who came back and had to pack the personal effects of their friends who had shared the same tent until they had caught the bullet or stepped on the mine. The one death was always more powerful then. Because somewhere there was the bottomless screaming insistence that the silly fucker was still there. He's just hiding. Come out you bastard. And the hideous feeling of trespass from simply picking up the material appendages of a life. The clothes. The articles of shaving. The letters holding soft voices that had turned to cries. And the awesome sense of superiority felt by the living. No matter how imposing the man had been, no matter how ferocious or how brilliant, he was instantly reduced to some unspoken pathetic stature when the others gathered to talk about him. The dead could not talk back. The dead were helpless. And every word of sorrow from the living rang softly with the ultimate superiority.

Barney wondered if someone was clearing away the personal effects of the Lone Gook. Or were the friends and the family still waiting for him to return? From the courtyard there was the sound of aimless footsteps on the tiles. Barney could make out the silhouette of a man who walked back and forth and then receded into the stairway. Woody sat up, prepared to do battle. He was sure it was the Polish colonel. Woody and the Poles had mutually declared the war of the peace-keepers. The Canadians and the Poles were fed up with each other.

Earlier that same evening Woody had stood at the entrance to the third-floor courtyard and sniffed the air. Cologne. Cheap cologne, the kind worn in abundance by Colonel Wzcninski. Woody had drunk just enough Canadian beer to decide that the Polish colonel was an interloper on the third floor. He sniffed his way through the potted palms and saw the Polish colonel standing stiffly in front of Donna's door. In Colonel Wzcninski's hand was a bunch of freshly picked flowers. His hair was meticulously greased back. His uniform was pressed to perfection. He cleared his throat several times and was about to knock on the door when he turned to see Woody standing beside him. Woody was a disheveled mess. Woody beamed an idiot's grin at the colonel and apologized for the loud belch that escaped him. In his hand was a ragged collection of hastily assembled flowers, most of them dead. Colonel Wzcninski stared at Woody in astonishment and then muttered some threat in Polish. Woody broadened his idiot's grin and then slowly reached out and knocked on the door. Get away! hissed Colonel Wzcninski. Woody knocked again. The colonel stiffly swatted at his arm. The colonel was beginning to perspire. His face was showing patches of crimson and he half turned to leave. The door opened and Donna stood staring out at them. She looked from the colonel's flowers to Woody's and began to smile. The smile was returned in varying degrees of stiffness. Woody looked at the colonel, who was now bright crimson and was muttering something in Polish from the side of his mouth. Woody then thrust his ratty bouquet of dead flowers at Donna, who accepted them with a puzzled smile. She looked over at the colonel. Woody also looked over at the colonel. With lips set in a thin quavering smile, he presented his bouquet of flowers. He bowed as he presented them. Woody also bowed. Donna began to laugh. Woody also began to laugh. The colonel remained for a moment with the thin crooked smile frozen on his face and then he too began to laugh in a dry, mirthless manner. Donna thanked them both and then after an awkward hesitation retreated into her room. The door closed. Colonel Wzcninski's laugh ceased immediately. He stood staring at the door with blank eyes. Then he erupted into a torrent of Polish insults and took a swing at Woody with his fist. Woody ducked and backed away, laughing. The colonel chased Woody all over the courtyard yelling terrible curses in Polish. The battle continued up the stairways with the fourth floor against the ninth floor. Colonel Wzcninski disappeared long enough to get drunk on the Polish vodka with which his peace-keepers were supplied. Woody did the same with Canadian beer. He was interrupted in his drinking by the sight of Colonel Wzcninski clanging his way down the hall. The colonel was wearing the ceremonial cavalry saber of his grandfather. He drew the saber, invoked the glories of the Polish cavalry in two languages and began teetering after Woody. Tears streamed down his face at the memory of Donna and what might have been. In the days of the cavalry it would have been different.

The battle of the peace-keepers flared up and down the stairs and hallways of the Catinat. The one dingy elevator became a no-man's-land. Others joined in. Miller the lieutenant from Saskatoon raced through the halls yelling revenge for his orchids that had been pissed on by the drunk from Cracow. And Joyal the medic from Quebec was knocked senseless by a five-day-old loaf of black bread.

Woody decided that a strategic retreat was in order. He had fled to the safety of Barney's room, where he could sit out this altercation with the civilized accouterments of beer and good jokes. But now the sound of footsteps on the tiles in the courtyard told him that perhaps Wzcninski was about to consummate his spiritual alliance with the Polish cavalry. Woody crawled out of the room on his hands and knees. He hid behind the potted palms until the man emerged from the shadows again. Woody got to his feet and crept around the palms. Suddenly the man was not there. Woody waited and then retraced his steps. He stopped, drawn up by terror. There was a metallic flash of light. And the sizzle of a blade cutting the air. At his throat was the honed steel tip of a long knife. The face behind the blade moved out of the shadows. The smile of rotted teeth confronted him.

It was Bannon.

I'm good, ain't I? said Bannon. Only when Woody nodded did Bannon remove the knife from his throat. Barney stepped out of his room and told Bannon to put the knife away or else go up and fight the Polish colonel with the saber. Bannon grinned. Hey funnyman, Bannon said. Howya doing? Have I told you that I have a brother who's a funnyman like you? He plays the carnivals. Barney gave Bannon a beer in spite of the looks from Woody. Barney invited Bannon into the room and made him feel welcome. He kept handing Bannon the Canadian beer until the rotted teeth were framed in a drunken grin. Barney let Bannon talk. About the war and the way they should be whipping asses instead of the other way around. Some meat rack going on up at Dak To, I tell you! And about home and the way that he and his brothers would get drunk in the little Kentucky towns near his home. They were righteous times I tell you. Beat the crap out of any of them who took to fighting with us. Bannon's drunkenness soon subsided into bleary recollections of home. He talked of hunting in the hills and the steel leg traps they used for some animals. Barney decided that Bannon himself was like one of his steel traps. Sitting there quietly, looking harmless. But the tiniest of impulses could trigger the irrevocable. The mental jaws slashing shut and the predestined swirl of sharpened metal.

Barney waited to ask the question. Why are you here? Bannon chuckled, wagged his finger at Barney and opened another beer. You know why I'm here. Because of room number 39. The colonel's lady. Bannon pulled an envelope from his combat jacket. A message from lover boy, he said with a grin directed at Barney. During the next hour Barney kept passing beer to Bannon, who sank into a maudlin confederacy with his drinking companions. Barney hoped that Donna would not return early from whatever performance she was at that night. And that Bannon would forget about the letter now lying on top of a case of beer.

It was the Polish cavalry that sprang the trap. The courtyard reverberated with the clanking of the ceremonial saber and the call to arms of legions long dead. Colonel Wzcninski stumbled first to the door of Donna's room muttering invocations of love that remained unrequited. Then he threw himself in the direction of the light from Barney's room. When he saw Woody sitting in the doorway, some hoof-driven cry of glory sounded within him. He lurched toward the door, drawing his saber. He swung with the saber but succeeded only in decapitating a potted palm. He steadied himself for a second assault. But something was wrong. Through the emotional fog of vodka and national honor he peered out at someone else coming at him with a knife.

Someone with rotted teeth that formed a hideous smile. The man slashed with the knife. It was all the colonel could do to fend off the slashing with his saber. The colonel began jabbering in Polish. Fear chilled him and sobriety seized his mind. But his reflexes were still awash with vodka and the other man was quicker, much quicker. The knife slashed at him. Blood shot from his arm. And again from his cheek. The rotted smile blasted a whinnying laugh at him as it feinted in one direction and then another. The colonel staggered back through the palms, spurting blood and crying for help.

Bannon had leaped out of the room at the sight of the saber. Barney had not known what was happening until Woody threw himself across the floor and the cold clash of metal sounded from outside. Some instinct caused Barney to grab a full bottle of beer as he ran into the courtyard. Bannon was a blur of homicidal motion. Barney ran toward the colonel, who was desperately trying to flee. Bannon leaped in front of Barney and a sudden ripping noise came with a thin spray of blood. Without any degree of conscious thought Barney stepped closer to Bannon and with a calm smooth motion flung the bottle of beer at Bannon. The bottle seemed to explode just above Bannon's ear. He went down as if poleaxed, hitting the tiles with a clanking noise. Bannon lay utterly still with the beer fizzling and bubbling around his head. Colonel Wzcninski teetered above Bannon, clutching at the places where he was bleeding and telling himself that it was his superior swordsmanship after all. The Polish cavalry had been avenged. He lurched off through the potted palms.

Barney took away Bannon's knife. Then they carried him downstairs and out through the back door to Nguyen Hue Street, where he always parked Isaacs' car. They dumped Bannon inside the car and waited until a military police patrol passed by. They told the military police that they had found him beside his car. He had obviously been beaten up by local thugs they said. The military policemen agreed and took Bannon and the car off to safety. Back in Barney's room Woody picked up the letter from Isaacs that had been left on the case of beer. Let me make things simple for you he said grinning. You would like to open the letter. As an official peace-keeper it's my duty to investigate violations, atrocities, and general carryings-on. He began to read with a theatrical flourish:

Darling—

I cannot be with you this evening. The brigade has serious problems. I may be at the front (if I can find it) for a day, perhaps more. I have missed you more than I can tell. I shall see you within a day or so.

All my love—I.

Woody stared at the note and whistled softly. He reminded Barney of a big blond schoolboy reading the teacher's mail. I didn't know Isaacs was like this, said Woody. Later, the war drew closer. The soft thump of the artillery shells became more insistent. The sky to the east of the courtyard was ghostly white with flares. Barney watched Donna return just before curfew. He waited for several minutes and then knocked softly on her door. She opened it with the same startled look and told him that it was impossible to see him tonight. It's possible, said Barney. The brigade chauffeur was here and left a message. No one else will be here tonight.

They sat in her room talking. She told Barney she was pleased to have someone to talk with. Barney believed what she said because the haunted look had disappeared from her face. By the soft light of the flares there was laughter and warmth that came from her eyes. She talked easily about her home in New Mexico, about her songs, and about the strangeness of Saigon. Soon they were laughing together. Barney shared with her some of the jokes that he had saved for future performances. Jokes that he had hoarded like treasures ever since Sam Senior had told them to him years ago in the dingy room at the Edison Hotel. She confided in him her worst fears of singing off key. And he told her of the time in the Catskills when he had dried up onstage. They laughed together, entranced by each other's presence and the magic that was somehow in the night.

From the courtyard there were footsteps and Barney felt the magic instantly die. She stopped in midsentence and waited for the footsteps to pass. The laughter had left her eyes. You were afraid it was Isaacs weren't you? Barney asked. Yes I was, she said. But not for the reasons you think. You see in some ways I control him. As untactful as it may sound, it is true. He is in love with me. Utterly, hopelessly in love. I'm beginning to think it is the kind of love sometimes felt by very powerful men much to their own surprise. It probably only lasts for a while because like other things in their lives it is part of the act of conquest. But if there is no conquest it becomes almost obsessive. And it is they who are the conquered.

Barney waited for her to laugh. Or perhaps wink as if it was just a conspiratorial little joke they were sharing. But her voice was soft and even. She stared directly at him. The pale light of the fading flares fell around her face. She did not turn away. I'm really not sure I want to hear the intricacies of your love affair with Isaacs, said Barney. It was he who had looked away. I'm sorry, she said. I've never talked about this to anyone else. But it is all a part of why I came here to Vietnam.

And I've also never talked about that to anyone, she said in a soft voice. The reason I came here was to kill Isaacs.

There was the same warmth from her eyes that never left him. Right now I wish I could think of a punch line, said Barney. They sat for several minutes saying nothing. The distant artillery was the only sound until she spoke again. Until a year ago the center of my life was Kalman. He was the man I lived with for three years. They were the only years of my life that have really meant anything to me. He had a kind of craziness that could make me laugh when I didn't want to. He was one of those people who was so sure of himself in a quiet way that he could walk into a room and make people feel at ease or make them laugh. That was how I met him. I was singing with a group that was playing at one of the little clubs in Los Angeles. We had been told that a record producer was coming to see us. It was pandemonium. Everybody was frantically rehearsing and fretting about the order of the songs. And we were constantly looking out for some guy to show up wearing gold-plated love beads, blow-dried hair, capped teeth and a Gucci silk shirt. Instead Kalman showed up. He looked so normal he was out of place. He introduced himself as Kalman—which was all people ever called him. Somehow his last name had become his first. We had some pretty high-strung egos in that group. But within an hour he had them cooled out and was getting them to perform better than they ever had. It was all done calmly. No tantrums. No strutting around letting everyone know how important he was. Instead there was a quiet control that came from inside. It was the kind of control that seemed even greater when he admitted his mistakes. And then made jokes about them. The night after we met him, the group gave its best performance. Everyone felt they were performing for him. It was a turning point for a lot of people. We got a contract and had a couple of modest hits before the group broke up a year later. Some of them went on to be big stars. One of the girls went to Broadway. And I stayed with Kalman. At a time when marriage was becoming almost unfashionable in California we got married. Among the other joys in those years was the freedom of not following fashions. Kalman had tried smoking dope and decided he was better off without it. He could sit in a recording studio with all the others wiped out and just tell jokes that would keep them giggling to themselves for hours. The only thing truly fashionable about Kalman was his age. He was twenty-five when I met him. He was a big success in a business where every recording company had its boy wonder. But he never worked for any of those companies. He worked for himself, producing records for singers he wanted to work with. And when he wasn't working he would often spend hours playing the piano at home. He was fascinated by what Stravinsky had done in the early nineteen hundreds, when he composed *Firebird* and *Rite of Spring* and most of the critics had hated them. Kalman admired Stravinsky. It was Kalman's great aim to compose the rock equivalent of *Firebird*. He would sit at the piano for hours composing and playing. It was his great sanctuary. But the times he was most truly alive were at the concerts.

It was sometime after the Monterey festival that he really became well known. All the big groups and singers wanted him to work on their albums. Jimi Hendrix. Jefferson Airplane. Two of the Beatles approached him. But he also had an offer of a different kind. It was from the Army. He had already been given one deferment and he probably could have been given another one if he had really tried to get it. For two months we talked as little as possible about the future. We went down to the beach at Santa Monica almost every day. It was he who was making me laugh. And when I look back on those days it was really the laughter that got us through it all. In a quiet way he became even funnier than he was before. But underneath it all he was scared. I could tell by watching him sleep. And then one day we kissed good-bye. He got on a plane and went to Fort Benning in Georgia. We saw each other once more just before he went to Vietnam. It was only for three days up in San Francisco. It was terrible. We were both so unnatural. He tried to make me forget about what was happening by making me laugh. But somehow it was a different kind of laughter. He lasted just over six months in Vietnam. He was killed somewhere in the highlands. In those six months he sent me dozens of letters and gradually I was able to understand what it was that he was saying to me in those letters. There was some kind of argument with the brigade commander. The commander took a dislike to him and pushed him into ever more dangerous combat missions. In his last month Kalman was ordered out on jungle patrols where very few of those who went out ever came back. It was just a matter of time. It had become a test of will between him and the brigade commander. The brigade commander was determined to break him. But he wouldn't break. Instead he taunted the commander. Not in any open way that would have gotten him court-martialed. Instead he used his humor. Kalman made jokes that got back to the commander and infuriated him.

That commander was Isaacs, she said.

The flares were fading. Barney could barely make out the contours of her face. As he listened to her talk of the man she had lost, Barney realized that he was hopelessly in love.

Todlachen, Barney said. He explained what it meant. Yes, *todlachen,* she replied. Laugh till it kills you. She reached out for the package of letters on the dresser. I have kept these with me constantly. Perhaps longer than is wise. But they are all I have left of him. When the news came I spent weeks in some kind of half life. Everything was a fog. All I remember of the funeral was the flag being rolled back and strangers in army uniforms saying things that they had said before to other widows.

I went back to performing. First dancing. Friends got me work on television shows that needed dancers. Then I began singing again. But it was never the same. I didn't care about it anymore. I lost one agent, who told me to call him when I decided I wanted to work at being a star. I played my share of Holiday Inn lounges making velvet sounds and getting business cards with room numbers written on the back of them. But I didn't care. I had just stopped feeling anything. I hardly saw any of my friends. I had no interest in going out with other men.

One day somebody at my new agent's office asked me if I would be interested in going to Vietnam for a few months. Big money, they said. My new agents would have me singing on street corners if their commission fee was big enough. They were asking all of their performers about Vietnam. They were turned down by even the most broken-down cocktail pianists. Everyone said no—except me. It was a way of escaping and being closer at the same time. I was away from all the memories of home. And yet somehow it was a way of hanging on to something I knew I should let go of.

When I got here, Milligan gave me his standard watch-who-you-sleep-with speech, patted me on the ass and asked if I was free for dinner. After I said no he became very cool and sent me off to play Bien Hoa. That was when I first saw Isaacs. He was walking out of one of the buildings as we drove past. I knew it was him instantly. I had seen a photograph of him in TIME magazine while Kalman was still alive. But seeing him in person made me realize something else. I realized I had seen him before. In San Francisco. He was the man who had waded through a rock concert that Kalman had helped stage, yelling insults at Abbie Hoffman up on the stage. I remember thinking then that the man was ferocious—that he could have killed Abbie Hoffman with his bare hands. And when I saw him that same chill went right through me. But that was when the idea first came to me. That I had it in my power to say Kalman darling I shall avenge you. I couldn't stop watching Isaacs on that first day. An eye for an eye I thought to myself over and over again. I came back here to Saigon after the show and read Kalman's letters and decided that I must go ahead with it.

The second time I performed out there I was aware that he was in the audience. I could almost feel his eyes. Then he sent his driver backstage with a note inviting me to his office for a drink. I was about to accept. It was the perfect chance. But something inside me crumbled at the thought of being alone with him. I remember that anger. Those eyes. I made an excuse to myself saying that I wasn't ready to do what must be done. I told his driver to say that I was not feeling well and please express my regrets. I fled back here to the hotel. All the way back I felt myself talking silently to Kalman saying I'm sorry my darling. I will do it. I promise. When I got back to the hotel there was already a large parcel waiting for me outside the door. It was flowers. And a note from Isaacs asking me out to dinner in Saigon the next night. I didn't even take the flowers inside. It would have been like taking *him* inside. I left them outside in the rain. There was a monsoon storm that night. I sat up all night listening to the rain and wondering how my life had gone so berserk. Sitting in a dark little room in the middle of a war with a plan to kill someone. By morning I had begun crying. I realized it was the first time I had really cried since Kalman's death. It had all just stayed inside for all those months. I cried for hours and hours until I finally fell asleep. When I awoke it was almost sunset. Outside my door there were more flowers. Another invitation appeared the next day. It was all very courteous and formal. But within the elegant flow of the handwriting on that invitation I could almost feel the force and the power that was reaching out toward me. And the more I politely rejected the invitations, the more I controlled the source of all that power. The power that had killed Kalman.

When I finally did go out with Isaacs it was to a restaurant on the river in Cholon. It was a place where it was unlikely we would be seen by anyone who knew him. It was hard to remember that we were in the middle of a war. There were other American couples who were dancing to music from a small orchestra and outside if you looked in one direction there was only the lantern lights from the small boats bobbing along the river. In the other direction they were unloading ammunition. In a strange way he was charming, almost relaxed, without any of the overpowering insistence behind his invitation. He did not talk about the war like everyone else there seemed to. I began to realize that he was the kind of person I've only met a few times in my life. Someone so sure of themselves, someone so in control, that they have no need to impress anyone with tales of past glory. It was very gentle and pleasant. I went into the washroom and took the pistol from my purse and stared at it. Then I started to shake uncontrollably and became violently ill. Later when he took me home everything was very proper and polite and when I got back in here I just sat for hours thankful that the evening was over. More flowers came. And small notes saying things in a way that somehow seemed too anxious for someone like him. I acknowledged none of them. But I began to notice that my bookings were almost entirely for Bien Hoa. When I asked Milligan about it all he would tell me was that someone high up liked me.

Be thankful he kept telling me. It could be worse. It could be Brooklyn. After a week I went out with him a second time. Again it was all very secret in a small restaurant where no one would see us. I had justified this second time to myself by saying that because I was losing my nerve, I needed time. And I needed to find the right place to kill him. That night there was a change in him. He seemed more intent on pleasing me. It was as if he had too much time to think during that week and had become desperately afraid that I would reject him. It was then that I became aware of the purely clinical element of power. The more I rejected him in a subtle gentle way, the more power I had over him.

But it was like having power over some wild and unpredictable force of nature. It becomes a fight for survival. To lose that power, to give in, is to be destroyed. That night we drove back here in his official car. There had been a guerrilla attack on one of the barracks near the cathedral. We were stopped several times by military police and once we had to make a detour around some fighting in the streets. That night the war seemed to be all around us. I had never seen so many flares in the sky and the sound of the mortars was closer than ever. It took a long time to get the old Vietnamese night watchman to open the sliding steel door downstairs. The watchman was afraid it was guerrillas who were knocking. We walked up the stairs to the courtyard and on the way I was telling myself that Isaacs was about to be turned down once more. But by the time we got to the door I realized that I was terrified. All my control had vanished. I was somehow in the grip of an awesome force and I could not tell if it came from within me or from him. And suddenly I was lost and being swept along, grasping for whatever destinies I had told myself were left. It was he who took the key and opened the door. There was nothing about him that physically forced me. But all choice was gone. He had suddenly become terrifying to me. It was when I felt his hands sweep across me that I was afraid I might break down totally. But we made love for hours. A mad insatiable love fueled by a kind of obsession that had seized him. And because I was the center of that obsession it became for me a desperate lunge for survival. And there was no chance just to be passive and let this madness of his surge around me and within me until it was spent. That would have meant submission. Destruction. And I was the one who had come over here to destroy. So that night became something more than lust and something less than love. When he left just before dawn he was exhausted. And also just the slightest bit desperate. Because I had held on. There had been no conquest.

When he left I lay here for a long time wondering what was happening to me. I kept on whispering to Kalman saying I'm sorry my darling. I shall win a victory for you. I promise you I will. But strangely I could not remember his face until I took out the photograph that I always keep. It was then I realized the destruction on both sides and I fell asleep telling myself that it was all madness, sheer madness.

For over a week I refused all invitations and canceled all my bookings at Bien Hoa. I told myself that I had to get away from *him*. But one night he was here when I returned. I was angry at the thought of him waiting for me, almost hunting me. It was I who was the hunter. Again the inevitable happened. But when it was over and he had departed I realized that it was now an obsession on both sides. I too was seized by something I could not or did not want to control. There was no way I could simply decide not to see him again. That way I would be the one who was hunted. I would be yielding to my fears of him. I could always go back to America but I told myself that would be a defeat.

So I let this strangled affair pull me in. I am not very proud of what I have done. And I want to end it.

They sat for a long time in the faint light until Barney asked how she would end it. She shook her head and said nothing. Why did you tell me all this? asked Barney. I have no one else I can talk to, she said in a voice so low that he could barely hear her. And ever since Kalman died I have never really talked to anyone. Not in an honest way. Not until tonight. I have wanted to be with you like this for a long time. But I was afraid because of what I am doing. She stood up beside the window. Another flare had dropped in the sky. There was the same startled expression that Barney remembered from the first time he had seen her. It was as if she were about to flee. By the light of the flare Barney could see her eyes darting as if searching for a place on which to rest. Her figure was a silhouette against the night sky. . . . . .

. . . . . Make her laugh, Barney tells himself. Make her laugh at the very worst of it. And he reaches out in the way he knows best with a kind of humor that talks of Isaacs and even—even of Kalman! For Isaacs will, he claims, have him dropped behind enemy lines if he finds out he is here. To entertain the troops of course. *Their troops*. There is the first trace of bewildered laughter on her face. It has taken hold. And so into the sacred memories of Kalman. The laughter freezes and falls around her in shards as Barney talks of Kalman. Can you imagine Kalman's delight, he asks, seeing Abbie Hoffman and Isaacs screaming at each other and knowing he has found the rock equivalent of *Firebird*? In the dim light he is sure he sees a smile. And so Barney continues until there is laughter, real laughter, and by the time the flares in the night sky blend into the first light of dawn there is a kind of joy within the room as Barney reaches out to her, drawing her in toward him. But even though there is joy, the voices within Barney cannot be silenced and they shout questions that he wants to drown out with the laughter. Yet still the questions come and demand to know: Does she or does she not still intend to kill Isaacs? *Todlachen!* whispers a mischievous old voice in reply and Barney laughs with her as they fall together across the bed. . . . . .

. . . . . *Kill Isaacs?* There are thousands of them down there trying to kill Isaacs as his helicopter skids through the rainy dawn skies while the jungle below blisters with rocket fire. It is the worst battle so far. The brigade is being butchered in bits and pieces by an enemy they can hardly find. An enemy so elusive that every attack seems an assault on phantoms. And so the word has come down from MACV: Retreat. *Retreat?* The word has buzzed and raged in Isaacs' mind all night as he has yelled and argued with the strategists, computer men, assorted generals and men with faith in numbers on pieces of paper. By the first light Isaacs is cursing his fates and wondering where in the hell of history there are places reserved for the rotted souls of commanders who preside over retreats. And he curses the cold and the rain that pours through the open door of the Huey gunship that shudders under a direct hit and the gunner shrieks and clutches at the blood that bursts through his flak jacket. Other hands pull the man inside at the moment when he is about to pitch forward and dangle from his safety harness belching blood onto the jungle three thousand feet below. The pilot pulls the Huey up but Isaacs bellows over the voices and orders the pilot to drop lower, far lower, and skim the treetops all the way into Dak To. In the middle of the blood and the screams of metal and voices Isaacs thinks of Donna and wishes to God he were with her for there is some need, something even more than a need that torments him and her face has flashed before him in the most absurd of situations. And now at three thousand feet with the snipers of history closing in around him and the rains and the rocket fire lashing at the jungle covering from opposite directions, Isaacs leans out and curses at the skies. . . . . .

. . . . . *Retreat?* drawls the eighteen-year-old in Graves Registration back at headquarters in Bien Hoa. This ain't no fuckin' retreat. It's sale day at the meat market is what this is. They're getting sent back in itty-bitty pieces. The eighteen-year-old in Graves Registration is exhausted. Ever since the battle at Dak To began, the bodies have been sent back to him after being identified over at Admissions and Disposition. For three days he has slept little. Over and over he writes Killed In Action—KIA—on the official forms taking great care to make sure that the right form goes with the right coffin. But sometimes he thinks What does it matter which name goes where? It's all giblets he tells himself. Death is all around the eighteen-year-old. It is now his profession and until six months ago he had never known death except when his grandmother passed away back in Tuscaloosa, Alabama. Now he is sure he even smells of death. He has begun to make jokes about death. And about the dead. Outsiders are often outraged by his jokes. Poor taste. Disrespectful. Disgusting. But the eighteen-year-old from Tuscaloosa tells them all to go fuck themselves. Nothing will stop him from making his jokes. They are his survival. His sanity. He does not know why he needs his jokes but he knows they are part of him now. Over the large door through which the forklift trucks pass carrying the metal coffins out to the transport planes, he has hung a large sign reading *KIA Travel Bureau*. And under an enlarged photograph of coffins being loaded onto a plane he had taped a headline from his hometown newspaper *Vietnam Troop Withdrawal to Continue*. But now he stops writing Killed In Action on another form and watches as more bodies come in. There are dozens of them, maybe hundreds in this batch. Who knows? Who will ever know? The eighteen-year-old begins to laugh. His laughter bounces off the metal walls of the warehouse. He is sure the dead are laughing with him. The clattering laugh of a thousand corpses all around. A thousand dead jaws clacking away. Clack-clack-clack-clack-clack! The eighteen-year-old throws the official forms into the air and yells Victory! Another battle won! The others in the warehouse stop what they are doing and look at the hooting, thigh-slapping crazy who yells Victory! over and over again. Some of them say he has gone over the edge and others are angry because he is always pulling idiotic stunts like this. Victory!? But the eighteen-year-old laughs and laughs and does not care what they think for he knows the secret of this war: the more bodies he gets shipped to him the greater the certainty that the general will find some way of claiming that the battle had been a victory. They will not use the word victory of course. Instead there will be an *extended containment of the enemy offensive* or perhaps it will be a *sustained contact operation*. Anything that can be jargoned out in army newspeak to avoid the obvious proclaimed with epic simplicity by every jungle-rotted filth-ridden soldier, *They fucking well greased us*. Clack-clack-clack-clack-clack-clack-clack-clack. And the eighteen-year-old from Tuscaloosa shouts to the growing stacks of dead men that victory is theirs! Victory! For they are not really dead! They are *personnel sustaining maximum response to impact*. Victory! over those tactless lucky bastards, those jungle-rotted, filth-ridden but still living buddies who note that *those fuckers carved him a brand-new asshole*. Eternal life bestowed by the army bureaucracy. Or if not exactly life, at least a kind of nondeath. Dead men can't be choosers. Clack-clack-clack-clack-clack-clack. The eighteen-year-old is told to stop laughing. STOP LAUGHING IMMEDIATELY! It is an order. There will be a military arrest unless the order is complied with this instant. There is disrespect being done to the dead! But the eighteen-year-old cannot stop laughing and slapping his thighs. . . . . .

. . . . . The dead . . . . .

. . . . . says Snider, his bony head poking up into rain, pronouncing each word like the thudding of a distant shellburst. He is on the other side of the base, talking to a helpful flight sergeant. Snider's eyes gawk out of his emaciated head. His cameras hang under his poncho. They are somehow heavier. Like useless globs of metal pulling him down, far down. Snider has just been told that he can fly into the slaughterhouse of Dak To on one of the Hueys or the Chinooks that are trying to get through. There would be just enough room for him on top of the ammunition. The ammunition? Snider remembers the ammo-laden Huey he had once seen take a direct hit at one hundred feet. The fireball shook the earth under his feet and he was a kilometer away. And so Snider copes with his ground zero image of being turned into a cinder and presses forth with nervous questions about getting out again. Pictures for LIFE. Deadlines. Editors in New York. And all that sort of thing. Unlikely. You'd have to stay replies the flight sergeant. The returning choppers are stacked full of . . . the . . . dead. . . . .

I see, says Snider trying to sound desperately regretful. But the truth—and he knows it—is that he is terrified. No longer is Snider the First Off, Last In photographer who clings coolly to helicopters that fly into whatever hell happens to be available. No longer are his nerves strung with ice. For now he knows fear. Ever since the darkened C-130 on the runway with the mortars dropping. That one tiny moment of fear; like the smallest sip to an alcoholic. Fear takes over, utterly. And Snider is awash with it now. He is useless. Deadlines, and all that sort of thing, says Snider deciding that the real story this week is Bob Hope. The great comedian is to land once again in two days' time and not to be there would be senseless. It will be a LIFE cover for sure. Or at least a three-page spread. So Snider convinces himself that Bob Hope will be better than Dak To and he climbs onto the motorcycle he has ridden for three years and heads back to Saigon. The roads are wet and he rides more slowly than usual. He is careful. Very careful, because fear has filled him like a cancer. It has eaten at whatever shielded him, whatever set him apart from other men. And now everything seems filled with danger. The trees. The stretches of tall grass. The tin hootches being drummed by the rain. He comes to a part of the highway washed away by the rain and he makes a slow cautious detour onto the side of the road thinking that he will use Ektachrome on Bob Hope. And then the road erupts under him in a deadly geyser of molten earth. The land mine has been meant for a transport truck not a motorcycle and the force rips Snider from one last blur of consciousness and hurls what is left of him far into the air spinning . . . . .

. . . . . like the rain in the battle at Dak To, spun off the whirling rotors of the helicopters and whipped into the faces of those still alive enough to grope through the storm and the mortar explosions. It is all a mad pinwheel of rain-blurred motion and in the middle of it Isaacs stands watching as his evacuation orders are carried out. A strange calm has settled across him. His men have seen it before and have come to rely on him for this calmness in times of great peril. The times when other men became fragments of jabbering emotions. But Isaacs does not think of danger now. He thinks only of the terrible word flung through the fog with the images of his stumbling desperate troops: Retreat. Isaacs walks across the cratered landing zone as if it were a country pasture. His mind is on the next battle. It will be different he vows. Not like this bloody fiasco, stage-managed by army bureaucrats back in Saigon. Xuan Loc will not be like this he tells himself. There will be no retreat at Xuan Loc.

But here it is chaos. A salvage operation carting out human wreckage and all Isaacs can do is keep the damage to a minimum. Too many of his best troops are being slaughtered. And the best troops will be needed for Xuan Loc. But now the enemy fire is too intense to get any more than a few men out to safety. They will have to dig in and wait for the weather to clear. He gives the orders to divert the incoming helicopters south to where the battle is not so intense. South to the highland city of Pleiku . . . . .

. . . . . which has shuddered under the direct assault of war for five endless days. Mr. Thomas peers dourly from the window of his mission just outside Pleiku and knows it is a sign from Him. A sign that the Lord has spoken. Thy will be done! The windows shake as the artillery barrage on the other side of Pleiku begins again. Mr. Thomas is thankful he did not leave for Saigon to meet Lawson. They were to have met two days ago at the Catinat. Mr. Thomas was to have finally read the articles that Lawson was writing. Finally in the pages of the *Herald Tribune* the world would know of the struggle in His name being waged in the humble mission at Pleiku. But Mr. Thomas had seen a sign, a vision in the night, that told him not to go back to Saigon. The sign was his old car parked in the yard outside the mission house. His old car had blown up three nights earlier. Mr. Thomas had peered out at the flaming wreck and rejoiced. It was obviously a sign from Him. A sign saying Don't go. It never occurred to Mr. Thomas that his car had been hit by a stray shell. Nor does it occur to him now that the artillery barrage has changed somehow. He sinks to his knees and asks divine forgiveness for thinking impure thoughts—thoughts that the Lord could perhaps show favor on his humble mission in Pleiku by arranging for the accidental bombardment of the Baptist mission on the other side of town—after the Baptists had been evacuated of course. The Baptists were too big. Too wealthy. A little bombardment would be good for them. He prays to the heavens for a nice little bombardment. But the world around Mr. Thomas suddenly explodes! At first he thinks that heaven itself has erupted. He runs from his old colonial mission house just moments before it is blown to bits. In the briefest of moments it is transformed from a structure with form and texture and history into a steaming uncoordinated abstract of junk. He cannot believe it. He stands in the yard like Lot's wife viewing Sodom. His eyes are like silver dollars. He talks but no sound emerges. He tries to move but cannot. For several minutes he stands in the yard in front of the settling dust. His mouth keeps moving. And finally a sound emerges. It begins as a squeak. Then it ascends to a shriek that can be heard over the artillery. It is the Baptists! He shakes his fist and screams hatred at the Baptists! They are the ones behind it all. He knows that the artillery gunners must be Baptists. He runs around the yard vowing vengeance. The world will know of this perfidy. The *Herald Tribune* will print the story! The full account of this atrocity will be emblazoned across the front page. The Baptists will be exposed for the soul grabbers they are. But it is too late for all that because . . . . .

. . . . . in the third-floor courtyard in the Catinat, Lawson is bellowing at the door of his room holding a bottle in one hand and a telegram in the other. The Vietnamese cleaning ladies grab their pails and scurry for safety. They have seen the siege of the third-floor courtyard before. Lawson's already florid face is beet-red from the exertion of howling incoherencies at the telegram crumbled in his pudgy hand. The telegram is from New York. It tells him that the *Herald Tribune* has ceased publication. Regards. Lawson is suddenly a journalist without a newspaper. Liquor dribbles down onto his correspondent's suit. The suit is under even more pressure than usual to contain Lawson and the seams groan against his bulk like the rigging of a ship in a gale. The siege of the third-floor courtyard rages for the early hours of the morning until Woody comes looking for Barney but instead finds Lawson. Lawson has decided that the answer to all his troubles is a wife. I need a wife, he tells himself over and over. Someone to straighten things out. Home-cooked meals. Clean socks. And through the gin-soaked thought processes he wrings out the decision to set off for the brigadier's whorehouse. There should be no trouble finding a wife there. Or maybe two if a spare was needed. Lawson lurches across the courtyard leaving Woody looking for Barney, who is nowhere around. Barney is not in his room. Nor is he in Milligan's. Or the hotel restaurant. But Woody does not think to look . . . . .

. . . . . a few feet away in Donna's room the light streams through the windows and Barney opens his eyes and looks up as the soft voice asks him if he wants to get

up. He smiles and shakes his head. Donna lowers herself to
kiss him gently and her long dark hair falls around him like
a cloak. He runs his hands across her back and draws her
closer to him as she was when they had fallen asleep. Barney feels suddenly overcome by an unusual emotion. It
creates a warm and gentle laughter and he hugs Donna for
the sheer joy of feeling her body against his. It is a warmth
he can barely remember. It comes from somewhere in his
past, almost from beyond memory, and with it comes a
release—a release from something unknown that makes him
want to cry as well as laugh. He is barely aware that it is the
first time in years that he has laughed simply out of happiness. Instead of humor. The difference between the two is
the linchpin of his life but in the ecstasy of the moment all
that is lost. . . . . .

Jokes

TWELVE

The following day Barney walked for hours through the streets of Saigon. In whatever city he was in, he would walk until he felt he knew at least one area of it well. It was his research. Long ago he had decided that making people laugh was partly a matter of sharing a common experience with them. He had walked through midtown Manhattan and parts of Montreal with Sam Senior. He had watched Sam Senior sniff jokes out of the air like a retriever. A remark from a waitress. The way a policeman talked. How people wore their clothes. It was all research material for Sam Senior and a week, a month or a year later it would suddenly slide out in a droll, offhand manner that would catch his audience off guard and make them laugh all the more because of the way it affected their own lives.

Saigon was mostly colors and noise stuck on top of one another. The old façade of French life in the Orient had long ago been replaced by the American presence. But the dynamics of the three cultures warred among themselves to create a kind of madness that somehow made sense to Barney. Broad tree-lined boulevards created decades ago by French colonial civil servants homesick for the cafés of Montparnasse were now crammed with new American cars that wound around the black-market street vendors who laid their freshly stolen new merchandise out on blankets. It made perfect sense. Barney walked through the moving maze of Le Loi Street where puny cycle drivers pedaled against the bulk of passengers two or three times their own weight. Tiny Citroën taxis painted blue and yellow darted among the army vehicles and black Fords with armed escorts. He walked back past the Central Market, through the awesome odor of mass rot. It was an odor that seemed to seep up through the entire city, but after a while foreigners ceased to notice it. It took the market to shake their olfactory tolerance level. Over near the cathedral he turned back toward the river walking past the Continental Hotel with its fading elegance and its slightly elevated sidewalk café which provided an excellent view of the beggar with the gnarled legs. The beggar slithered back and forth along the sidewalk on his hands trailing his useless legs behind him. Barney had long ago decided that this was a beggar with a sense of marketing. He had aggressively staked out his territory on the sidewalk in front of the Continental's café. No other beggar dared intrude. He wore only short pants, leaving his withered legs exposed. Conscience money flowed. A packed lunch at the Continental was to the beggar what an American freighter in the harbor was to a black-market thief.

Across from the Continental was the Caravelle, the only really modern building in Saigon. The Caravelle was the hotel that had provided Barney with some of his best material. Its occupancy rate was something aspired to by hotel executives around the world. It could charge practically any price and never have an empty room. The Caravelle was crammed with journalists. The biggest networks and publications hired rooms on a yearly basis and schemed to fi d ways to take over the rooms of other networks and publications. The desk clerks were all becoming wealthy. When he was not performing, Barney would sometimes spend the evenings at the bar on the top floor of the Caravelle. It was always packed with journalists from a dozen countries. The bar had become legendary. Some of the toughest journalists who could not get into the Caravelle claimed that news in Vietnam was often made by one drunken reporter receiving a briefing from another drunken reporter at the bar. The same claim was often made by senior military officers whose exploits were reported in anything less than the glowing heroic terms of their own press releases. Such officers had long ago written off reporters anyway. Most of them were either seditious creeps or drunks. Not at all like their own reliable objective aides who wrote the press releases. The reporters at the bar in the Caravelle would become very indignant at even the implication that news was made in this manner. They became most indignant after they had consumed several drinks and formed their next day's article from conversations with other reporters at the bar.

Barney spent hours observing the newsmen at the bar. He began breaking them down into types. The strangest were those who wore the war around them like a flak jacket. It never left them. They were the ones who would mentally disappear whenever the distant artillery shelling lit up the night horizon behind the rooftops of Saigon. They were the liberated crazies, the ones who would write strong condemnations of war but secretly loved it. The war was the missing jigsaw piece of their personalities. And the missing piece was cut from the purest fantasy. It was cowboys and Indians, playing guns, cops and robbers. And the word *glamour*. It was hell, it was despicable, it was murderous, but it was also glamour. There was no way they could go back to covering the state legislature and elections. Not after the war. The war had wormed its way into the darkest part of them and nestled there forever.

Then there were the polyester warriors, the ones who stayed in Vietnam just long enough to interview a few war-chewed officers, watch the distant artillery shelling light up the sky and buy at least one custom-made correspondent's suit. When they returned home, the distant artillery shelling would have become the battle they were involved in, and the correspondent's suit would be worn just enough to let other reporters know they had been to the war.

There were other men with the gentleness of saints, who had devoted their adult lives to photographing one war after another and yet somehow seemed untouched by it all. There were a few female reporters who were always aware of having to prove that they were as tough as the men. In their hotel rooms most of them had long telegrams from their editors telling them to stick to human-interest stories. Orphans. Hospitals. Life at the embassy. Etc. . . . The women made sure it was known how much they resented these telegrams. There were other newsmen who loved Saigon simply because it was not the suburbs outside Cleveland or New York or Paris or Melbourne. It was not like home at all. There were no commuter trains, parent-and-teacher meetings, mortgage payments and car repairs. Most of them wrote weekly letters to their wives telling of the musty accommodations, poor sanitation and long hours. Most of them had one or more beautiful Vietnamese girls with whom they slept. The girls were often very young, sometimes perhaps a little too young. But then this was not like back home. This was war. Most of them loved the war. They loved it more when they did not have to be really involved in it. They preferred to get telegrams from their editors telling them to stick to the human-interest stories. Orphans. Hospitals. Life at the embassy. Etc. . . .

Barney used his research trips to the bar of the Caravelle to create characters whom he used in his routines at the Club. One was Wallingford C. Stone III, heir to a chain of newspapers across America. Wallingford C. Stone III was waiting for his father to die so his name would be at the top of the masthead. In the meantime he was fulfilling his obligations as a respected multimillionaire who accompanied other multimillionaires to Vietnam in order to receive firsthand in-depth high-level discussions with military leaders and get laid. As Barney told it, his official purpose was to set the public back home straight. He did this in a column entitled *A Stone's View.* Barney's tales of Wallingford C. Stone III being taken up to a front-line position by exuberant senior officers was an experience that every member of his audience had observed. Upon reaching the front-line position, Wallingford C. Stone III had one simple desire: He wanted to get the hell out. As quickly as possible. People got shot there. Long ago he had decided that he was too rich to die. His immediate reaction was to buy the helicopter which had just flown him in. Then he would simply order it to fly out. The company could always use another plane. Just clean off the army markings and it would be fine.

The continuing adventures of Wallingford C. Stone III became an almost weekly feature of Barney's act. In certain areas of Vietnam some of the more elegant news executives could not understand why they were called Wallingford by the troops. Barney had created other newsmen characters. One was René, the grizzled little French TV cameraman who was captured by the enemy and then released. But René knew his rights. He refused to let them set him free. René realized that after three days of capture he was being paid on continuous overtime. René did everything possible to avoid freedom. He was no fool. He was on triple time. In Paris, René had been a Marxist and had fought for liberation of any kind. He spent his captivity making sure his captors did not liberate him and computing his overtime pay. He had decided he would stay captured for a year. That would enable him to buy a chateau outside Paris with his overtime pay. The first thing he would do is fire all the help. They were sure to be Marxist. Every day René promised his unwilling captors jobs after the war. Gardener. Cook. Chauffeur. Whatever they wanted. But no overtime.

Barney's newsmen characters came directly from the bar at the Caravelle. He regarded himself as a reporter of a different kind. He was reporting on the reporters. But he was using jokes instead of facts. Sam Senior would have understood. It was a little like the true old time burlesque. Sometimes it was more fun to be a participant. On this afternoon he decided to accompany the newsmen who reluctantly left the bar at the Caravelle and walked across the square to the daily event that had become known as the five-o'clock follies. The five-o'clock follies was the meeting between the military and the press. The military sent out their best young press information officers to stand up on a stage with maps and charts and lie about what was going on in the country. Most of the time the young press information officers did not know if they were lying or not. They were simply playing the military Christians to the lions of the press. The men who actually decided what should be said never appeared up on the stage. They were too smart for that.

Barney walked into the briefing theater after quickly showing the military press card he had stolen from Lawson. The guard at the door waved him through. The reporters inside were either slouched in their seats or scribbling quickly as a young officer spoke from the stage. Most of the reporters seemed haggard and dissipated. The young officer seemed to be polished. He almost shone. Everything about him was starched and crisp. Not one hair was out of place. He called everyone *sir* and never showed any signs of emotion. The question period was almost over when Barney shot his hand into the air and when recognized by a nod from the stage fired off his question in the staccato manner of the reporters. Barnett W. Lucas. Idaho *Times-Gleaner*, he said. All the reporters had to identify themselves and their affiliation before each question. That way the press officers could listen to the tape recordings and mark down who was friendly and who was not. Question regarding 173rd Airborne at Bien Hoa, said Barney tersely. Right sir, said the young officer, go ahead. Why, asked Barney, are the enemy casualties in that area listed at several thousand for the past month when the whole province is shown on your chart as being 98.4 per cent pacified? The young officer smiled. Obviously, he said, because the enemy has moved troop concentrations into that area. Ten minutes ago you said that all the enemy was up north at Dak To, said Barney. The other reporters sat up like hounds testing the air. The young officer showed a moment of uncertainty and asked to refer to his notes. The reporters referred to their notes. Questions soon began overlapping. How could so many enemy be killed when according to the figures there was almost no enemy there? Who compiled the figures? *Invented* the figures? The young officer became angry. It was the first time anyone had seen him angry. He glanced offstage to the other officers, who were too smart to be where he was. The reporters loved it. It was the show they had been hoping for. But suddenly the young officer realized where he had seen Barney. That man's a comedian! he roared. Then put him up on the stage, yelled one of the reporters. He belongs here, shouted someone else. Laughter broke out across the theater. Papers were thrown into the air and the guards were called in.

When Barney returned to the Catinat, Isaacs' black staff car was parked outside. He went upstairs. The third-floor courtyard was quiet. All the doors to the rooms were closed in the coolness of the early evening. A few lights were on. Donna's room was in darkness. Barney circled the courtyard and then went into his room. Before he had switched on the light there was a sizzling noise outside and then a thud against the door. He opened the door while the knife that was embedded in it still quivered. Bannon grinned through the twilight. He wore a big bandage that gave his head the shape of a light bulb. Thought I'd play a little joke on you, he said. You're a funnyman. You like jokes. Bannon laughed and stepped up to the door to pry the knife free. You got me last night he giggled. Goddam but you got me. Must have gone down like a cut pine tree huh? My fuckin' head felt like you'd stuck this thing in it, he said holding up the knife in the light and laughing through his bad teeth. Barney was sure the laughter came through those bad teeth in black little clouds of rotted air.

Bannon did not seem angry about what had happened to him the night before. It was all part of being in the war. But I'll get my chance, he grinned. All's fair. Ain't that what they say? He threw the knife against the door with a burst of ferocity. It whistled through the darkness catching the light as it went, a metallic lightning bolt that slammed into the door sending out an explosion of splinters. Bannon regarded his craftsmanship with pleasure. Hey funnyman, you been screwing the colonel's girl? he laughed. You been poking the old sow ain't you?

Barney said nothing. Bannon began to laugh and slap his thighs. Oh funnyman I know what you been doing while the cat's away. But you can't fool old Bannon. Nosir. Not old Bannon. I can tell 'cause they went for a walk out somewhere. I drove him here and he was like a rutting goat. He didn't want no walks. He wanted to do some serious stud farming. Like they've always done. But no she wants to talk. Now why would she all of a sudden want to talk? Bannon laughed and tugged at the knife in the door. Nope, you can't fool old Bannon.

There were voices on the other side of the courtyard. They were low, almost whispers but the footsteps on the tiles were clearer than voices. It was Isaacs and Donna. They were visible through the palm trees only for a moment. Bannon took great delight in watching Barney's reaction. Maybe old Bannon can be fooled, he said. Barney tried to show nothing but knew he was failing. Behind the palm trees there was the sound of a door opening and closing. And then silence. Well how about that? grinned Bannon. They've gone inside. Barney was thankful it was dark. He felt his face grow red from a kind of anger that he wanted no one to see. He wanted to go over to her door and make an idiot of himself by kicking it in and yelling all sorts of mock-heroic catchphrases that in a different era would have meant a duel at dawn. At least it would have been resolved in those days. Now there would be just a lot of indignation on all sides. The door to her room suddenly opened again and Isaacs left quietly. He was alone. Bannon's eyes went wide. Ohmigod he muttered. He kicks my ass if I'm not at the car when he is. He grinned at Barney. Maybe you can't fool old Bannon huh?

Several minutes later Donna emerged carrying her wardrobe bag. She stopped and looked over to where Barney was sitting. We're performing at one of the clubs just up the street, she said. We've got a new act we're trying out. Good luck, said Barney. They looked at one another from across the courtyard for a moment and then with a quick uncertain smile she left.

Barney sat outside his room as the night noises of Saigon settled into the courtyard. *Todlachen* you idiot, he muttered to himself.

A familiar wheezing sound came up the stairs into the

courtyard. It was soon followed by a bulbous silhouette struggling with two oversized suitcases. It was Sheldon. He stopped on the landing gasping for breath between teeth that clenched a long dead cigar. On his head was a crumpled golf hat. Pinned to the hat was a big button that read *Hey baby—Your place or mine?* Sheldon wheezed and huffed up a few more stairs and then saw Barney watching him. Hey kid, he yelled in his thickest Brooklyn accent, you a statue or what? Pretend you're one of my fans. Gimme a hand willya. Before my truss comes off and whiplashes both of us.

Sorry, said Barney. But from all the noise I thought someone was bringing an iron lung up here and— And someone had welded it shut, interrupted Sheldon. Hah hah very funny kid but don't fool with my lines. Now then where the hell is this room number Thirty-A. Sheldon held up the room key squinting at it and wheezing. Thirty-A is taken said Barney. That's Snider's room. Not any longer it ain't kid. It's my room now. You and I are neighbors now. Can you spare a cup of flour? A joke kid. A joke. What are you standing there gawking at? My fly open or something? Sheldon pushed the door of the room open and reached for a light. Barney stood in the middle of the courtyard. He got killed kid. The poor bastard got killed. Ran over a mine on his motorcycle. He's in a zillion pieces now. Like a pizza. So don't look at me like that kid. You understand? If I didn't get the room someone else would. Gimme a hand.

Sheldon switched on the light and looked around, stunned. Jesus, it's a goddam zoo in here. In the years that Snider had rented the room no one else had ever been allowed inside. No one else had even seen the inside of the room. Cleaning ladies had been instructed not to enter and to leave the clean sheets and towels outside the door. The room was a spider's web of glass tubing. It was the kind of glass tubing used in laboratories. The glass tubing ran over Sheldon's head, down the length of the room and into beakers, flasks and test tubes. On a counter were dozens of plastic vials filled with pills. Barney emptied one of the vials and sniffed at the contents of a pill. He grinned and held it out to Sheldon. Try one he said, it'll make you laugh at your own jokes. Sheldon looked utterly intimidated by the room. He sniffed at the pill. It's some kind of dope, said Barney. Maybe LSD. Sheldon jumped back as if even being near the powder would send him off babbling. On one wall there was a full-length mirror and beside it were pinned photographs of Snider. In the photographs he was wearing the uniform of an army general. The uniform hung on a hook not far from where Sheldon was standing. In the photographs Snider's eyes had a glazed, lost look. His bony head protruded up from the shoulders of the uniform as if it had somehow been screwed in at an improper angle.

Hey kid, muttered Sheldon, staring fearfully at the photograph, was this guy missing a few parts? Sheldon's eyes seemed to follow them from the photograph. The same phosphorus eyes that had stared right through people in life were chasing Sheldon around the room. Spooky, he muttered. Hey kid you got any space in your room? Just for a few nights? Till I can get this zombie's playpen cleared out. Barney grinned and shook his head. Sheldon looked desperate. Listen kid I'll get you tickets for Bob Hope. He's performing tomorrow. I know Bob. I can get you a seat right beside me. In the front row where you can see up the skirts of the dancers. The pussy seats we used to call them. Come on kid. You can't leave me in this place. Sleep with the light on, said Barney.

Very funny putz, said Sheldon as Barney left. Cripplekicker, he screamed. He grabbed a vial of pills and threw it at Barney as hard as he could. Take two after every meal, he yelled. The vial of pills sailed past Barney's head and landed by the stairs. Barney turned back angrily. But Sheldon suddenly looked as if he were on the verge of tears. All his angry blustering had vanished. Without his blustering the world would walk firmly over Sheldon and then kick him onto the junk pile of frightened souls. It was his protective shield. Barney suddenly understood Sheldon. He wanted to feel sorry for him. But feeling sorry for Sheldon now would destroy him. It would turn him into one of life's frightened souls. So Barney yelled at him instead. It was the only way to help Sheldon. You throw things like you tell jokes, Barney shouted. You never hit the target. Sheldon whimpered resentfully with hound-dog eyes. And don't tell me that you know Bob Hope. The only time you ever met Bob Hope was when he walked through Hanson's fifteen years ago. And you missed him because you were on the phone to your agent asking why you weren't getting any work. Right? Like hell, said Sheldon defensively. I know Bob. He and I used to work together. Oh yeah? said Barney, I didn't know he waited on tables in the Catskills. Very funny smartass, snapped Sheldon, regaining some of his normal belligerence, but I will have you know that I worked with Bob in films. Yeah, yeah, said Barney, trying to act bored, in *The Road to Bali*. Right? Everybody at Hanson's heard about it a million times. They said you played the part of the road.

Hey kid, yelled Sheldon. Come round tomorrow. I'll give you some lessons. And if you're nice I'll let you look at the jokes I throw out. Barney laughed at Sheldon. The laughter made him even angrier. Barney walked out into the courtyard. Another vial of pills whistled over his head. Try them as suppositories, yelled Sheldon. Fart your way to dreamland.

Later that night the vial of pills was responsible for making the third-floor courtyard a battleground of
competing nightmares. Lawson kicked the event off with a
low moan that became a shriek. He was dreaming that he
was being beaten by his latest wife. His latest wife was the
Vietnamese bar girl in the Bon Accueil whom he had met
five hours earlier. He had stopped there with Woody to plan
the raid on Brigadier Mosby's whorehouse. It was a strategy
meeting that had definitely peaked early after Woody and
Lawson momentarily cut their losses and fell in love with
the same bar girl. The bar girl wore a miniskirt and made
sure that she bent over to serve the drinks at the table next
to theirs. Every time she bent over, Lawson found himself
staring at a wide expanse of smooth yellow nylon. I'm falling in love with her ass, Lawson announced triumphantly.
After his third scotch he fell face forward into the expanse
of yellow nylon, and proclaimed eternal love in words that
were too muffled to hear. The bar girl laughed and began
slapping his face between her hands to bring him back into
the world of the living. Before she brought him back, she
quickly made change on his drinks and cheated him out of
six hundred piasters.

It was staring into that joyously laughing face and feeling the sting of his cheeks that Lawson loved. But in his
nightmare there was no joyous laugh. No tingling sting. Instead there was a jabbering that he could not understand.
And a dull relentless pounding across his body. He called
out in his sleep. And moaned until he woke up and
shrieked. He shrieked because he was totally naked and
some dark-haired woman was spitting curses at him in some
language he did not understand. He had never seen the
woman before. She was not even his latest wife. The woman
was hysterical with fury. She wailed at him with questions
that he could not understand and beat across his head like a

drummer doing a solo. Lawson bellowed and fell off the bed trying to escape. She began breaking things over Lawson, who was desperately trying to remember what his latest wife looked like. All he could remember about her was a wide expanse of yellow nylon. He could not remember her face. Maybe this was his wife. But what language was this she was speaking? It was not Vietnamese.

The woman was the receptionist at the Italian embassy. She was in the middle of a tirade against men. The receptionist at the Italian embassy was only twenty-two but already could feel herself growing old. It was a thought that would not have occurred to her back home in Calabria in the south of Italy. There she would have been too busy with her fourth child. The receptionist at the Italian embassy had begun the evening with Colonel Wzcninski. He had been courting her for months, showing up at the embassy with flowers, and his hair slicked back like Rudolph Valentino. At first she had rejected all of his offers. But every day flowers kept coming. The reception area of the Italian embassy soon looked like a florist's shop. After a while he began sending her plastic flowers. They would last as long as his love he told her in a note. She finally accepted his invitation in the hope of making her lover jealous. Her lover was the First Secretary of the embassy.

Everything in the receptionist's life was blissful until she followed her lover to Vietnam, where he had just been posted. By the time she arrived, he had decided that an oriental mistress was what he had really been looking for all his life. The First Secretary had fallen madly in love with one of the girls at a bar on Tu Do Street.

From the moment she left the embassy with Colonel Wzcninski the receptionist knew she had made a mistake. She hated everything about him. His cologne reminded her of decaying straw. His trousers were too short and his an-

kles were skinny. And his gallantry bored her. They talked
to one another in broken English. He talked incessantly and
all she could make out was something about the Polish cavalry and how he had just won a saber duel with some American. She wanted to go back to the apartment the embassy
had rented for her. But her roommate also worked for the
embassy and could be bribed by her ex-lover to tell him
what time she got home. So she was determined to stay out
all night. Even if it was with the Polish colonel. She was
hoping her lover would fly into a jealous rage.

Colonel Wzcninski was overjoyed when she accepted
his invitation to look at the flowers in his apartment in the
Catinat. The flowers were plastic but he was sure that
would prove of little consequence. But after they entered
the lobby of the Catinat she wanted to throw up. The
thought of being alone in a room with Colonel Wzcninski
made her almost desperate. She had the sudden image of sitting in his bed watching him undress. She was sure he was
the kind who would meticulously fold his trousers and hang
them up while she was watching. Not at all like the First
Secretary, who left an amorous trail of clothes from the
kitchen to the bedroom, and all the while muttered breathless incantations of eternal love. Colonel Wzcninski flashed
his best smile as he reached out and grasped her hand in the
darkness of the lobby. He was almost strutting with authority as he led her up the stairs toward the fourth floor. She
was slightly in front of him on the stairs when she felt his
hands on her hips. She slapped at him but he took it as a
sign of love and began running his hands up from her hips
to her breasts while saying something about the old days of
the Polish cavalry. He grasped her left breast and chortled
Charge! in Polish. She wished that her hypocritical brothers
in Calabria had been there at that moment to defend her
honor. Her brothers were forever talking about their sister's

honor. They would die for it, they said. Let one man so much as lay a hand upon her. Her brothers were forever following her all over Calabria hoping to defend her honor, and pinching the asses of other girls whose brothers had sworn to defend their honor. Murder for honor was a cottage industry in Calabria. The receptionist at the Italian embassy wrestled loose from the grasp of Colonel Wzcninski just long enough to turn and bring her knee up swiftly the way her brothers had taught her. Her knee wedged momentarily in his groin. Her brothers had been right after all. Colonel Wzcninski's eyes suddenly seemed to spin in different directions. He clutched at the wall. A jagged smile quivered across his face. With a glassy stare he croaked a few words about the old days in the Polish cavalry and walked with pigeon-toed, halting steps up the stairs toward his room.

The receptionist from the Italian embassy adjusted her dress and looked around. The stairway passed through some kind of courtyard. In the faint light she noticed a shiny object at her feet. It was a plastic vial containing pills. They looked like sleeping pills. Suddenly an idea came to her. She put the vial of pills in her purse.

An hour later she sat in the chair in Colonel Wzcninski's room still holding her thighs together while he huffed and wheezed trying to pry them apart. She had successfully resisted his every attempt to make love to her. He had tugged and struggled to get her onto the bed. But she was almost as big as he was. She had kicked him over the edge of the bed and run back to the chair. He had eventually appeared, dazed and perspiring, from the other side of the bed and then rushed at the chair. He heaved against the chair trying to push it closer to the bed. She dug her heels into the floor and pushed back against him. The chair with her in it clattered back and forth across the room. Finally he collapsed, exhausted. He could not understand this woman. She did not want to leave but she did not want to make love. It must be some kind of game. To make him prove his manliness. Maybe this was the way they did it in Italy. No wonder the Italians lost so many wars. Their men were all exhausted.

With a quavering flourish he stood up and looked at the object of his affection. She glowered at him. She was radiant in her fury. He decided that it was just her Italian way of showing that she loved him. He opened the door of his room and bellowed gallantly for the sergeant from Cracow to bring more wine. All night he had opened the door between attacks and bellowed orders. He was sure this would impress her. After the wine arrived he resumed his exhausted quest to part her thighs. He knelt in front of the chair pulling and tugging until he sank back almost delirious with exhaustion. This explains a lot about the Italian economy, he told himself. He reached for his glass of wine. Within minutes he was bouncing off the walls. The hordes had broken loose with his mind. The room lit up in a million stars that burst in colors he had never seen before. The stars were created by one of Snider's pills that had been secretly dropped into his glass by the receptionist from the Italian embassy. The pills were from the plastic vial she had found in the third-floor courtyard. It was the vial that Sheldon had thrown at Barney.

The receptionist was terrified. He lurched all over her, jabbering and tearing at her clothes. He seemed much stronger than before. She flung open the door and the sergeant from Cracow fell into the room. Behind him were a dozen Polish officers hoping for mass rape. She fled along the corridor. Colonel Wzcninski staggered after her bellowing orders through the starbursts. He was ordering her to stop and undress.

She ran down the stairs to the third-floor courtyard. Every room was dark. But the door to one room was wide open. She ran into the room where the door was open. As the call of the Polish cavalry sounded incoherently behind her she closed the door. The courtyard outside echoed with shouts. Lights went on in other rooms. Colonel Wzcninski jumped around like a man on a pogo stick while his men tried to hold him down. He yelled at them in the only Italian word he knew. *Stupido! Stupido!* From the other side of the courtyard came the shriek of another man, having a nightmare. *Ladies and gentlemen—Bob Hope!* shrieked the other man over and over. It was Sheldon. Listening in the darkness of a strange hotel room the receptionist from the Italian embassy suddenly knew what she wanted: she wanted to be having her fourth baby somewhere back in Calabria. She wanted to leave this insanity that she had been lured into. In a moment of clarity so precise that she was later to think she was seeing a vision of the kind the priests had said came only to saints, she realized the root of all her problems. *Men!*

It was *men* who had used her at every turn. They had paid bribes for the use of her body. They defended her honor while pinching her ass. They taught her piety while bartering her morals. They had promised marriage and then left to go home for dinner. They had lured her halfway around the world to hear the news of their latest love. Her father. Her brothers. The priests. The slobbering old men at the office. The First Secretary. This man from the Polish cavalry. It was a conspiracy—a male conspiracy to use her and cast her aside like a rag doll now that she was twenty-two and growing old. She suddenly saw an image of herself as a suffering saint. But this was replaced by another image of an avenging angel. The saint and the avenger warred within her until Lawson decided the holy scenario with a pronouncement.

The pronouncement was *Alice for christsakes put that down!* Lawson was moaning in his sleep again. The receptionist from the Italian embassy had not even been aware of another presence in the room in which she was hiding. She barely made out the figure of the man lying naked on the bed. Lawson looked like a beached whale. His stomach protruded and quivered in the faint light. His lips parted and came together with sputtering little noises that faded into low whistles. His legs twitched, sending masses of deathly-white flesh rippling like jelly. *Alice!* he screamed. *Put it down!*

Thank you! Thank you! You've been a beautiful audience! came the cry from Sheldon's dream across the courtyard. The sounds from outside filtered into the room as she circled Lawson. The babbling of the colonel faded as he was carried up the stairs insisting that his horse had been stolen. She circled Lawson with the pure serenity of one without options. Her destiny was before her. With a beatific calm, she gazed down at Lawson's bloated white nakedness. Her twenty-two years were welling up in her. Her four unborn babies were murmuring. The priests were pinching her ass. *Men!* She leapt on Lawson, thrashing and pounding with her fists. *Alice!* he screamed. *You've been just marvelous!* yelled Sheldon from across the courtyard . . . . .

. . . . . for in his dream Sheldon is awash with adulation from the multitudes who have come to shower him with their love and their grateful laughter. In his dream he has become . . . Bob Hope!

THIRTEEN

. . . . . but at that moment, in those the darkest hours of the night, the still hours when his mind sees shrouds over all that is living, Isaacs reads his invitation to attend the private party being held in honor of Bob Hope's visit to Vietnam. It is to be held after the performance tomorrow afternoon in Saigon. But Isaacs cannot think of laughter. It is something remote from him now, like an appendage that has withered and been left behind on some forgotten path. He has returned from a defeat. A shattering bloody defeat that has spilled lives out across the highlands around Dak To. Even now the transport planes lumber into the night loaded with metal cases, each with eight handles, a flag tied on top and what had been one of his men inside. Losers. The ignored of history. The thought drives him out of his office, out to the area near the runway. He has not slept in almost one full day but the fuel of raw nervous energy drives him on. It is an energy wrung from overheated inner generators turning on their own momentum. He cannot stop. Everything is in motion within him. The fear of being history's cipher. And a raging against the insignificance of this war—*his* war. He walks through the darkness inwardly seething at the mad irony of it all.

But on this night there is a second rage that has descended like nettles across his mind. It is Donna. The memories of his first glimpse of her are played out like phantoms in the blackness before him. In his mind he sees her glide across the stage and then vanish on the runway. A transport plane roars past, shaking the earth and the air around him, climbing into the night sky with its cargo of silence, the hundreds of souls locked within their metal cases. But *she* flashes past him with those haunting dark eyes that he sees in the darkness. More than anything else at this moment, more than history itself, he wants to reach out and draw her into him. Casting off this careening emptiness. It is roaring within him, dominating him. She has become an obsession in her elusiveness. Everything in his life has been a quest for control. Over others. Over an enemy. Over the forces of nature. Over himself. Everything can be brought into a kind of order. But there is no order to his emotions now. He has ventured out unprotected, far out into emotional terrain that is for him uncharted. He has taken every step in the hope that it would be the last. In the hope that *she* would stop and gently yield and become the part of him that was now empty.

But it is too late. Isaacs wanders through the night raging at what he feels for her. He has begun to *need* her. And always she dances away from him in some way that does not yield to any kind of order he knows. He can feel her eyes just as he felt them during the worst moments at Dak To when the human wreckage of a battalion had fallen around him. Then he had seized the chaos out of the cries and the blood and by force of will had pounded that wreckage into a kind of order. Even there he forged an order, a control. And even there he had thought of her and been stunned by those thoughts.

Isaacs has walked past the end of the runway. From the darkness comes a nervous voice ordering him to halt. Easy son, he says. It's your commanding officer. A deathly-white shaft of light suddenly flashes upon him. Then the nervous voice of the sentry. Yessir! The light vanishes and Isaacs walks further. The nervous voice calls out after him saying, Sir I wouldn't go out there sir. They've been attacking the perimeter sir. But Isaacs hardly hears the sentry. He walks out toward the perimeter and it occurs to him that here too he is unprotected. He carries no weapon. He walks out to the edges of the barbed wire. Behind him the sentry calls out again, telling him that it is dangerous out there. But the voice seems distant and there is a euphoria that has overcome Isaacs. It is the sudden exhilaration of walking into an unknown that could destroy him.

Isaacs begins to yell into the darkness. There is an enemy out there somewhere and he taunts that enemy. He walks along the barbed wire calling out at the darkness. Screaming at it. Daring it to try—just try and destroy him. It is a lunging rage that erupts and bellows into the void. He comes to a part of the barbed wire that has been cut and he runs through onto the windward side of the peril, laughing and raging at whatever or whomever is out there.

Before him now there is nothing but the blackness of the Vietnamese night. It is its own kind of uncharted terrain. And it is silent. There is not a movement, not a sound. For that moment it is under his control. He has taunted it and won. A kind of order has been imposed upon it. *His* order. He sinks to his knees exhausted and in a flash *she* dances through the night. . . . . .

. . . . . and from the sandbagged sentry post the sentry peers out and wonders what in hell is going on out there. He sees Isaacs yelling into the night. Only two nights ago, that night had zapped the sentry with enough terror to leave him tingling for days. The guerrillas had come silently out of the darkness. So silently that he had heard nothing until they were through the barbed wire and almost upon him. He had screamed and cursed and prayed and emptied his .50-caliber machine gun at that terrifying silence. Yet still they crawled from the darkness like creatures from his worst fantasies. The last one had died only inches away from the sentry's tiny sandbagged fortress. Every few nights something would happen. And now this crazy bastard is wandering around looking to get his ass shot off. The sentry decides that the stories he has heard about Isaacs' fearlessness are true. They'll never believe him he decides, when he tells them about the colonel taunting the gooks outside the barbed wire in the middle of the night. The sentry is thrilled by Isaacs' heroism. . . . . .

. . . . . but out beyond the perimeter Isaacs is kneeling on the ground and doing what he has not done since he was a boy. He is weeping. He is embarrassed and afraid of anyone seeing him. But he cannot stop weeping. . . . . .

. . . . . while in her room at the hotel, Donna sits up in bed and stares out at the lights of the courtyard. The noises from outside have made it impossible to sleep. At intervals all night long, there have been strange shouts and arguments. For the moment it is quiet. Too quiet. It is at such times that a kind of loneliness settles in but it is of her own choice for the moment. Hours ago she had made excuses to Isaacs when he had said that he wanted to stay with her. But somehow the excuses were too obvious and it showed in his eyes. There was the slightest shadow of desperation that fell across his smile and she had known that he was now twisting slowly and painfully in the wind. And now she only wants it all to end. It has gone too far . . . but her thoughts are interrupted by the strange cry *Ladies and gentlemen: Bob Hope!* . . . . .

. . . . . and that afternoon Bob Hope will step out in front of thousands of young soldiers the way he has done for decades through all the middle years of the twentieth century whenever America has been in a war, and often when she has not. Bob Hope has been good for America. He has made her citizens and her troops laugh through the best and the worst of those years. And America has responded in one of the ways that she does best. She has made Bob Hope rich. Fabulously rich in a way that the nickel-grabbers back at Hanson's could not even begin to imagine. And in America he is better known than anyone except perhaps the President himself. The oval face with the sloped nose and the mischievous eyes has virtually become a national emblem. No one in all of America's history has achieved such fame and fortune simply by making people laugh.

But this afternoon something goes slightly wrong. Bob Hope stands there in Saigon on a crudely fashioned outdoor stage with a corrugated tin roof telling jokes to the khaki multitudes. Many of the soldiers in the audience are the sons of the soldiers who laughed at Bob Hope's jokes when he played Europe twenty-five years earlier. But that was in the war against Hitler and now it is all slightly different and, in some strange way that he cannot quite put his finger on, slightly wrong. For the sons are not the fathers. And there is no Hitler as a galvanizing enemy. There is a different mood to his audience now, almost resentful. It is as if his audience is silently signaling that he, Bob Hope the fabulously wealthy comedian, the friend of Presidents, the supporter of this war, is a part of the reason why they are in Vietnam.

He sees the strangeness first in tiny bits of show business anarchy. Some of the dancers in his troupe break away from the rehearsed routines and thrust their upraised arms into the air with their two forefingers forming a V. In the old days, the days of gallantry and Winston Churchill and ready-aye-ready the V meant *Victory*. It was hope and fervor and patriotism. But now this spark of anarchy flashes through the audience and arms shoot up like lightning rods catching the message and returning the V sign and now it means none of those things. Now the V sign means all that is anarchy in the eyes of the generals. It means Fuck the Army, and Peace, and War Sucks. Bob Hope watches it all from the wings and takes note of this strange mood, so different from the G.I. Joes of another generation. But to hell with it. Laughter is laughter he decides. And sure enough when he is out there it all starts off like the old days and the laughs come as they always have. . . . . .

. . . . . And from the sixth row, Sheldon is thrilled. He sits baking in the sun, wearing a newspaper hat on his head and sweating from every possible pore. For no one else would he endure such discomfort. But it is worth it. Just to see Bob's timing. Incredible! His every raised eyebrow or mock grimace. Or the pursed lips that come when a joke dies. They are such perfect devices, like a craftsman's tools instantly called upon to hone a certain mood, to enhance a laugh. So enthralled is Sheldon that he begins to mime those pursed lips, those mock grimaces, without knowing he is doing it. For at that moment he and Bob Hope are one. The laughter is *his* laughter. But then something goes wrong. One of the jokes goes wrong, for when Bob Hope mentions that he has talked to the President there is loud booing. It is a comic minefield and Bob Hope quickly retraces his steps with just a flicker of concern. But the tone has been set and in an instant the jokes are mentally reshuffled as the booing subsides. Sheldon is astounded. He is furious. Perspiration pinwheels from his bulging face as he looks around to see who is booing. It is sacrilege. It is like pissing on the altar, he tells himself. . . . . .

. . . . . But these the middle years of the century have turned the antennae of humor in a direction slightly different from what Sheldon has sensed. The laughter itself now is slightly different. It has become part of the arsenal, a weapon directed against the high and mighty. And just as overzealous lieutenants leading their fearful men out on glory-ridden suicidal patrols are now being found shot in the back—*fragging* it is called—so are national leaders being fragged by explosions of laughter. The Little Tramp is fighting back.

The Little Tramp! From the genius of Charlie Chaplin in the early years of the century had come the most universal of all the comic characters. With baggy pants and ragged coat the Little Tramp is forever being pitched onto the scrap heap of life. Around the world the multitudes had roared with a laughter that can only come from having been pitched onto the scrap heap of life. Chaplin's humor in his movies catches a common thread and the world sees itself as the Little Tramp, dusting itself off, struggling for decency and living under the whim of the mighty. It is a kind of image that emerges naturally enough from the First World War when the troops were entertained with the gentle music-hall humor and then sent off to die in unquestioning waves. Twenty thousand in one summer's day at the Somme. A million casualties there in five months. Ready-aye-ready. And out of that abattoir comes the Little Tramp, for who knows better than he that sooner or later someone

of high position will be around to enunciate the central doc-
trine of the century:

Annihilation is in your own interest.

and what else is there to do but dust yourself off and try and
get through it all with a sense of decency? If it comes to a
choice is it not better to die laughing? It is, after all, a
laughing war. . . . . .

. . . . . but Sheldon cares for none of this as Bob Hope
regains his comic stride. Sheldon looks around thrilled as
the laughs resume. Bob is in good form today. He wonders
where Barney is. He should be here. To watch the master
work and study his timing. God what timing. He cannot see
Barney anywhere. That's the trouble with these young comedians he tells himself. They never do their homework.

But Barney is fifty kilometers away . . . . .

. . . . . where he stood in the hot dusty breezes beside
the runway watching a tragic ceremony that was part of
the paratroop tradition. Standing on the runway was an
army chaplain intoning mournful funeral rites. Beside the
chaplain were Isaacs and most of the high ranking officers
of the brigade. On the runway, lined up in eerie rows, were
the boots of the men who had been killed at Dak To. Just
the boots, nothing else.

Watching the boots was like watching ghosts. Barney
expected the boots to move or shift their weight from one to
another on the blistering asphalt. In his mind he saw row
upon row of phantom soldiers standing in the boots muttering impatiently about the way these goddam chaplains can
drag anything out. And he saw row upon row of metal cases
with the phantom soldiers clawing to get out. Shrieking
tearfully that it was all a mistake. That it should have been
someone else sealed in there for eternity.

The heat was intense. Tiny whirlpools of dust spun in hot funnels of air. The sky was bleached white by the sun. The air was almost too hot to be breathed. A crowd of soldiers watched the ceremony. Each one had stared at the row of boots and had the same thought. Each had tried to see which were the boots of his friends. And each had for an instant seen his friends standing there swaying in the heat waves rippling off the runway. One man was weeping silently. Others were staring down at their own boots lost in some there-but-for-the-grace-of-god-go-I wonderland of gratitude. Most were just staring blankly off into some inner infinity. Barney watched them as much as he watched the boots. He wanted to know what the others were thinking. He wanted to know if anyone else there was watching the fearful disposal of the ingredients in a social experiment. The aim of the experiment had been to create history. It had failed. Now another experiment would be tried. Some of the ingredients were standing beside him in the heat listening to their own thoughts as the chaplain droned on. Barney wanted something outrageous to happen. Something so outrageous that it would stun the ceremony to a halt. And bring laughter, tears, anger, anything to shake loose the benediction of sorrow. He wanted it all to be mad and Irish. He wanted it to be a wake. Where the dead were regaled in wild stories and the sorrow and pain came out in its truest voices of laughter. Anything but this. He wanted some mad mechanical genius to have fixed up devices that would make some of the boots twitch. Or begin to tap impatiently in the heat. Or make a pair of them walk away. He stared out into the white heat and saw the chaplain peer fearfully over the Bible in mid-vowel.

And Barney laughed to himself as he alone saw the boots turn and slowly sneak off down the runway.

FOURTEEN

On the afternoon after the ceremony on the runway, Isaacs held his longest baseball practice. He had left the runway walking around the long terrible row of the boots of his dead paratroopers and headed straight for the practice. He had walked across the arid dusty plain beside the runway, under the hot white sky of the afternoon. The images of defeat had baked into his memory. The metal caskets. The rows of boots. The nasal intonation of the chaplain. He wanted to be rid of it all. To cleanse himself of a sense of loss.

Baseball was his sole diversion. His one quiet passion that could be pursued while war and chaos swirled around him. Other men played golf, whored, went hunting, played chess, dabbled in astronomy or joined a choir. Isaacs coached baseball. He had once made what was almost a clinical study of all the other sports and found them to be in some way lacking compared to baseball. Only baseball possessed the measured symmetry and structure in the way it was played. The finely tuned precision of a man throwing a ball which could travel in an infinite number of permutations of velocity and rotation. The subtle strategy used in the advancement of a man from one base to another. And the always present possibility of sheer force combining with exquisite skill to blast a baseball out of the stadium. As a boy Isaacs had spent most of his summers doing little else but playing baseball. The worst year of his youth was when he was on a team that finished in last place. He hated losing. He tormented the weaker players who made errors that cost them the game. Several of these boys quit and Isaacs was not sorry to see them leave. Survival of the fittest. Isaacs believed in Darwin's theory of natural selection in all elements of life. He studied the lives of the baseball greats. Many of them were intemperate, opinionated, unreasonable and overly demanding. That was what made them great. Greatness and decency seldom meshed. When it became apparent that he would become a better soldier than a ballplayer he decided that his hobby would be managing a team. He began to study the lives of the great baseball managers. The old portraits of Connie Mack with his Philadelphia Athletics showed a man with eyes as dead as charcoal and a face like a Jesuit in pain. But a winner. And John J. McGraw, who looked out of the old New York Giants photographs with a rapacious smile that seemed to speak of illiteracy and meanness. Another winner. Most of the teams Isaacs coached had been winners.

At some of the worst moments of the war Isaacs could be found standing on the dusty baseball field coaching his team. For an hour, sometimes two, he would patiently work at the task of forming the utterly raw material into a unified human machine capable of responding in a roughly predetermined manner. Then he would return to the business of fighting the war with a renewed sense of elation. The baseball practices were his elixir, his one cleansing indulgence.

Soon he would display his team at the New Year's festivities at the American embassy. As the target date approached, the entire team drew together. The sense of inept joy that had marked their early practices was gone. Now there was a slightly grim fascination with their own growing skill. From second base Minh would pound a pudgy fist into his glove and jabber pidgin English encouragement to the pitcher. No longer did he burst into tears of embarrassment when he made an error. Me no number ten now, he would say. Me number one, he grinned, his chubby face growing rounder as he smiled. Kanh the tiny infielder had finally learned not to fall over backward when the ball was hit to him. He was the kamikaze of the infield. He would throw his body in front of the ball rather than let it go past. He had made spectacular catches, usually ending up sprawled on the ground with his hat fallen over his eyes. The hat was the smallest size available yet still it was too big for Kanh. And Kien the tall skinny pitcher permitted himself one exultant whoop when he threw his first curve ball to Isaacs. Then he settled in to the task of perfecting this curious process which made the ball seem to change direction in mid air. They were all experiencing what Isaacs decided was a growing pride in their own abilities. It was what was needed for the whole damn country. Give 'em something to be proud of, he would say to the team coaches, and then watch all the other problems get solved.

The team was waiting for him, even though the practice had not been scheduled until half an hour later. Recently they had begun showing up early without being escorted by their parents. It was Tan the cool first baseman who would round them up and bring them there early. Tan was a born leader. He had a kind of certainty that remained when the others faltered. And anything short of victory created a metallic quality in his eyes. He hated losing. No lose team! No lose team! he would jabber in the practices. Once, Isaacs had seen Tan's mother, a graceful woman somehow out of place with the roughness of the peasant life around Bien Hoa. *Bonjour madame* he had said and she reacted in a startled manner as if a part of her past had suddenly rushed at her. *Bonjour monsieur le commandant* she had whispered uncertainly under her breath, averting her eyes. Isaacs knew then that his theory was correct. Tan was the child of her romance—her marriage?—over a decade ago with one of the French soldiers who had been in Vietnam before the Americans. The genetic design of that liaison was stamped upon Tan's features.

The heat of the afternoon had created a stillness across the base. It shimmered off the runways and the sand. There was a deadness to everything. Even the sounds seemed sucked up by the heat. In front of Isaacs his baseball team waited patiently under the shade of a canvas tent flap. Behind him in the receding distance two soldiers removed the boots of the dead paratroopers from the runway. The soldiers were now just two silent specks of shimmering muted color, moving in a kind of slow motion. Only Isaacs broke the stillness, striding, almost running across the whiteness where the sand and the sky merged.

He arrived at the playing field, his uniform wet with perspiration. The team sat under the tent flap silently waiting for him to speak. The three coaches he had taken from the ranks of his brigade knew instantly that it would be a difficult practice. One of them, a sergeant who had played first base for a team in Texas, asked if they should bring out extra drinking water but Isaacs seemed not to hear him. He walked back and forth in the heat as if his thoughts were congealing into sentences that were difficult to utter. Number one! he said finally, his gaze sweeping the team and settling on Tan. Isaacs' face was florid and beads of sweat spun from his forehead as he moved. We are number one, he said loudly. You, me, same-same okay? He pointed back and forth from the team to himself. The boys on the team peered up at him with varying degrees of comprehension.

No lose never! he said. He continued pacing in the heat. He spoke in impassioned phrases laced with Vietnamese words. He spoke of glory and history. He spoke of the immortal Babe Ruth of the New York Yankees. And he spoke of General Pershing, who lived at the same time.

The coach from Texas stole a glance at the third-base coach, a leathery army veteran from Florida who could still throw a baseball farther than anyone in the brigade. *Babe Ruth! General Pershing!* Spare us. The third-base coach hated Isaacs even more than the coach from Texas. But the job of coaching was one of the softest in the brigade. No chance of getting shot up. Coaches were treated as endangered species by Isaacs. But god help the coach that turns out losers. It was the front lines wearing a fluorescent bull's-eye for losers. The third-base coach had long ago figured out the framework of his life. He was in the Army because he did not want to work for a living. The only drawback to the Army was that it occasionally went to war. The third-base coach did not mind war as long as he personally was not involved. Being a third-base coach was much preferable to being point man on a patrol. People got shot on patrol. The third-base coach saw life through tired cynical eyes. If this maniac wants to whip these little gooks into a team, no problem. It would keep the little gooks from becoming big gooks and zapping Americans. And it would keep one Florida ass off the firing line. Play ball!

Isaacs had arranged for a surprise. He nodded to the coach from Texas, who walked over to a jeep and removed a big cardboard box. The box was opened in front of the team. They began to cheer and whoop with glee as Isaacs held up one of the baseball uniforms. The uniforms had been specially made back in the States. They were made from gray flannel and on the back of the shirts in red lettering was the word *Airborne*. Shoes and T-shirts and pants flew into the air as the boys scrambled to try on the uniforms. Only Tan did not join in. He seemed pleased with his uniform but did not try it on as the others were doing. He held the shirt up and then as if not wanting to displease Isaacs he put it on over his other shirt. The pants and socks he left in the cardboard box.

For the entire practice, played in the deadening heat, Tan wore the two shirts. Both were soon drenched with sweat. Isaacs thought it strange but said nothing. Tan always had his reasons. Tan was his favorite. For almost two hours the flurry of red and gray motion was all that broke the stillness of the base. The shouts of the boys and the incessant urgings of Isaacs were swallowed in the heat and then disgorged as muffled noises.

Barney watched. Beside him Sergeant Lover sat in the shade of the canopy outside the Club spitting parts of toothpicks and squinting into the distance. Gonna be problems, he said in his slow stretched-out drawl. You can always tell what kind of shitstorm we're in for just by watching his practices. If they're long and frantic it means we're in for trouble. Barney and Sergeant Lover watched for several minutes in silence. Then Barney looked at him and grinned. Then you're in for trouble, he said. Sergeant Lover just stared off into the heat. He spit out another end of a toothpick. No kidding, he said.

They sat under the canopy as if the heat were a storm and they were waiting for it to pass. In his cool laconic manner Sergeant Lover began talking once again of the old days. The days when Isaacs was just a junior officer grateful for the quiet advice from the toughest career sergeant in the brigade. The stories of the old days were not so much part of a conversation between Barney and Sergeant Lover as they were a release of secrets. The stories were released carefully, one by one. Sergeant Lover was a man who controlled his emotions. Emotions were dangerous. They were unpredictable. He had long ago decided that emotions were what caused men to do ridiculous things in battle. Emotions could get a man killed. And even in simple fistfights the man who controlled himself usually controlled the fight. Serveant Lover had long ago strung his emotions so tightly over a mental frame that any resonations were imperceptible from the outside. Yet with the tautness had come a brittleness. What could not bend could only break. Sergeant Lover's army record had a two-year gap in it when he had suffered a breakdown shortly after returning from Korea. He had gone inwardly berserk months before it was apparent to others that he was not readjusting to peacetime life. When the last of his emotional strings finally frayed and snapped it sent entire pieces of his personality crashing around him in one violent amnesiac weekend. Cars were stolen and wrecked during high-speed chases. Fights were picked with strangers in bars. Guns were used. And once a knife. A prostitute was kidnapped and released halfway across the state, shrieking through the streets of a small town. The Georgia State Police drew circles on a map. Fort Benning was at the center of the map and little red pins marked reports of Sergeant Lover incidents. Early on the third morning thirteen state troopers surrounded him and were prepared to kill him at the slightest excuse. He gave them no excuse. He sat on the step of a motel room behind a partly opened aluminum screen door and cried. Sergeant Lover cried steadily for days. He was taken first to jail and then to an army hospital. After much persuasion and a few bribes, the state troopers were disposed to drop the long list of charges and let the Army handle its own. The man who persuaded them was Isaacs. Isaacs had entered the jail and stood silently staring at his toughest sergeant, who sat slumped in a corner of the cell weeping uncontrollably. It was an image that did not mesh easily with the awesome memories of a cool veteran giving encouragements to terrified recruits in the worst battles of the Korean War.

Because of Isaacs, Sergeant Lover was not thrown out of the Army. For two years he recuperated in various army hospitals across the country. When he returned to Fort Benning, the glue that held his mental processes together had bonded sufficiently to permit him the same calm exterior he possessed before his breakdown. The slow grin was the same. The cool blue-eyed stare was the same. But much had changed. Isaacs had leapfrogged ranks and was now a major on his way to becoming a colonel. There was no longer the same relationship between them. Isaacs was polite instead of warm. No longer was he the junior officer in need of advice from a battle-hardened old pro. Isaacs was busier now. There was not time for old friends. There was time only for history. Sergeant Lover had at first tried dropping in on Isaacs the way he had in the old days. But in a dozen subtle ways it was made clear to him that the old days were over. An appointment was needed. Or maybe next week when it would not be so busy. Or, wasn't there work to be done with the new recruits? All the soft edges had been honed away from Isaacs. There remained only the flint-hard, sharply defined surface of a man who feared little in life. At least little that he would admit to. Sergeant Lover had adjusted quietly but uncomfortably to his new status. Then over the months that followed, the discomfort had become resentment, seething in the distant reaches of his thoughts, far behind the impassive eyes and the slow curling grin. He grew to hate Isaacs because of the old days that were forever gone for reasons that he could neither believe nor understand. But not once did he reveal his feelings. His emotions were once again neatly in place and strung tightly. Control. He was in control of his emotions and whatever went on in the depths was masked by the tough coolness of the surface. It was a surface that had been made easier to maintain by the Vietnam War. For Sergeant Lover the war had been a release. The battles and the whoring—which had won him his name—had eased the pressures along his mental fault lines.

It was only when he encountered Isaacs directly that the smile grew thin and the silences became longer. He watched the baseball practice and thought for a long time of another baseball practice. You know, he drawled, I remember when that sonofabitch held a practice in just this kind of heat. It was back at Fort Benning with a team made up of Georgia kids. Farmboys. Crackers. He almost drove them into the ground this one afternoon when it looked like we were going to war. It was when the Russians put missiles into Cuba and President Kennedy was threatening god knows what if the missiles weren't taken out. We were on full alert. Everything that moved and breathed all over America was on full alert. It looked like we might even invade Cuba. Everyone else was working themselves into a lather. So what does that bastard do? He holds a baseball practice. And I remember thinking then as I was watching those farmboys almost drop from the heat that the practice wouldn't have been half as long if Isaacs wasn't all excited about the upcoming glory of an invasion. He was in a foul mood for a whole week after the invasion was called off. And it took the farmboys the whole week to recover from that practice.

A couple of years later he did the same thing when the Marines were sent into Santo Domingo and it looked like we'd be parachuted in after them. The heat was worse than this and one of the infielders passed out like a rock right on the field. Isaacs stood there yelling at the guy to get up and play ball. But it was no use. The guy was in dreamland. Exactly what is going to happen out there, he said, flicking a toothpick out toward the baseball field. Through the ripples of heat, the boys could be seen dancing back and forth between the bases or chasing after the balls. But now there was a slow-motion quality to their movements as if the heat was bearing down upon them. Their shouts were now just sporadic monosyllables. The coaches were on one knee, watching with towels hanging down around their heads. Only Isaacs moved and shouted as he had an hour ago, a staccato presence on the shimmering white plain.

A car emerged from the distance, stopping at the baseball field. It was Isaacs' staff car. They could see Bannon get out and stand beside it. Sergeant Lover spat pieces of toothpick disdainfully. Bannon should be nailed up somewhere out there and left to dry, he said. Half the guys in this brigade would love to find him walking with his back to them on some jungle path. In the distance the practice came to a momentary halt as Isaacs went over to talk to Bannon. Then he leaned over and talked to someone inside the car. Sergeant Lover's eyes narrowed. I had some friends that got killed because of that weasel, he said. They were the poor bastards who went on the patrol with him when he freaked out. He turned into a cringing jibbering idiot and they died because of him. His howling must have squeezed every goddam Vietcong into that one forlorn little jungle patch. Chopping our guys to pieces with cross fire. And *he* survives. And gets to be Isaacs' chauffeur. Damn, if that didn't turn a few minds inside out. That bastard.

Isaacs' staff car drew closer, undulating through the heat waves, a mass of black and chrome that took shape as it approached the Club. It stopped at the stage door farther along from where Barney and Sergeant Lover sat under the canopy. A rear door of the car opened and a woman hurriedly got out. It was Donna. She walked inside without looking at Barney, who tried not to show the turmoil suddenly unleashed with him. The car cruised toward Barney and Sergeant Lover and stopped. Bannon grinned out at them from his air-conditioned serenity. With his rotting teeth he reminded Barney of a slightly demented Halloween pumpkin. Well, well, Bannon said. The funnyman and G.I. Joe. Is he teaching you how to be a hero? he said to Barney. Or are you teaching him how to laugh? Bannon giggled at his own form of humor. Neither Barney nor Sergeant Lover showed any reaction. Hey funnyman, Bannon called out through the opened part of the car window, did you see the piece of ass that just got out of the car? Bannon laughed again and then leered through the window making his eyebrows move up and down. Betcha you were worried funnyman when you saw her get out of this here car? The colonel's car. Figured he'd started shaggin' her again didn't you huh. I know what you and her been doing. Old Bannon's seen you at it. But it's okay funnyman I just picked her up at the bus depot at the edge of the base. Before she fainted from the heat. So don't get all upset, he grinned.

Both Barney and Sergeant Lover were utterly still. They just stared at Bannon, who stared back and grinned and snorted. Hey, said Sergeant Lover finally, you got a flat tire. Bannon got out of the car and kicked the tire. It ain't flat, he said, his lips closing across his brown teeth to form a tight crooked little line of indignation. It ain't flat at all you asshole. It's a joke, said Sergeant Lover staring at Bannon with cold hostile eyes. Ha-ha, Sergeant Lover said in a flat voice. We're teaching you how to laugh boy. Don't call me boy, snapped Bannon. Why not? asked Sergeant Lover. It's the most polite thing I can think of . . . boy. You better be careful, said Bannon. I can make it tough for you G.I. Joe. I know about you wanting to be more important. I hear about it from the colonel. About how you and he used to be friends. I hear it all while I'm driving. Fuck the colonel, said Sergeant Lover in a voice so calm it was barely audible. Bannon chattered righteously. I'm gonna tell the colonel. I'm gonna tell him and then—

Sergeant Lover's right fist flew forward as if it had been triggered. It caught Bannon on the side of the head, pitching him backward into the car. Sergeant Lover hardly moved while Bannon clawed his way around to the rear of the car, whimpering and yelping threats. Sergeant Lover remained placid as Bannon staggered to his feet. He walked around to the rear of the car and began cuffing Bannon the way a cat would play with a trapped mouse. Bannon backed around the car. I'm teaching you how to laugh boy, Sergeant Lover told him as he cuffed him again on the shoulder. I know all about you, hissed Bannon. With the same calm stare Sergeant Lover whispered, No you don't boy. And again the fist flew, this time knocking Bannon over the front of the car.

When the practice ended the uniforms of the boys were soaked and steaming. The coaches were all close to being ill. The third-base coach had wrapped a wet towel around his head and was fighting to keep a gagging sensation from overcoming him. He hardly heard Isaacs bellowing through the receding heat at his chauffeur, who for some reason was getting up off the ground. It was growing dark. The first traces of the evening coolness wafted over the coaches and the team. They all sat on the ground in a communion of exhaustion. Isaacs walked away in the direction of his lurching chauffeur. When he was out of earshot, the third-base coach summoned the strength to mutter one word. *Maniac!* he said. The third-base coach was beginning to think that maybe being on the front lines—wherever that was in this war—would be preferable to what he had just been through.

The third-base coach sat propped up in a chair just outside the Club cursing Isaacs. Pershing! Babe Ruth my ass! he had muttered to himself. Give the little bastards guns instead of baseballs. Then we can settle this matter in grand style. Yankees 9 Gooks 0.

FIFTEEN

That night Barney walked out onto the stage of the Club with the images of the boots on the runway still in his mind. He stepped into the charged air of rebellion and shattered all middle ground by saying I want to talk to you about casualties.

There was an instant silence.

It was the kind of roaring ominous silence that precedes the onslaught. The reek of violence swelled from beyond the footlights. There were hundreds of them out there, hundreds who had just stepped in from the slaughters of Dak To and the vibrations of death and fear shot out from them as if a part of them was still living in it.

Barney stared into the smoky glaring circle of the spotlight and told them the truth. He told them that for the first time he was stepping onstage without really knowing what it was he would be doing. He told them he had spent the afternoon thinking about the ceremony he had seen on the runway. And about his thoughts of wanting the boots to begin walking away from it all. Then he reached behind the curtain and brought out a pair of battered army boots. They were his only preparation for the performance. He held the army boots up into the spotlight. The darkness in front of Barney burst with murmurs of amazement. The sight of the

boots set off the part of them that was still living through
the slaughters. It was the raw nerve of memory that had
sent them shrieking out of their sleep, the instant replay of a
friend's death and the shattering confrontation with their
own uncontrollable fears.

On the stage Barney could sense the violence. But there
was no turning back. He put the boots down on the stage.
Then he stepped back, out of the spotlight. Only the boots
remained in the ghostly searing glare of the spotlight. Barney waited in the darkness. The murmurs ceased. For the
first time in its existence the Club was both filled to capac-
ity and utterly silent. The outlines of the hundreds of soldiers were etched in the faint paleness of the peripheral
glare from the spotlight. It was a massive still life. Smoke
from cigarettes seeped up like mist in valleys. The occasional movement of an arm or the turning of a head broke
the stillness and made it even more ominous. Barney was at
his ultimate moment. It was the moment of being on the
edge. Of being forced to leap or else plunge into the abyss.
It was the moment he had forced for himself again and
again. But never like this. Never with death to overcome.
With the image of death on one side of the footlights and
the survivors of it on the other. The thrill and the terror of
the moment held him in the purest of fears. The moment
was unconnected to what had passed before and he had no
idea of what he would do next.

He too became part of the stillness for that instant when
he clutched the microphone knowing he must wring laughter from the hostile darkness and the images that silently
screamed from the two boots. In that instant, time warped
the way it is said to refract for those who are dying and see
their life pass before their eyes in the flicker of the last second. In that single last second Barney saw Sam Senior at
Hanson's where the comedians would sit for hours steeping

in desperation that drove them to be funny. And he remembered Sam Senior on one afternoon when no bookings had come in for the tenth day in a row. Sam Senior sat over the same cup of coffee for hours watching the world through somber eyes. His features seemed to sag like wax left too close to the heat. And then suddenly a voice escaped from him. It was the voice of one of the other comedians but it came from Sam Senior's mouth. The voice was arguing with another voice that also came from Sam Senior. The other voice was that of the owner of Hanson's, who had a thick Danish accent. The owner was yelling at the comedian for taking so long to drink one cup of coffee and taking up profitable space in a booth. Soon everybody in Hanson's was laughing. Even Sam Senior. Later Barney asked him why he did not do more voices. Bah! mimics, snorted Sam Senior. They are dangerous. They become devices if you rely on them. Only once in a lifetime does a comedian ever need to mimic. And sometimes not that much. If you ever have that one perfect moment you will know it he said.

Into the still-life darkness of the Club a cry cut loose with an eerie chill. *Whooooooooooooooeeeeeeee!* Particles of madness shot through the minds of an audience that thought they had heard wrongly. It could not be! But again came the cry. *Whoooooooeeeee!* It shot down spines, set hair on end and parched throats. For a third time came the cry and then the laconic drawl that was so familiar yet so chilling. *What does these mothers think we are? Making us stand heah in da heat. Does they think we is a collection of niggers?* It was LeRoy! The infamous LeRoy of the infamous Yankee Spies. The black man's black man doing his nigger routine. Cutting through it all. Flying in the face of the winds of phony deference with his sho-nuff, feets-do-yo-stuff slyly cynical routine that left him taller in the eyes of everyone around. But it was all wrong. LeRoy was not tall

at all now. LeRoy was dead! *Sheee-it man! We quit pickin'
cotton years ago. But now dey got us standing here on this
man's runway while dey is a-wailing prayers over us. And
dat chaplain—he is definitely God's cheerleader. Best time
he ever had I swear.* But LeRoy had been blown to pieces at
Dak To! Everyone knew LeRoy was now just a number on
last week's casualty list.

But the boots became LeRoy. In the breathtaking
stillness a thousand and more eyes fastened upon the boots
and created LeRoy. He grew from the boots in the pale
glare of the spotlight. LeRoy was alive again! *Will you stop
bitching LeRoy?* came a whimpering voice. Amico! The
chubby little paratrooper who was always being teased
about his size. Amico, whose jokes cracked them all up.
Amico, who could laugh at his own physical proportions:
Hey sarge can I have two parachutes maybe? Or: *Sometimes I get worried you guys want to use me as a bomb, not
a paratrooper.* Amico, whose round Neapolitan face could
contort into a crooked smile that in itself was funny to look
at. But Amico no longer had a smile. Amico was in the helicopter that blew up outside of Dak To. *LeRoy I'm hungry.
I'm sick of standing here in this dumb ceremony. I want
food. Fooooooooooooooood!* In the boots on the stage they all
saw Amico standing there grinning at them. For who else
could make the word food sound like a love call?
Foooooooooood!

And then it happened. Someone laughed. It was a spon-
taneous laugh, loud and genuine. Whoever it was, he had
laughed at Amico before and now he was laughing at him
again. Amico was alive and standing there in front of them
mooing his call for food the way he always used to do.
There was another laugh from somewhere at the back of the
audience. And then others laughed, and for some it was a

release, tinged with a kind of fear that they may never stop laughing.

Amico what is with you huh? We is standing here on this runway with all these people making speeches about us and saying prayers and hallelujahs and amens and all that shit and all you can think about is food. Man I just wanna get out of here. I'm dying of this heat—

LeRoy don't use that word.

What word?

The one you just used. You know—what the heat is doing to you.

Well hell man I can't help it. My feet are killing me.

Your feet are . . . killing . . . you?

Yeah man my feet are killing me.

LeRoy you and I gotta have a talk.

Other laughs came as the two boots on the stage took on more life. The laughter cut into the invisible cloud of violence that hung through the darkness. It was taking hold.

In the darkness Barney was transformed. He had almost ceased to exist. He was the receptacle of life for the characters who clamored to exist again for this one moment, their voices springing with ghostly precision from Barney's mouth. Amico and LeRoy. And then Henderson the funny-looking farmboy whom everybody teased because he wrote letters twice a day to his girl friend. Boyd the brigade bookie who took bets on everything and Stankowski who was always grouchy and funny at the same time. All of them suddenly alive again through Barney and all of them shot to pieces in the fighting at Dak To. Their voices floating through Barney's mouth from the distant darkness of the silent metal cases that were now at that moment approaching the Pacific shore of America at thirty-two thousand feet.

Hey Boyd Whatcha doin'?

Figuring the odds LeRoy. You want in on the action?

With what? Shoelaces?

Eight to five that the chaplain will do his yea-though-I-walk-through-the-valley-of-death number. Three to one that some of those gumbos in the audience over there will start bawling. And even money that the colonel will make his big Men it's tough for me to have to preside over this speech.

That fucking colonel's gonna get our asses shot off.

Like I said Stankowski, you never were a straight-A observation man.

It was exactly the kind of bantering that had occurred around the mess tents and the Club for months. Even the talk about Isaacs seemed so natural although it was coming from the stage over a microphone and was causing the press relations men to look anxiously at each other and the major to glance over to the doorway beside the stage hoping that he would not see Isaacs standing there in the shadows. But Isaacs was there. A vague outline in the darkness. Arms folded and feet apart. The major could not see Isaacs' face and was thankful. He wondered again why Isaacs did not just ban this comic who was creating such a disturbance.

On the stage the boots were now Amico again. He was hungry and hot and wanted the ceremony to be over so they could all get something to eat. He hoped they weren't going to sing hymns. That would be too much. Suddenly from the audience there was another voice. A soldier had stood up on one of the tables in the center of the Club. He was middle-aged, not very tall, and had a face that showed both defiance and defeat at the same time. A career sergeant. He stood up into the spotlight and began to sing *Auld Lang Syne*. After a few bars of the song Amico's voice ceased speaking. The audience fell silent, unsure of what was happening. The soldier on the table was singing loudly, emotionally. His eyes closed and his arm began moving back and forth as if pumping the tune out.

Should old acquaintance be forgot
And never brought to mind
We'll drink a cup of kindness yet
For the sake of auld lang syne!

The spotlight narrowed onto the soldier on the table. It was no longer on the boots. Out of the smoky mist and darkness other men rose up onto the tables. Other voices joined in. Of its own kind it was a communion, a linking of the living with the dead, and the force of the song bonded them all into one overwhelmingly emotional moment. It was past and present together. Spontaneously row upon row of men, some tough and embittered and others utterly drained, locked arms and sang as loudly as they could. Some wept and others laughed. The younger soldiers who did not know the words made sounds that somehow sounded like the lyrics. Others remembered fragments of the song from the television every New Year's Eve. What they could not remember they made up.

Barney looked down from the darkness of the stage. Before him swayed hundreds upon hundreds of soldiers. Their singing resonating through all that held him up, through all the lives of the men who had died and whose voices were leaving him now, forever. The singing continued after Barney had disappeared behind the stage curtain. The other acts who were scheduled to perform after him did not go on. For a while they stood around occasionally peeking through the curtain, uncertain what to do. Barney sat in a corner, exhausted and almost unaware of his surroundings, hearing the singing but not really listening to it, conscious of the others only as blurs of colors in the darkness. Gradually the other performers left. Barney remained, sitting silently as the singing faded into a faint and lonely refrain. Sometime after it had stopped he was aware that Donna was standing beside the curtain. That was a very big gamble, she said. We were standing back here holding our breath. I don't know if congratulations is quite the right word. It's always the right word, said Barney.

From beyond the backstage came a staccato click of regulation dress shoes on the concrete floor. A soldier following orders given intemperately. The click came nearer until the curtain parted. The major who always wondered why Barney was not just thrown off the base peered at them. Beg pardon ma'am and a quick tip of the hat. Probably from a military family. The quick anxious eyes in the round soft face of the eternal second-in-command. He stopped in front of Barney. The colonel wants to see you he said.

Barney just stared up at him mutely. The silence unnerved the major, who had been programmed for instant response. He doesn't have much time. More silence. Then as if to explain it all, the major blurted, Look we're very busy over there. The third-base coach of the baseball team has just been found murdered.

Maniac! It was the last word anyone could remember the third-base coach ever saying. It was a few hours later that he was found dead. He was found propped up in a chair just outside the Club. Several people claimed to remember seeing the third-base coach sitting in the chair smiling at them as they went into the Club. It was only later that they reflected that perhaps the third-base coach was already dead when he was smiling at them. After all it was dark.

The third-base coach died of a knife wound. It was a clean almost neat wound that began at the base of the neck. It was a wound caused by a long thin knife. It was later determined that the third-base coach died sometime shortly before Barney began his act in the Club.

SIXTEEN

Barney opened the door to Isaacs' office. The room was in darkness except for pools of light at the far end. Isaacs stood in the light, leaning over a map table. He looked up quickly, his eyes like gunsights following Barney into the room. In the stark light, his face appeared craggy, almost hawklike. I saw your performance. Very impressive, Isaacs said in a voice as dry as dust. Barney walked over to the map table never once allowing his eyes to leave Isaacs. His exhaustion was falling away from him. The tension of the moment shot through the vacuum. It was a moment he had expected. Wanted. Like magnetic opposites they fixed upon one another. Barney stopped on the other side of the map table under the lights that reacted conversely upon him. The light erased the remaining traces of exhaustion on his face. He appeared younger, almost boyish. He was sure that Isaacs was waiting for him to avert his eyes and shuffle off like the major, who had nervously shown him the way to the office. At last Isaacs cast his gaze down upon the map on the table. Do you know what this is? he asked.

Would I be wrong in saying it's a map of the jungle? Barney asked after looking at the map colored almost entirely in green and stitched with coordinates and military designations. Isaacs looked at the map lost in distant thoughts and then snapped his head up drilling Barney with the same fiery stare. Yes you would be wrong. This is the final outpost of civilization! Isaacs said. He picked up a marker pin and inserted it under a name on the map. The name was *Xuan Loc*. Barney looked at Isaacs to see if he was serious and was aware that Isaacs immediately caught the flow of his thoughts. I'm trying to show you something that perhaps you may not be able to understand, Isaacs said in a quiet hard voice. I'm trying to show you that this is where we have to make a stand. We have been pushed back too far. Can you understand that? The question was uttered as a statement. A taunt.

Why there? said Barney. Hah! snorted Isaacs. You think like the rest of them. You think in linear terms. It doesn't matter where the hell it is. It can be here! There! Timbuctoo! Fifth Avenue! It's not only the place that matters. It's the *time*. We have been pushed not only too far, but too long. And this is where we happen to be at this moment. He pointed at Xuan Loc on the map. This is now the outpost of our civilization. Just because we are here now. And *now* is the critical time. We can wait no longer. So this is where I make a stand.

What about the thousands of dumb grunts who get shot up in the name of your vision? said Barney. Have you let them in on the secret that your jungle briar patch is now a jewel in the asshole of civilization? Isaacs rose up disdainfully. It is the price of history, he said. We are the Romans, and there are Carthaginians all around us.

Why are you telling me this? asked Barney. To give me material for my next show? Isaacs laughed in a dry, mirthless way. I'm just trying to prepare you, he said. I'm preparing you for a realization that will make all your jokes a little more difficult. And I can't wait for you to find out what it feels like to be a killer, said Isaacs.

Barney stared at him blankly for a moment. Are you trying to tell me I'm going to kill someone? he said.

That's exactly what I'm telling you, said Isaacs with a slight, correct smile. And *then,* I want to hear your jokes.

Good luck to you, said Barney.

And once it's all over you're going to thank me for it, said Isaacs. Only then will you understand history.

History is one group of people convincing another group that annihilation is in their own interest, said Barney. Isaacs sustained his correct smile. Marvelous, he replied. Just marvelous. Your job is to make jokes about it. I understand that. Believe me. We all have our roles. Even the court jesters.

Barney became more serious. He sat down in a chair and looked at the floor. You know, Colonel, he said, I used to worry about that. I never knew how to answer the people who asked me why I wasn't banned from the base. Why you didn't order the guards to stop me at the gates. If I was so scathingly funny why didn't Isaacs react? I used to wonder. Then I began to worry that perhaps I was serving a purpose. Your purpose. Like a court jester kept around to distract the bored. Someone who gave those poor bastards a few laughs to cool them out before you sent them off to get shot up in the name of history.

But you know something? I don't worry about it anymore. Because in a choice of weapons I'll take the jokes. And right now—after tonight—you would too. You didn't call me in here for a history lecture. You called me in here because you're still hearing the laughter. You can't get it out of your ears.

The smile remained fixed on Isaacs' face. Probably, he said. Though I will never admit it to any of my aides. My aides like to agree with me before I finish talking. You know the kind. They have also wondered why I did not ban you from the base. But I made a mistake once before with a comedian. A man named Hoffman. A filthy, foul mouthed long hair. It was at some goddamned peace rally in San Francisco. I got angry. A mistake. When people laugh at you the worst mistake you can make is to show anger. It is like blood to sharks. I vowed then that next time would be different. And it is.

A button on his desk was pressed and the door at the back of the room opened quickly. Several military policemen entered . . . . .

. . . . . and Barney is placed under arrest. It is all done smoothly, efficiently. There is not a trace of anger. Isaacs leaves the room and allows the nervous major to inform Barney that he is being detained because of the murders. Someone has pointed out that whenever a murder occurs on the base the comedian is there. So are five thousand other people says Barney as he is taken off to the base prison. Shoelaces and belt and all traces of identity are removed and then there is the small cell of darkness. At first there is only silence and the sweet smell of marijuana that comes from the guard's room after a while. Then in the gathering light, the outline of another prisoner. Hey man, says the soft drawling voice. You drew the lucky number too huh? It is Sergeant Lover. Arrested for assaulting the colonel's chauffeur. Shoulda caved his empty skull in, Sergeant Lover says slowly. You should be behind bars he yells at the nineteen-year-old military prison guard who is now so stoned that he can only look out at them through lolling eyes that see—*see* the music from the Armed Forces Vietnam radio, 50,000 watts of pure color. You're a criminal, you hear me, yells Sergeant Lover in disgust. What has the Army come to? he mutters. Thieves, perverts and dope fiends. . . . . .

. . . . . but his tirade is interrupted by noises from outside. Trucks are rolling. Helicopters are descending. Soldiers are in motion. The base is alive! The noises of action are everywhere. But it is the middle of the night when all is usually still. Sergeant Lover and Barney peer through the bars of the jail window. Here it comes man, murmurs Sergeant Lover. Oh dear god here it comes! . . . and across the base the name is repeated: Xuan Loc. *Xuan Loc?* The might of the thousands of human and metallic components is being alloyed into a massive machine of war. An entire brigade is in motion in these hours long before dawn. The base glows with the light trapped under the low hanging clouds. Supply convoys are formed. Headlights like malevolent eyes peer through the darkness as the huge trucks are loaded with rockets and shells and food and oil enough for a siege. The convoys will roll out at first light while the troops are flown in by helicopter. The voices in the night cut through the roar of the machines. The voices are tense, almost angry. They know it is to be big. Very big . . . because word spreads that the hospital is being emptied. Whenever the truly bloody sieges are expected only the desperately wounded are allowed to remain in the hospital. At such times a hundred, perhaps two hundred beds are emptied, ready to receive the wounded. It is the inevitability of those beds, empty, starched and silently beckoning that spooks the troops. A forecast of pain and death. The number of beds emptied is supposed to be a secret but somehow it always gets out. And now the word flashes across the base driven on by a barely harnessed telemetry of fear. *Six hundred beds!* The disbelief turns to anger. Then the ratchet of fear is turned and the notches click by in collective thoughts. The emotional pitch of the entire base is driven up to the limit. Silent soldiers eye their friends and wonder who it will be. Who will get the beds and who will get the metal boxes. Oh dear god don't let it be me. The thought rises in unison until it becomes almost audible above the fumes and roar of the machine. . . . . .

. . . . . Oh dear god says Sergeant Lover, Didn't I tell you huh? This afternoon? I've seen him do it before but never like this. Now you know why you're here, he says to Barney. He can't risk you joking about this, man. Barney turns back to the light from the guard's room. Hey star-gazer, he yells. Come here. The stoned jailer moons his reply with an idiot's happy grin. Far out, he says. Far out. Sergeant Lover shouts at the guard. You can't even talk sense when you pump that shit into yourself. Faaaar out! comes the idiot reply. You and Captain Blood— The guard stops and tries again. You and Captain Blood . . . is all he can say. In some dope-clogged groove his mental needle is stuck. Who the hell is Captain Blood? yells Sergeant Lover.

SEVENTEEN

Captain Blood? A hero. A glorious daring myth who wins the women and knows no fear. For Captain Blood there are no images of empty hospital beds. Captain Blood is the old movie that was showing on the Armed Forces television network earlier in the evening as the nineteen-year-old prison guard was getting stoned. Captain Blood was filmed over three decades earlier. Because of the movie, a young actor named Errol Flynn became a star. It is a movie about pirates and all that is good opposing all that is bad. Errol Flynn is the hero. He is good. He is . . . *swashbuckling* is the word that is always used. And for decades the devilish leer of Errol Flynn had carved notches in the hearts of his audience. Errol Flynn was pure Hollywood. He was handsome. He was famous. And now he is dead. But his ghost lives on in Captain Blood . . . . .

. . . . . because at this moment, in these hours before dawn, there is yet another ghost of Captain Blood who is awakening in Saigon. It is Errol Flynn's son. In the darkened room Sean Flynn rises and gropes for a light. There is the mask of the father under the face of the son. Sean Flynn has grown used to comparisons, which he ignores now. As a very young man he had starred in movies, second-rate films like *The Son of Captain Blood*. But all that is behind him now for Sean Flynn has changed professions and become truly—the word might be *swashbuckling*—in a way that his father never was. For Sean Flynn, still in his twenties, has become a journalist. A war correspondent. He lives in the jungles that are not movie sets. The bullets are not blanks. The explosions are not special effects. And there is no take two. The transition is appropriate for in the years of Vietnam it is the journalists who are the mythical figures. It is the journalists who are the stars. In the marches on the Pentagon, the burning of huts in Vietnam, or the radical-chic parties of New York, the new journalists position themselves in center frame. Sean Flynn has made no mistake.

For in the years of Vietnam, good and evil are forever relative and the journalists ravage the old-style heroes. The world soon fills with midgets on thrones of the mighty. There are no leaders. No giants. No titans. For under the searing light of these new stars the journalists, all of the old order shrivels and is proclaimed dead, struck through the heart with the pen of subjectivity.

. . . . . as Sean Flynn finds the cord for the light that clicks on erasing the darkness with a dull glow. He is confronted by the clutter of the room. Cameras and lenses slung from pegs. Combat jackets piled on top of civilian clothes. Jungle boots still stiff with the mud of some past fire fight. All of his clutter is functional. There are no trappings. The war has a way of stripping things bare and it is a monastic bareness that Sean Flynn finds more opulent than all of the movie sets of his childhood. He begins the sleepy ritual of dressing for war in the predawn darkness. There are no swords, no guns, just cameras. It is a ritual he will repeat until the day he sets off with a friend, riding motorcycles into the bitter darkness of Cambodia. Riding motorcycles into war! *The Son of Captain Blood!* . . . will never be seen again. He will be swallowed up in the savagery and meanness of the Cambodian invasion. Sean Flynn will simply disappear. Presumed to have been gunned down in some jungle. Or captured on some dirt road and taken off to be executed. Bad comparisons can be made. It is like a movie without the final reel. It is a script without an ending. But it is a hero's death in the new order . . . and perhaps preferable to the finish of his father, who died awash with liquor, nursed by his latest teen-age mistress who he hoped would ward off the ravages of the mythology that he could not live up to. . . . . .

. . . . . But on this morning Sean Flynn sets out on the deserted streets of Saigon under curfew. He has heard that something big is happening. There is an operation moving out of Bien Hoa. The 173rd Airborne. Sean Flynn trudges through the streets to the pickup point where the black Air Force Fords are waiting. He has only gone a few blocks when he is aware of another presence behind him. It is an old European automobile lurching through the silence. It is a Citroën 15CV, a French car made almost thirty years earlier, before the Second World War. There are still many of them in Saigon, relics of the days when the country was a French colony. The Citroën halts not far behind him. Sean Flynn watches as a young man clamors awkwardly from the car, cursing and muttering threats at the Citroën. The man seems much too tall to fit into the car, which Sean Flynn notices has an official flag mounted on the front. The man throws up the hood of the car and hammers at something attached to the engine. The man is wearing short pants and some kind of military jacket. The man returns behind the wheel of the Citroën, which lurches into life and then jerks to a stop beside Sean Flynn. You going somewhere? the man asks. Bien Hoa replies Sean Flynn. Me too. Jump in. And so Sean Flynn gets into the narrow old car and immediately notices that the back of the Citroën is filled with cases of beer. Canadian beer. The driver mutters an introduction. The name is Woody he says. Just Woody. I am here to keep the peace, he announces defiantly. The car races through the empty streets, past the fetid tin shacks by the river and out to the highway that leads to Bien Hoa. Sean Flynn immediately notes that there is a sense of urgency, almost fury, to this man Woody. His large hands seem to strangle the steering wheel. His bare legs dance on the pedals as the car jolts from one gear to another.

You in a hurry 'cause you've heard there's peace somewhere around here and you're afraid you'll miss it? asks Sean Flynn. The driver looks at him from the corner of his eyes. I thought there was peace everywhere here, he says. At least that's what I was told by the people I work for. There is just a trace of a smile. Sean Flynn decides that perhaps this is kindred spirit in uniform. He listens as the peace-keeper describes his profession with a madness that only the most sane can possess in the war. They trade professional stories. Absurdities. Laughter. Sean Flynn is offered a bottle of Canadian beer. And he is told the tale of the latest peace violation that this hulking peace-keeper is hurrying to report: A comedian has been jailed!

Sean Flynn looks at the driver wondering if a hasty reassessment is necessary. A comedian has been jailed?

EIGHTEEN

In the brigade prison Barney was making the guard laugh. The guard was now so stoned he would laugh at anything. Barney was almost getting to enjoy being in jail. The guard was his best audience ever. The guard was on his hands and knees seized with a terrible fit of giggling. Barney had decided to make jokes about the huge convoy that was forming outside. He told the guard a story about the drivers of the convoy getting lost and resupplying the wrong village. Halfway through the story Sergeant Lover put the pillow over his head and went to sleep. But the guard loved it. Barney was suddenly aware of another laugh. It came from outside. It was more of a mocking laugh. Climbing onto the cot Barney looked out and saw Bannon staring at him. Bannon's head was once again bandaged. In the faint light his head looked like a skull, the skin stretched too tight across it and the rotted teeth being the final evidence of decomposition. When he laughed it was as if dust came from his mouth. Hey funnyman, Bannon leered in his twangy drawl, what's all this about you committing murders? He whinneyed a laugh. At the sound of Bannon's voice, Sergeant Lover was standing on his cot in a flash. Well, well, grinned Bannon, look who's here too. Ain't this a sight! Shouldn't mess with the colonel's chauf-

feur. The colonel's chauffeur has a way of getting you dumb
lifers in the shit. Bannon laughed. You ain't going to be out
getting laid for a while, he said. Don't count on it robot, said
Sergeant Lover. They're gonna need me more than they're
gonna need you. Sergeant Lover spoke in a quiet, inten-
tionally patronizing voice. His sureness irritated Bannon,
who felt *he* should be the only one to be patronizing. You
assholes, yelled Bannon, feeling even worse for letting them
know he was angry. You better worry about more than
murders, he hissed. Hey funnyman, he said, look! He
pointed over to Isaacs' personal compound, where a light
had been burning all night. Your lady friend's in there!
With Isaacs! Bannon laughed in mocking triumph. Hey funnyman. Imagine what's going on in there. Huh? . . . . .

. . . . . but there is nothing going on. Except for
Isaacs angrily pacing through his living quarters. He has
just returned from a search. In silent, contained desperation
he has stalked the width of the base looking for Donna. To
the troops who saw him, it was a commander's last-minute
inspection. A final assessment. But it was none of that.

After the performance at the club Donna had waited for
him as he had asked. And when he returned to his quarters
he had found her sitting quietly in the darkness of the small
porch. He had asked her to go inside with him. Now, on *this*
night, he no longer cared if she was seen with him. Not
now. When history was moments away. The beginnings of
Xuan Loc were all around them. The noises. The orders
called out in the night. The lights at an hour when there
should have only been darkness. She had hesitated at a moment when no one else dared hesitate. The night around
them was driven by a single will. Every mind, every machine, was responding to *his* will. It had decreed destinies,
even death for hundreds. He had waited, sitting beside her

in the half darkness, watching her eyes seem to search for a resting place. He suddenly felt awkward in her presence. Almost overpowered. He felt there was a clumsiness to his own presence that might crush what he desired simply by reaching out for it. At that moment her hesitation became for him something touching, perhaps gentle. For a moment her long dark hair hid her eyes and he almost held his breath wanting to touch her. But when she turned to face him he could not comprehend the cool certainty in her eyes. The fleeting unsure glances had vanished. It was as if she had stepped onstage shedding fears like a cloak. In the soft light he saw her as being beautiful in the way that he always remembered from the performances. There was a classic serenity to her, a serenity that had seemed almost impenetrable and for that reason alone he was drawn to her.

But she had ended it in the simplest of ways. She shook her head and with a few words left him inwardly grasping for composure. I do not love you, she said. I wish you well. But it is over. I'm sorry. He felt as if the breath had for an instant left him. He waited for her to avert her eyes as if her will had faltered. But she did not. He waited for her to smile as if perhaps it was just some lapse of humor. There was no smile. She stood up and again said that she was sorry. And at that moment when the will of thousands was bending in harmony with his she cut through it all with a few words and a murmur of good-bye. Isaacs reacted from impulses fathoms beneath all that he had ever understood about himself. He reached out and grasped her arm pulling her back toward him. Within him, all that separated tenderness from fury was the finest of emotional lines. She resisted his force for the briefest of moments that it took for the line to be crossed.

He forced her back onto the porch, somehow certain that it was all a mistake. She cried out for an instant but her cry was lost in the roar of the passing machinery and vehicles. It was all wrong but only for the moment. She *would* change. She *would* love him. She had to. She struggled against him but powerful arms had encircled her and drove her swiftly back inside the doorway and . . . . .

. . . . . in the blur of motion Donna looks up at his face that has become a series of masks. Her fears become a form of pity as he pleads with her not to go. Not to leave him. Not now. But they are not pleas in the truest sense for she knows there is no alternative. She can either yield or be forced. She is driven farther back inside the hallway. His hands and arms tighten around her and with it all comes the barrage of pleas that she wants to shut out. But her every glimmer of resistance is smothered, overpowered. He is relentless. She fights not to give into her fears and break down under the force that engulfs her. It is her feelings of pity for him that save her. For with the pity comes a flicker of superiority. For the quest is for possession of what she knows she will not yield.

There is a moment of exhausted silence. But for her it is over. Her fears have left. She knows what is inevitable and nothing he can do will destroy her. She looks at him with a cool, even stare. She does not intend to mock him. But at this moment anything less than submission is mockery.

The final vestiges of control crash around him. He forces her back through the hallway, still pleading, still telling her that he loves her, that it *will* change. But now she does not resist. Now her passiveness is a resistance more overwhelming than all of his force. She is flung through another doorway and onto a bed. He is upon her in an instant and she senses in his desperation a curious attempt to be gentle because a part of him still believes it is all just a mistake that will pass when she regains her senses. She lies perfectly still as he kisses her and begins to undress her.

His whispers have become fragments of words and desperate phrases. She barely hears them for at that moment she sees only Kalman and knows that this will be the last time she will remember him in this way. For Kalman—beloved Kalman—is about to be avenged and the words she hears now are the words to which she had once loved and embraced and laughed. Isaacs kisses her with a racing fervor, sweeping across her body. The words pour out in a torrent as he brushes across her breasts and down into the warmth of her thighs. She lies perfectly still. The room is dark, but from outside lights move and dart across the walls. He rises above her, his hands across her arms, and he knows that *now* he would even prefer her to resist. To fight back. Next to love, he wants, needs a resistance. Anything but this.

But she stares up at him. The last pieces of her clothing are crudely removed, and again the harshness of his hands almost begs for resistance. Her legs are pulled across the bed under him and then raised. It is all a mistake he is saying. It will change. It will; it will. He moves across her quickly. He thrusts and for an instant there is a tiny tingling pain. She looks up at him. Again masks. They contort into whispers and pleas and the rhythm of his body intrudes throughout hers. There is a building anger. A driven insistence. The overpowering of all that can be won by force.

But none of it can be won. She has already yielded a physical part of her, discarding it from her emotions like a chrysalis. She just lies there showing no response. Nothing. She stares at him as he looms over her thrusting furiously in dominance and defeat. It has been a tactical assault. She has been simply real estate. But there is no possession. No conquest. All that was desired has slipped away to other territories. Emotional guerrillas. He trembles within her and around her and the onslaught of his words is seized at that moment by a tiny cry. It is a cry of submission.

He settles across her. There is a stillness. A silence. Then he slowly rises from her. He lies on his back beside her. Lights play and twist across the ceiling. They are the only movement in the room until slowly, deliberately, she gets up from the bed. She searches for her clothes and silently dresses. As she is about to leave Isaacs whispers from the bed. Goddam you, he says. She leaves as . . . . .

. . . . . into a dust-choked darkness of Bien Hoa, Woody clattered among the assembling convoys in the battered Citroën. He had arrived at the main gate honking the horn imperiously at the machine guns that were trained on him from the tiny sandbagged fortresses. All the way to the base Woody had played gracious host, offering Canadian beer to Sean Flynn. As usual for Woody whenever he hosted a party, he drank far more than the guests. Woody flung open the car door and stepped into the floodlights. With a careful flourish he fastened the Canadian flag and the banner of the International Control Commission onto the flag standards on the hood of the car. Then he turned on his heels and jammed his arm into a spit-and-polish salute. On Her Majesty's business! he screamed into the sandbags in his best sergeant-major voice.

There was a silence and then a drawling voice came from behind the sandbags. What the fuck is this? Halloween? asked the voice. There was another silence which only slightly deterred Woody. He remained in rigid parade ground salute. Who are you anyway? demanded the voice. Woody's reply was almost barked. I am Woody and in my vehicle is Captain Blood Junior. We desire passage immediately my good man!

From behind the sandbags came mutterings. Captain Blood? And then louder: What happened to the legs of your pants? Somebody cut them off? Another silence. Woody slowly allowed his head to look down at the lower half of his uniform and then back up at the sandbags. Still he saluted. This, my good man, he yelled, is the uniform of Her Majesty's Forces from the Dominion of Canada. We are here to keep the peace. Kinda late ain't you fella? drawled the voice from the sandbags. In case you ain't noticed we got a war going on. My good man, snapped Woody, I don't care one whit for all your quibblings over technicalities. Who are you with your machine gun to argue with dozens of the world's foremost statesmen who signed the Geneva Accords and declared that there was peace?

You know what? asked the voice from behind the sandbags. What? asked Woody. I think you're a commie, said the voice. You better get your ass out of here before there's trouble. At that moment with unspoken teamwork Sean Flynn opened the door of the Citroën and clamored out with a case of Canadian beer. He lugged the case over toward Woody and placed it on the ground. Woody opened the case with a flourish and removed one of the bottles. Now my good man, he said, the Woodchopper and Captain Blood Junior will demonstrate the healing powers of this miraculous brew. This is not the watered-down ablution you drink here. Nor is it the foul Balmy-Bah which you pour into yourselves in your dissolute moments in the bars of Saigon. It is, my dear sir, a veritable oasis in this interminable desert. Woody then snapped the bottle cap off between his teeth and downed the entire bottle with one gulp.

From behind the sandbags a head appeared. It was the head of a young soldier with a long thin neck, a protruding Adam's apple, and a helmet that was too big. Woody reached for another beer, held it between two fingers, and then let it drop onto a rock. It shattered in a foaming explosion. Pity, said Woody. He dropped another beer. Hey wait a minute man! yelled the guard.

They passed through the gates with Woody singing the Canadian national anthem and Sean Flynn wondering just what kind of madness he had fallen in with. But all of his best friends were slightly mad in a very sane way. The Citroën lurched toward the lights of the airbase. Sean Flynn gripped the sides of the car. It seemed that Woody was aiming the car instead of driving it. The car skidded to a halt in front of a platoon of soldiers. Which way to the jail? yelled Woody. A soldier gave them directions. Marvelous! beamed Woody handing the soldier a beer. The future of mirth is at stake, he yelled as they roared off.

Shortly after dawn Woody positioned himself outside the brigade prison. He sat in full uniform on a folding chair. From the Citroën he had produced a large and colorful Cinzano umbrella, the kind used in European sidewalk cafés. He fastened the umbrella to a makeshift table. He sat behind the desk with his clipboard and began writing reports. By the time the sun was over the horizon, Sean Flynn had returned to visit Woody. He had decided that perhaps there was as much of a story in what Woody was doing as in what the rest of the brigade was doing. Barney watched through the bars. Shortly after Sean Flynn returned, a press relations officer showed up. What are you doing? asked the officer. I am writing an official report on a violation of the peace. What peace? asked the press relations officer. What violation? asked the nervous major, who had been sent over from Isaacs' office.

That violation! bellowed Woody, dramatically pointing to the prison window where Barney watched: Barney stared out at them, hollow-eyed. He moaned and then slowly sank out of view. That man has been tortured! It's perfectly evident, yelled Woody. He has not been tortured, retorted the major, who was rapidly depleting his already thin supply of composure. Inside the prison Barney looked over at Sergeant Lover and shrugged his shoulders. Sergeant Lover shook his head and rolled his eyes.

Not only has he been tortured but he has been arrested for making people laugh! Clearly a violation of the peace, said Woody. There is no fucking peace, yelled the major, pointing to the runway. You see those helicopters? They're jammed with men going off to fight. To kill. To die! You see those trucks? They're loaded with enough ammunition to blow this shithole off the map. We're at war you idiot! The major's face was red and eyes were bulging. My dear sir, intoned Woody in his most supercilious voice, dozens of the world's foremost statesmen who signed the Geneva Accords once declared—and still maintain—that there is now peace and I am here to report on violations of that peace. At that moment, Barney clamored up into view for a few seconds, moaned, and then sank down again. He has *not* been tortured! hissed the major. And even if he had it is none of your goddam business. Now leave this base. Woody peered up at the major. Have your man bring over some mineral water will you, he said with a faint smile. With a twist of lemon.

Woody remained sitting under the brightly colored umbrella for the entire morning. The sight of the tall young officer in the strangely truncated uniform attracted other curious journalists who had arrived because of the huge Xuan Loc operation. Several times the major appeared in the window of the brigade headquarters. Once Isaacs could be seen looking through binoculars. Later, Isaacs left in a helicopter for the hour-long flight to Xuan Loc. When he returned in midafternoon the large colorful umbrella could still be seen from an altitude of three thousand feet. Brigadier Mosby soon arrived at the brigade headquarters. He stared in amazement at Woody and then disappeared inside, where he made profuse apologies for the ludicrous conduct of one of his men. While Mosby was making his apologies Woody removed his contingency file from the car. The contingency file had been carefully compiled over a period of months. It was to be used for just such an occasion. He left the file on the table as Mosby approached.

Barney watched through the bars. Woody winked. Barney could see the brigadier approach, containing his fury until he was close enough to lash into Woody. The brigadier looked to Barney as if he were on the verge of some sort of seizure. Woody stood up, smartly saluted and endured Mosby's wrath for several minutes until offering him a seat at the makeshift table. For what purpose? snapped Mosby. To look at these terrible forgeries sir, said Woody. Forgeries? asked Mosby. Yessir. Someone is obviously trying to forge documents that would do you harm. I just found them. Woody opened his contingency file. In the contingency file were enough documents to have Mosby cashiered from Her Majesty's Forces. There were photocopies of the purchase agreements of almost all the bars and brothels that Mosby secretly owned. The agreements were first made out in the name of a fictitious Vietnamese purchaser. Then other agreements were made out from the fictitious purchaser to Mosby. Brigadier J. A. Mosby, D.S.O., C.D., was far too much of a career officer to make an exemplary larcenist or crook. Everything had to be done by the book. He stared at Woody's contingency file and slowly sat down.

Mosby had hired an old Vietnamese lawyer in Bien Hoa to draw up the necessary papers. The old lawyer was decrepit. He had a wispy beard that struggled down from his chin to form a goatee. The old lawyer tried to be very French. He had lived in Paris for three years. He spoke a form of French that no one could ever understand. When he concluded drawing up the necessary papers for Mosby he expected at least a bottle of good wine for his efforts. He received nothing. He concluded that Mosby must be part British. British crooks were always the worst. British crooks never wanted to admit to any wrongdoing. The greater their larceny, the greater their sniffing superiority. French crooks were much preferable. They gleefully admitted their crimes to their associates. Even philosophized about it. And most important, they offered bribes to keep their associates quiet and content. Wine. Money. A better job. The French knew how to make the best out of corruption. The old lawyer kept copies of all Mosby's transactions. He kept them in a battered leather briefcase that he carried with him even when he went to sit in the brothel that Mosby had just bought. He liked to sit for hours in the brothel and observe. It was like being a latter-day Toulouse-Lautrec. One day he died in the brothel. The woman who managed the brothel for Mosby gave him a proper burial and kept the briefcase. She disliked Mosby as much as the old lawyer. The woman who managed the brothel was a friend of Woody's. She gave the papers to Woody, who laughed and laughed as he read them. Then he brought her a case of Canadian beer.

While looking at the contents of Woody's contingency file, Mosby's mouth drew into a thin line under his mustache, which he tugged at. I see, he said several times. I see. He looked up at Woody, who had adopted the look of a faithful hound dog. Mosby's eyes were like caves. Obvious forgeries, he muttered. He walked quickly back toward his waiting staff car. The nervous major stood nearby. Mosby snapped at him as he passed. Clear-cut violation of the peace! Then Mosby drove away at a high speed.

Four hours later Barney was released from the brigade

prison. He would not leave until Sergeant Lover also was freed. It was decided by brigade headquarters that there was the possibility of a minor international incident unless the matter was ended swiftly. Too many reporters were asking what was going on. And the sight of a foreign army officer sitting under a Cinzano umbrella was too difficult to hide. Isaacs had left the matter in the hands of the major. Isaacs was now totally obsessed with the details of Xuan Loc. Over half the necessary troops had already been deployed there during the first day. Under the weight of the responsibility the major had almost gone to pieces. He quivered like a tuning fork as he announced that all charges had been dropped.

Barney grinned at Woody, who merely shook his head. I think I should have left you in there, he said. They piled into the battered Citroën and drove away from the prison, where the guard was once again stoned and staring at the pretty lights of the airfield. As the Citroën drove past the brigade headquarters, the major ran out and breathlessly flagged them down. I've been asked to inform you that the brigade still has a high regard for your talents as an entertainer, said the major. Barney looked from the major to Woody and back again. What the hell are you talking about? Barney asked. You have been selected to begin a new policy of Armed Forces entertainment, the major announced. You have been chosen to entertain the troops out in the field. Where out in the field? asked Barney.

Xuan Loc, said the major.

NINETEEN

Barney's release was the cause for great celebration. The celebration was held at Brigadier Mosby's brothel in the town just outside the airbase. It was filled with soldiers who were either celebrating the fact that they were not being sent to Xuan Loc or those who were going crazy on their last night before being shipped off to Xuan Loc. A few of the latter were seized by a kind of manic desperation. Images of death hung in front of their eyes no matter how hard they laughed. They drank too much and fell in love with the whores, whom they promised to marry upon their return.

By the time Sergeant Lover arrived, he was already in his best form. Within two hours of his release he had become a serious contender for the Clean Truck Award. On the road between Saigon and Bien Hoa he had taken an army truck to four car washes. They were part car wash and part brothel. While the young boys washed his army truck, the whores took care of Sergeant Lover in the nearby shack. Sergeant Lover considered it one of the most important cultural innovations of the war. He often wondered why no one in America had thought of the idea. If there were drive-in restaurants like Colonel Sanders' Kentucky Fried Chicken, why couldn't there be *Sergeant Lover's Car Wash!*

emblazoned across America? Sergeant Lover planned to get rich with the idea when he got back to America. In the meantime he continued doing extensive market research. He arrived at the brothel celebration with an impeccably clean and still dripping two-and-a-half-ton truck. Most of the Canadian beer had gone by the time he arrived and Barney had organized another meeting of the remnants of the Yankee Spies. LeRoy was dead, and three other members of the Yankee Spies were already in Xuan Loc. But in LeRoy's memory they met to celebrate the best violation yet. Shortly before he died LeRoy had handed Woody his latest Violation Report. LeRoy had copied onto a Violation Report an account of the invasion of Normandy in the Second World War. The account was complete with all the original code names and names of the towns in France which were captured. Woody had taken the report and handed it in. Three days ago word had been received that the report had been routinely approved by some bureaucrat in the peace-keeping organization.

In the middle of the ceremony Barney realized that Woody was nowhere to be seen. He left the Yankee Spies, who were in a conspiratorial fervor, planning to sneak in an account of American astronauts landing on the moon as an example of another violation. Barney walked along the balcony that stretched around the second floor of the brothel. The balcony overlooked what once had been a large garden. Beyond the garden were high stone walls constructed years ago by some wealthy French colonist who wished to shut out the un-Gallic realities of the little town around him. Mosby's brothel had seen better and more chivalrous days. It still had the superficial grandeur of the colonial mansion that it once was. But in its present use, style was not a consideration. The once elegant salon had been partitioned by flat slabs of wood painted white. The ornate furniture had yielded to army-issue metal folding chairs. Heavy boots had ravaged the once gleaming floors. Neon lights were everywhere casting a sickly glare upon clients and whores alike. On the second floor there was a large starkly lit room. In the interests of efficiency, hospital curtains had been hung around each of the dozen beds. The curtains had been stolen from a military hospital. The beds were also stolen. They provided the room with a distinctly clinical aura. It looked like a hospital ward. The first owner of the brothel had decided that instead of building dozens of small private rooms for the whores and their customers it would be better to have them all in one large room separated only by the curtains. It would be easier to keep track of what was happening. When the original owner, who was Vietnamese, had sold the brothel to Mosby he had proudly emphasized the room as a major selling point. Mass production, he had stated. Very American. Efficiency comes to whorehouses. High volume. Low overhead. On a busy night, the large white room resounded with grunting, moans and breathless cries. Under the stark neon lights, soldiers and whores lined up waiting for a free bed. The whorehouse was big business.

Barney searched for Woody along the crowded balcony and in the white room. There was something about the white room that Barney always found depressing. For all of the forced enthusiasm of the soldiers, it was a place where illusions died under the weight of reality. Satisfaction was found only in the expectations. And the whores seldom seemed to fit the stereotype. There were only a few who approached their profession with a voraciously cynical mask of enthusiasm. Most of the whores seemed overwhelmed by their surroundings. The spirit seemed driven out of them. A kind of loathing flickered in their eyes.

Woody was nowhere to be found. He was not in the white room, nor was he in any of the other rooms of the old mansion. The Citroën was still parked just inside the gates. No one remembered seeing Woody for hours. Barney knew what the problem was. Woody was off somewhere having another one of his identity crises. Woody had identity crises whenever he spent too much time around the American soldiers. Seeing the American troops doing what soldiers are supposed to do made Woody question his own role in life. He would become morose and decide that he was a soldier who would never be a soldier. He would spend his days wandering the world with a clipboard. A bureaucratic referee. Barney found Woody sitting in the back of Sergeant Lover's freshly washed truck surrounded by beer bottles. I'm doomed, said Woody sadly, I'm a failure. Who needs a soldier who's never a soldier?

It was on that night that Barney cured Woody's identity crisis for months to come. Barney became the brains behind Woody's greatest military triumph. Barney provided Woody with the perfect strategic target that could be besieged and destroyed by an invading force. The target was Brigadier Mosby's brothel.

Barney also provided Woody with an army which he could command. He drove Woody four kilometers down the road to the local South Vietnamese army base. The South Vietnamese and the Americans were allies. But often their armies hated each other. The Americans regarded the South Vietnamese as lousy soldiers. The South Vietnamese regarded the Americans as bullies who stole their best women. In the area around Mosby's brothel, the feuding was particularly bad. The South Vietnamese army had often tried to invade the brothel, while their allies, the Americans, were in there with their best women. The South Vietnamese had always been repulsed by a defending force of sexually fervent Americans who resented the interruption. The walls around the grounds of the brothel had been reinforced and heavy metal gates had been installed.

With Woody watching suspiciously, Barney sat down with the South Vietnamese military commander, in a dimly lit room that was filled with torn maps and smelled of cooked fish. The South Vietnamese commander was a small man with tiny resentful eyes. Several of his aides crowded into the room. One of the aides translated Barney's remarks. Barney told the commander that his friend the peace-keeper had decided that the brothel was a detriment to peace among the two great allies. Therefore the brothel should go. But allies could not attack each other because then they would not be allies. The allies would be at war with each other. But if the attack was led by a peace-keeper then technically it could not be war, said Barney with a sly and faint smile. He waited as his statements were translated to the commander in the glottal sing-sing of the Vietnamese language. The commander showed not a flicker of a response. His cold eyes shifted from the translator to Barney as he asked a question. What do you want me to do? was the translation. Give this peace-keeper enough troops to declare war, said Barney.

The commander made a remark over his shoulder and his aides began to giggle. He made another remark this time with a smile. His aides began to chatter and make obscene gestures. Barney looked over at Woody, whose eyes were widening. You're crazy, said Woody.

Woody was brilliant. In the name of peace he declared war and destroyed Mosby's brothel. He began with an artillery bombardment of the back wall that enclosed the grounds around the brothel. From the first order he gave to commence firing he felt a thrill unlike anything he had ever known before. Watching the back wall being blown to pieces, he knew how Napoleon got started. Most of the

American troops fled through the side gate. A few tried to make it to a small tower that had been built for just such attacks. It was a perfect sniping post. But the tower . . . . .

. . . . . erupts in a fireball before the defenders can reach it. But within the whiteness of the hospital curtains there are those who are blissfully unaware of the maelstrom outside. They are those who simply want their money's worth. And squirming, terrified whores or not, they do intend to get fair value for their hard-earned dollar. But beyond the white curtains, chaos has taken hold of the white room. Soldiers and whores in various stages of dress are racing for the door as the clatter of shelling echoes through the room. But in the middle of it all there is a cry—one beatific cry that cuts through the shrieking roar of war. It is a cry of one who is hearing the word of the Lord. It is Mr. Thomas! He sinks to his knees murmuring hallelujahs and is immediately bowled over by a fleeing whore. It is a sign from Him! Mr. Thomas knows it. It is a sign that the Lord is punishing him for allowing himself to be brought into this den of iniquity by that sinner and fornicator Lawson. And groping for his glasses, Mr. Thomas rues the day that he ever cast his pure lot with the bloated Lawson. And yet . . . . .

. . . . . it was Lawson whom he went to see immediately upon returning to Saigon after leaving the trauma of his shattered mission at Pleiku. If his ordeal was not worth at least a front page story in the *Herald Tribune,* then nothing was. And Mr. Thomas was determined to pursue the Lord's story with ferocity. There would be no more bottles of scotch. No more endless story meetings. *Now* it was page one for the Lord or nothing.

But it was not Lawson who answered the door to room 34. It was a woman. A young woman, almost as tall as he was, with short black hair and large suspicious eyes. She was the receptionist at the Italian embassy. The smell of cooking food wafted from the room. From inside, Lawson's voice called out welcoming him as a long lost friend. Lawson was luxuriating on the bed, dressed in his new Italian dressing gown. In his hand was a glass of chianti. Cases of the finest chianti, direct from the Italian embassy, were piled in one corner of the room. The room itself had changed. Lace curtains were on the windows. Pink and blue satin was everywhere. A large plastic crucifix hung over the bed. In a makeshift kitchen area, pasta was cooking.

But the Lord's page one story? Problems buddy, said Lawson grimly as the receptionist from the Italian embassy filled his glass with more chianti. The *Herald Trib* folded. But not to worry. The Lord giveth and the Lord taketh away, he said with a wink raising his glass. Mr. Thomas could take it no more. He went to pieces and began weeping and yelling about the Lord's wrath. The receptionist from the Italian embassy grabbed a large bullet-shaped stick of pepperoni in case he became violent. But Lawson calmed him down. He thrust chianti at him. He made promises. He held out hope. Free-lance said Lawson. That's where the action is now. I'm free-lance and that's better for you. Much wider circulation possibilities. Hell we could get the Lord's story in ten papers. Not just one. Mr. Thomas wiped the tears from his eyes, took a sip of chianti and said the Lord would probably like that. But . . . . .

. . . . . now the Lord is answering in fire and brimstone. Another explosion lands somewhere outside the chaos of the white room and Mr. Thomas gropes for his glasses knowing that the Lord is furious with him for drinking so much chianti and allowing Lawson to tempt him. There was a big story Lawson had said. Out at Bien Hoa. And Mr. Thomas crawls along the floor amid the racing feet and the shrieks and the ecstatic moans. He begs forgiveness from the Lord and again the roar of the attacking artillery is heard. He scampers under a closed white curtain, pokes his head up and there in the horrors of his myopic vision is the jiggling naked mass of Lawson wheezing his way to eternal damnation with one of the whores. Something within him snaps. His fists become the Lord's fists. He pounds and flails at Lawson. But the fuel of lust has carried Lawson to higher altitudes and with one chortling swipe, his beefy arm sends Mr. Thomas catapulting back into the bed behind the next set of curtains. Mr. Thomas is almost knocked senseless by the blow and as he gathers his wits he is aware of a strangely pungent warmth beneath him. He peers down and slowly recoils in horror. It is flesh! Warm mounds of naked flesh! It is a young Vietnamese whore who lies very still upon the bed. She wears not a shred of clothing. She is very still and for a moment Mr. Thomas is convinced she is dead. But a comatose murmur escapes her and he realizes she has only fainted. There is another artillery roar and Mr. Thomas claps his hands across his eyes and flees howling for forgiveness. The room is almost empty. An acrid smoke of explosives singes the air. A few soldiers are racing along the outer balcony. Mr. Thomas tries to stop them to explain that there is a girl in one of the beds who must be saved. Someone must help her! But no one heeds his pleas. They all rush past him. In a frenzy Mr. Thomas races back into the room and whips open all the hospital curtains. But no one is there to help. Not even the fat Lawson. They have all fled. There is only the naked girl. The very sight of her sends him to his knees in fear. Another explosion outside, this time closer. He is alone in the center of the huge white room, his chattering pleas for forgiveness echoing off the stark walls. The artillery behind him and a naked whore in front of him. Mr. Thomas does not know what to do. He prays for divine guidance because it is all too much for one mortal. First his mission at Pleiku and now this. Divine guidance comes. An explosion sends plaster crashing from the ceiling and Mr. Thomas races for the bed where the girl is being covered, with a fine white plaster dust. He must save her. But still the moment of *touching* her sends satanic fits through all that is holy within him. Actually placing his hands across those mounds of nakedness! Clutching her body to his! He leans against the bed, steeling himself for this, the ultimate damnable sensation. But the bed moves. He looks down. Of course! It is a hospital bed. On wheels! He chortles. He laughs. Wheels! God is good! He pushes the bed across the room, running, laughing with exultation.

But the bed is too wide for the doorway. He crashes into the doorway running at full speed. The bed collapses into a metal abstract. The girl is flung onto the floor. Mr. Thomas does not have a moment to think before he sees a man standing in front of him. It is a young man with a strange calmness to him and a smile that speaks of secret knowledge. It is Barney. Get her out of here, says Barney. There is urgency and tranquillity mixed in his voice. Mr. Thomas obeys. He grapples with the nakedness of the girl, clasping her warmth to him, feeling the softness of her body under the firmness of his hands. He murmurs the Twenty-third Psalm as he lifts her up and trundles off down the balcony into the darkness. Behind him the sky erupts in flame and he howls for forgiveness averting his head from the mounds of flesh that push against his face when he looks ahead. . . . . .

. . . . . And Barney continues his search of the rooms. They are all empty. He checks the downstairs darkness of what once had been colonial splendor and now is only a tattered remnant. Empty. A chandelier swings under the vibrations of the artillery. A picture frame crashes to the floor. Dust is falling like rain. He walks into the gardens. They too are now empty. He walks out through a gate, where he meets Sergeant Lover and three paratroopers who have returned with flak jackets and M-16s ready for a fight. Barney sends them back. An identity crisis he explains, and they act as if they understand. Woody as Alexander the Great. Woody as Patton. Woody as Rommel . . . . .

. . . . . and as Barney fires the flare into the night signaling the all-clear Woody stands atop a truck wearing his peace-keeper's short pants and a combat helmet. It is the first time in Vietnam that he has worn a combat helmet. He gives the order for his troops to stop shelling their allies. He peers through the binoculars at the destruction of the outer wall around the mansion. The rubble thrills him. At last! He gives the order to his ground assault troops, who race triumphantly toward the empty mansion. The South Vietnamese troops blast automatic weapons fire into the mansion even though no one is there to return the fire. Their commander stands next to Woody. He too is ecstatic. It is the first victory for his troops. They have not been able to defeat the enemy. Defeating their allies seems much easier. Much more rewarding too. Attacking the brothel will be good for morale. It will avenge all the whores stolen by the Americans. The South Vietnamese strip the mansion like a pillaging column of ants. Everything is carried off. Beds. Curtains. Stairs. Chandeliers. The booty of war. There are three casualties. An unpopular officer is mysteriously shot in the back, but does not die. A plundering soldier shoots himself in the foot while carrying off a live pig. And a sergeant is wounded when he races downstairs in the darkness moments after the stairs have been ripped out and carted away. The victors regroup behind Woody, who receives a second all-clear signal. With ultimate composure Woody surveys the scene. The tense silence enraptures him. It is his quintessential moment. He savors it, thrilled and wanting it to stretch to the infinity of his memory. His troops wait. The artillery is readied. The range has been computed to the meter. The silence has a music all its own.

Slowly Woody turns to his artillery and in a quiet measured voice that reeks of authority he says Gentlemen, commence firing. And in less than an instant the night catches fire with roaring blasts that shake the very air around them. Again and again the artillery cuts through the darkness and each blast is echoed by another one, even more terrifying, as the shells shatter Brigadier Mosby's brothel with explosions so spectacular that Woody's breath is almost taken away. The roof seems to atomize with a flaming roar. The center begins to buckle. But another blast arrests the buckling motion and an entire wall is shot outward. Before it can fall it takes a direct hit and explodes into molten rock. It is all over in seconds but in Woody's mind everything is happening in a beautifully languid slow motion. Every explosion is a ballet of war. There is a terrible grace to it all. Almost reluctantly he gives the order to cease firing. He stares out at the flaming rubble. The sudden silence sweeps over Woody. He has never felt so calm before. . . . . .

And then it is morning. A gentle mist hangs across what is now a clearing among the trees. Dew covers the ground. The sun sends shafts of light horizontally through the trees. Water buffaloes graze aimlessly. A dawn chorus of birds swoops through the stillness. And in the middle of the clearing there is now a massive pile of rubble. From the middle of the rubble protrudes an ornate staircase that winds elegantly up to nowhere. On top of the staircase sits Barney. He leans against the scrolled bannister watching the swooping birds. At the bottom of the stairs, Woody is sprawled on a tattered chaise longue that had somehow escaped being stolen or destroyed. Two cases of Canadian beer are balanced nearby. The cases are nearly depleted. Barney has talked all night with Woody. First there was the euphoria of victory. And now at dawn he watches Woody sink into a philosophical seriousness. Woody is on the verge of deciding that the staircase is a metaphor for life, winding ornately up to nowhere. But the metaphysical introspection is severed by the roar of a car. It is a car traveling at high speeds. The squeal of tires can be heard from a great distance away. The noise grows until the car seems to burst through the mist. It is an official car flying the banner of the peace-keeping forces. The car swivels to a halt and from the back seat a man seems to burst out of it. It is Mosby.

Horror is mutely etched upon his features. His eyes are saucers of disbelief and fury. His mouth gapes in strangled words. Atop the rubble Woody leaps up and freezes in a salute. The fury wells up within Mosby. It emerges as a sound. Not a word, or a phrase or an accusation. Just a throttled vowel sound that seems to go on and on. Mosby's face is quivering and scarlet. He points a trembling finger at Woody, who remains stiffly saluting atop the rubble. Woody suddenly seems to lose his nerve. The enormity of what he has done is focused in Mosby's accusing finger. Woody's eyes dart around the rubble. Mosby makes another attempt at articulating his rage. You! he screams at Woody. You! And then: You?

Yessir, says Woody still saluting. It was a peace-keeping

attack sir. One ally attacking another. I'll send you off to war for this! yells Mosby. Yessir, says Woody. There were no casualties sir. Mosby does not hear him. He is walking back and forth, prowling in a state of gathering shock. Do you know what you've done? he says several times, each time in a louder more desperate voice. There were twenty-two beds! he screams at Woody. Twenty-two! Each one averaging five salvos a night times seven days a week times fifty-two weeks a year! Thirty-nine-thousand-times-a-year! he yells jabbing each word at Woody.

From the top of his staircase leading to nowhere, Barney can contain himself no longer. He looks at Brigadier Mosby, D.S.O., C.D. Then he looks down at the rubble and thinks of the thirty-nine thousand times per year and begins to laugh. He does not mean to laugh but he cannot help it. He laughs so hard he begins to hoot. Tears roll down his face. Woody looks over at him and suddenly the laughter is contagious. He sees Barney try to speak through his laughter. All Barney can do is point down at the rubble and roar with laughter. Woody forces back a laugh. He is still saluting. But then he too buckles and shakes his head and then begins roaring with laughter. He laughs so hard that he can no longer stand up. He subsides onto the rubble. *Thirty-nine thousand* Barney roars pointing down at the steamy rockpile. But Mosby sees no cause for humor. A man has a right to retire with dignity, he yells at them. Have you no decency?

TWENTY

When Barney arrived back at the Catinat
Hotel it was nearly noon. The monsoon rains had begun
their daily onslaught on the city. For several hours every afternoon the rain would fall, clearing the streets of all but
the beggars who huddle under awnings and the occasional
battered little blue and yellow taxi. In the third-floor courtyard the rain clattered loudly on the tiles. Voices were
muffled by the downpour. From Lawson's room, now distinct with its ruffled lace curtains, came the voice of a
woman talking loudly and emotionally. In Snider's old
room, Sheldon paced the floor rehearsing new lines. Sheldon's door was open as usual. When he saw Barney he
called out, Hey kid, see Milligan. He's looking for you.
Sheldon went back to pacing out the elliptical circles in his
room. Barney opened the door to his room. It was not
locked. He pushed the door open slowly. In a chair reading
a book sat Donna. I didn't want to miss you, she said. I've
waited in here since last night.

For a moment the uncertainty returned to her eyes. The
flashing exuberance of her stage persona had flown. Barney
sat opposite her on the bed. She picked his unspoken questions out of the air. You know I was with him two nights
ago, she said. But it's over now. It was something I had to

do. To finish it. Barney looked at her with a wry smile. You have a funny way of finishing things, he said. What is there for me to say now? she asked. Trust me? Or: I don't want to talk about it? Or: I'll make it up to you? There was the faintest trace of a smile.

When I was spending my night in jail, said Barney, it was easy until Bannon sat under the cell window and began drawing mental pictures of what was going on between the sheets in the colonel's house. At that point it did become a prison. I was furious with myself for feeling so jealous. I wanted not to care. But I did. So in answer to your question, Yes I'd love to hear you say you'd make it up to me. Or that I should trust you. The only problem is I'm not sure I'd believe you or not.

You'll believe me, she said with all the coolness returning to her eyes. You'll be amazed how much you will believe me. She handed him a piece of paper on which was written: *Kid—see me. Urgent. Milligan.* This was tacked on to your door when I arrived. He's been up here looking for you twice. Barney crumpled the paper and walked to the door. You'll be here when I get back? he asked, trying to sound slightly casual. He knew it wasn't working. Trust me, she said.

Hey kid, where ya been? growled Milligan over the top of his bifocals. Out shelling whorehouses, said Barney. Very funny. Yessir, very funny. Work on it though kid. Milligan tunneled through the masses of papers and glossy photographs that covered the desk in his office. Outside in the narrow corridor of the Catinat a nervous young couple waited their turn to see Milligan. Jugglers, he said, shaking his head with both amazement and derision. Who the hell needs jugglers? he muttered. They went out with spats. Milligan burrowed through a different corner of his desk and chewed harder on his cigar. Been hearing good things about you kid. Weird things, but good things. At least I think they're good because they want you back all the time. Don't understand it though I gotta tell ya. 'Cause with all the shitting in the nest that you've been doing I would have thought they would have dumped you over the edge. He found a piece of paper and squinted at it. Yeah, he said. Yeah. When Milligan concentrated, he exhaled through his nose in short whistling bursts of breath. Yeah this is it. They want you to lead off a new program. Sheldon ain't gonna like this. They want you to go out into the field to entertain the troops. To some little joint in the boonies. Zu—Zew—Exewan.

Xuan Loc, said Barney. Yeah that's it, said Milligan. I dunno where the hell it is but it's big money kid. Big money. Getting like Vegas over here. If this goddam war gets any worse we'll all be rich.

Are you going? Donna asked before he could say anything. He closed the door, returning the room to shadows. Isaacs wants you to go out into the field doesn't he? she said. That's right. For one day, Barney replied. They want me to leave in two hours. She asked if he was afraid and he said quietly: Of course. She asked again if he was going and he gave the same quiet answer. I've known this moment was coming for months, he said. As long as I was living off the war I knew I would someday be drawn into it. Part of me has been almost fascinated by the thought. And another part of me has lived in dread of it.

Living in dread. She repeated his words slowly as if they were foreign. I think there is a part of you that will always live in dread. Of course there is, said Barney. That's why people become comedians. Laughter is dread turned inside out. I sat with my step-grandfather for hours and hours when I was a boy. Everyone called him Sam Senior. We went to a place called Hanson's, a café on Broadway in

New York. He would sit in there with all his friends and tell jokes. He was the funniest man I ever met. And then I used to see him an hour or so later alone in his hotel room. He was filled with a slow seeping kind of dread. Once I told him I felt sorry for him and he threatened to beat the day-lights out of me. Dread you live with, he yelled at me. It's our modeling clay. But pity, never. Drink poison instead, he would yell. It's faster and less painful.

He walked past her and she reached out and took his hand. Perhaps, she said. Perhaps. But I listen to you talk about going off into the war and I have a feeling that I'd al-most forgotten. A low, cold fear that has curled up inside me for two years. You keep making a mistake, said Barney. You look at me and you see your husband. No, she said. No longer. For a long time I did. I told myself that everything about you was like Kalman. At least all the things I loved about him. The shy way that he would walk into a room and then quietly take over. The way that his humor seemed to come from thin air. I kept seeing his eyes in yours. And the way you talked. But no longer. Not after two nights ago. I did not spend the night with him. But I was with him for part of it and then I left. What happened between us was not making love. It was a kind of rape. There is nothing in me that blames him for what happened. I have my own sins to atone for. But when it was over I was free. A ghost had been appeased.

They sat in silence. The monsoon rains were lessening. Barney watched the water rushing down in front of the win-dow. I'll be leaving soon, he said. She did not respond to him directly. Instead she said only that she had waited in his room through all of the previous night. She unbuttoned her blouse and removed it. She unfastened her hair from its dancer's knot on the back of her head. Her hair fell down around her shoulders in dark waves. They both undressed in silence and then lay across the bed, where he ran his hands gently across her legs and up to the curve of her breasts. She reached out, drawing herself closer. She hugged him, clung to him and pressed her lips to the side of his face with a joy that had suddenly broken out of a darkness. He drew her under him.

Blaaaaaaaaa. The strange raucous sound cut through the room. Barney looked around but could see nothing. Again the sound came. This time there was movement at the window, obscured by the heavy lace curtain. Then a pounding on the door. A face peered against the glass. Barney wrapped a towel around himself and went to the door. It was Sheldon. In his mouth was a pink paper noisemaker that unfolded when it was blown into. Sheldon looked up and down at Barney, who stood in the doorway wearing only the towel. Your fly's open kid, he said, puffing on the noisemaker which unfolded reluctantly. I'm busy, said Barney. I should be so busy, said Sheldon, peering around Barney. Who you got in there? The colonel's wife? Huh? Is that how you're getting all these big dates out in the boonies huh? Sheldon saw Donna hidden by the covers of the bed. Barney closed the door behind him. Sheldon's eyebrows danced and a leer crossed his face. He looked back to Donna's room. Hey kid! You old dog, you're drilling holes in number 39! I didn't think she was screwable. She's not, said Barney. What do you want? Sheldon was impervious to any form of insult or rejection. I wanna know if you need some help with number 39, he said with a laugh. Hey kid tell me, is she the kind where you gotta tie a board to your ass so you don't fall in? Huh? Sheldon laughed. Barney stepped back inside and had almost closed the door when Sheldon reached out and grabbed his arm. How did you get that big-money date at Xuan Loc? he snapped, his face drawing up into intense angry furrows. I got a right to know. I should have been out there too. You paying anyone off?

Barney grinned at him, slowly shutting the door in his face.

FIVE

Laughing War

TWENTY-ONE

Barney waited all afternoon to get on one of the helicopters. But he was told every flight was loaded with priority personnel and supplies. Finally the dispatch officer informed Barney that they had received a message about him. He was to leave at dawn. Barney remained at the base overnight. It seemed almost deserted. Almost everyone he knew had been sent to Xuan Loc. Entire tents, filled with personal belongings and cots, stood silently at twilight. There was an eerie stillness, occasionally broken by the needles of light racing down the distant runway. Barney found an unused cot in a tent. He lay in the darkness listening to the distant shelling. All the hostile shelling he had ever heard was always somewhere off in the distance. But tomorrow it might be different. Only for one day Milligan had said. Barney had heard Isaacs' voice coming from Milligan's curling mouth.

Barney lay on the cot and thought of Sam Senior alone in his dingy little room in the Edison hotel. How can you face the crowds if you're not alone sometimes? he would say. Sam Senior had spent much of his life alone. Many of the regulars who hung around Hanson's also seemed to be alone much of the time. The loneliness drove them to be funnier. Being alone had never bothered Barney. He was capable of being alone without being lonely. But now for the first time since he had been living in Sam Junior's house, he felt lonely. It was a loneliness that left him with a desire only to go back to Saigon, to home, anywhere where there were objects and people who were familiar. The terror of the road, Sam Senior used to call it. You give in once and you never go back out there. It spooks you too much.

In its most shattering sense it was the terror of the road that gave this war its seductive and deadly attraction for all those who were not forced to be there. Photographers, journalists, missionaries—and entertainers made a choice every day they were there. They could leave anytime they wanted. Or anytime they grew too afraid to venture out past the safety of Saigon. Merely surviving one more day gave some an exhilaration and a sense of purpose they had never felt back home when survival was unquestioned. And the unimagined terrors and fears of every new day was the booster shot of their existence, the metaphysical adrenalin that set their souls racing. But for each of them there was the fear of the black hole of emptiness that yawned out past the rim of the day they lost their nerve. The terror of the ultimate road upon which they all sped. Barney fell asleep, telling himself that he would stay in Xuan Loc for one day and no more.

At Xuan Loc the darkness was like a shroud. There was no moon, no stars. Lights within the fire base were kept to an absolute minimum. Isaacs made his inspection in the dead of night using a tiny pen flashlight. He moved like a cat. Sentries whose nerve ends were already shorting out from tension would suddenly find a tiny beam of light aimed at the ground beside them and a voice saying Everything all right son? The restless fear-charged card-players who could not sleep because of the nightmares of what lay out *there* would suddenly find another presence in their fetid sandbagged sleeping quarters. Isaacs was everywhere. He was the phantom of Xuan Loc. He never seemed to sleep. He moved to inner rhythms not heard by others. It was the drumming of history. Isaacs stared up into the darkness where the huge hills loomed unseen and knew that history was gathering. In those hills the enemy was massing. He knew it not just from the intelligence reports. He could *feel* their presence. It was a mystical communion and Isaacs would stand on the sandbag walls serenely facing into the darkness and the winds that were the whispering heralds of the next monsoon storm. He would stare into the darkness knowing that *they* were gathering into a force that would attempt to annihilate him. It was like a chorus of voices from the hills. The visions of the darkness thrilled him. Finally! In this one place, the years of his life were to fuse into a single moment of history. It was to be a turning point of this terrible war. This war that reeked of defeat at the soft white hands of the clerks who ran it. There would be no retreat. No strategic withdrawal later proclaimed a paper victory. Here they would stand. And if necessary die.

It was working as he had intended it to work. The enemy was present in great strength. The monsoon storm was coming and when it came there would be no possibility of withdrawing, as Saigon would inevitably order him to do when they found out he had lied to them. For Isaacs had committed military heresy and deliberately contravened orders. His orders from the computers and the generals and the analysts at Military Assistance Command Vietnam were to carry out operations at their direction over a wide swath of II Corps and III Corps. But Isaacs had stripped his other operations of troops. He had brought in entire battalions that were supposed to be left elsewhere. But when his actions were discovered it would be too late. The monsoon storm would be upon them and the enemy would have already made its move. And Isaacs no longer cared about the consequences at the hands of the clerks. There was no other choice. It was either the whimpering oblivion of the clerks or the glory of lone victory. The timid were the mutes of history.

In his crudely built headquarters Isaacs went over the maps and plans again. He knew the maps by heart. He had known them for months, just as he had known his strategy. The camp was silent. Isaacs tried to sleep even though he did not want to. For the moment, sleep seemed almost a waste. With the light still burning he lay on the cot in the small room. And against all the forces of his own will power he thought of Donna. The last terrible moments shot before him, his memory patching into a different circuit over which he had no control. He sat bolt upright with a tiny cry. The same cry of submission that had escaped him on that night. The anger and fear of that moment returned ricocheting against the foundations of all that had sustained him for days. He got up and walked around his small tent, which suddenly became a cage. He charged into the free air of the darkness and the comfort of knowing that *they* were out there ready to join him as part of a ceaseless unity.

The next day Barney came in on one of the first helicopters. It had taken off into the slate-gray skies and cut through the powerful winds that were molded around the curves of the jungles below. There were a dozen men, several large cartons and the gunner squeezed into the helicopter. The men were all ashen-faced, staring blankly out into the skimming jungle, as if they were waiting for it to bubble up with beautiful orange bursts like some deadly tropical fluorescence of ground fire that would shower them with its poison. The helicopter quivered under the force of the winds and cut toward an area where the ground seemed sucked up into the mists. It dove into the grayness and beneath them emerged the fire base. It was massive, larger than any of them had expected. It was a military city in the middle of nowhere. Xuan Loc International, yelled the gunner as the helicopter settled onto a flat area whipping the dew off the grass. A horizontal rainstorm shot into their backs as they scrambled out of range. Other helicopters dropped out of the grayness, fat metal locusts disgorging their innards, nervously bouncing on the ground, slamming words back into the throats of those who screamed unheard orders, staring malevolently with plexiglass eyes. There was never a helicopter landing in the field that could be called routine. All the hopes of those desperate to get out, and the fears of those spilling in were sucked into the rotor-whipped vortex of threshold noise and motion. A giant blender of tensions. The choppers were death and escape all rolled into one high-rev, surface-skimming package. The sight of a helicopter taking a hit was something that none of them could ever forget. Depending on the cargo and the hit, it could suddenly be transformed into a blooming ball of flame, wracked with convulsions that would, in the merest of moments, reconstitute its human and metallic components as a molten mass of shrapnel about to be spewed out at low altitudes, or it could take a hit that would be deceptive and drawn out, like the final moments of some creature that has lost its will to live in midflight. These were the hits to the engine or the flying mechanism. They were unnoticed from the ground until the chopper began to list or keel over in the air. They were the worst to watch because of the there-but-for-the-grace-of-god-go-I terror of seeing the crew realize they were doomed, clawing and scrambling at doors and windows, shrieking at controls that turned to dust in their hands as the horizon became a kaleidoscope, and spilling out like rag dolls flung to the ground below. For anyone who had ever seen it there was a memory-activated mental zoom lens into those screaming faces of the doomed.

Half an hour after Barney landed, a helicopter was hit. It was blown to pieces in the air as it came in between the distant hills to the east. The collective breath of the fire base was held as the wreckage dropped from the sky, a sinking friend too far from the shore to be helped. The helplessness drew in and was pumped out with fear. The thousands who stood watching tensed, waiting for the next blow. But it never came. There was just sience. Superstition jumped the circuit of exchanged looks. It was an omen. A sacrifice for what was to come. A part of the ritual. *They* are letting us know they are there. Fear shot through the fire base like a mad pinball chalking up scores of infinity, touching every player before guttering in edgy remarks that tried for humor where there was none.

Sergeant Lover came over to Barney. I'm here because I have to be here, he said in his soft drawl with its sharp edges. But if you ain't out of here by noon I'm gonna know you're crazy. He did not look at Barney. He stared at the distant plume of smoke and then walked away.

Barney walked through the fire base toward the head-quarters tent. From the far end of the base, the howitzers began firing at the hills. It had begun. The fire base became an anthill of intensity and purpose. Shells were uncrated, weapons cleaned for the third time. Patrols were formed. No order had to be given a second time. Fear was the drill instructor. Sandbags were being piled around the head-quarters tent when Barney arrived. He was surprised to see Bannon standing outside the tent looking lost without his car. The circles under Bannon's eyes were darker than usual. His eyes seemed unable to rest upon anything. Barney's presence seemed to make him even more nervous.

How nice of the colonel to bring his chauffeur along, grinned Barney. Are they flying the car in? Very smart funnyman, snapped Bannon, his eyes darting. Very smart. I'm getting out of here. I don't belong here. I'm going back on the next chopper. His words tumbled out, in a slightly manic torrent. Inside the headquarters tent, behind a folding table, sat the nervous major who had arrested him three nights earlier. The major seemed harassed, unable to focus on anything. There was some kind of time lapse between questions and the major's answers, as if all the nervousness had congealed around his reflexes. Where do I perform? Barney asked him. I'm not sure, he said finally. What time do I perform? said Barney. When the words sank in and returned, the major said he couldn't say anything at the moment. He was just waiting for confirmation of what was to happen. The colonel wanted to talk to Barney. Just wait a few minutes. Wait. The words came out as pieces. Outside Barney waited. Bannon paced out slow elliptical circles. The wind had stiffened. It whipped a rain so fine it was almost a mist. And it grew stronger.

The major called Barney inside and did not return to the tent with him. Isaacs was hunched over the table. He was the first person Barney had seen at the fire base who did not look nervous. His eyes never left Barney. He was smiling. There seems to be some misunderstanding, he said. The major tells me you were expecting to give a performance. Isaacs was conciliatory, almost soothing. Saigon does have a way of confusing things, he said. Too many clerks. I'm afraid a performance is impossible. I'm sure you can understand when you look around outside. Of course, said Barney. His every receptor lit up waiting for the ambush. Congeniality was the point man. He sat down opposite Isaacs and returned the smile. I wouldn't want to be in the way, he said. So if I'm not going to be useful I might as well leave

on the next helicopter. Without the slightest physical altera-
tion, Isaacs' smile somehow changed. It was a shift in the
spectrum of emotions with all the original colors still being
there. You've always been in the way. Ever since you first
had the stupidity to set foot on my base. But as I told you
before, I value control in most things, particularly in myself. The few times I've lost control have been disastrous. So
I waited. Until now.

Beside Isaacs was a rifle. He picked it up with the easy
familiarity of a craftsman reaching for one of his tools. This
is an M-16 he said. Full or semiautomatic. On full, you can
empty it in five seconds. Ask one of my men for a quick
course. He held it out to Barney. Isaacs smiled. Barney did
not move to accept the rifle. I can't wait to see you use it,
said Isaacs. And then once you've watched someone die,
someone you've killed, I want to hear your jokes about the
war.

You won't get the chance, said Barney. I'm taking the
next chopper out. Isaacs just shook his head. There are no
more choppers in or out, he said. The weather. We are now
isolated. He smiled and Barney matched him in smiles while
feeling his heart hammering into his chest as if it were trying to get out. He stared at the rifle in front of him and then
managed a smile. He shook his head. I think I'll decline if
you don't mind, Barney said. I am sure you recall how we
agreed on our last meeting that we all have our roles in life.
Barney turned and left the tent.

Bannon saw him and followed after him struggling to
keep his balance on the slick ground. You talked to Isaacs
didn't you? Bannon said desperately. When's the next
chopper coming in? Huh? Barney did not answer and the
questions were jammed at him again. There are no more
choppers, he finally replied without breaking his stride.
Bannon began to argue with him. Of course there are more

choppers, he said. That's a crock, man, he yelled at Barney. That's a goddam crock and what the fuck do you know about when there's gonna be more choppers. And I'm leaving here, asshole, he hissed. Bannon's face had constricted around his already prominent bone structure and turned strangely white as the blood stopped flowing. Barney kept walking but soon realized there was nowhere to walk to. There was only one end of the fire base and the other. Some of the troops called out as he walked past them. They made an attempt at humor that none of them could quite manage, as if the devil-may-care part of their remarks got stuck on the way up. Hey when do the jokes start? You gonna make 'em die laughing huh? Put on a show for the gooks man. It's all a load anyway.

He walked as far as he could until the roar of the nearby howitzers was painful to hear. Not far from the howitzers was a tent fenced in by canvas and bamboo. Lying on the ground, blindfolded, with their arms tied behind their backs, were two prisoners. From inside the tent came muffled shouts drowned out by the crack of the howitzers. Barney returned to the center of the fire base, where Sergeant Lover sat outside a bunker wearing a poncho and staring up at the hills. Across his lap was an M-16. Rain dripped from his helmet. As he often did, Sergeant Lover began talking to Barney as if he were in the middle of a heavy conversation they had been having for an hour. Yeah it's gonna be the rain, he said. If the rain stops just before darkness, they'll hit us tonight in case the storm lifts tomorrow and we can call in air support. Tonight, he drawled, and then said nothing for several minutes while they both stared at the hills. Barney wondered if Sergeant Lover was feeling the same fear being notched up in tightening bands across his chest. In the others he could look into their eyes that had become semaphores of memories of every stretcher case they had ever seen in this war. They would momentarily stop seeing themselves and others as humans, or men, or individuals or whatever it was and start seeing walking sacs of blood and steaming organs of various unpleasant colors and smells that were all held together by a very thin covering that could be broken very easily. It took just one medevac stretcher case and Oh dear god: not me! was burned into the brain like a mark from a branding iron.

But Sergeant Lover's eyes were impenetrable. They gave nothing. So you ain't gonna make it out, he said. Boy, you're gonna have a lot of new material for your act. They went inside the bunker, where Sergeant Lover found Barney a poncho. They sat on cots listening to the rain beat on the sandbags overhead. I was gonna ask you about what Bannon said the other night. Outside the jail. About the girl. The dancer that Isaacs got the hots for. Sergeant Lover said no more, as if he had already framed his question. So go ahead and ask me, said Barney, glad to talk about something other than what was going on out there in the hills. I have, said Sergeant Lover reclining on a cot. In that case said Barney, the answer is yes.

Why is it that I know her from somewhere else? said Sergeant Lover. Maybe photographs, said Barney. She used to be married to someone from this brigade. Sergeant Lover looked over, his gaze turned inward searching for a mental image. It came to him and he sat up with as much astonishment as he was capable of conveying. Of course, he murmured. I took photographs of her down from the inside of his locker after he got killed. It was Kalman wasn't it? Poor crazy Kalman.

TWENTY-TWO

The story of Kalman came out in quick frag-
ments, interrupted occasionally by the roar of the howitzers.
The rain had stopped. Words and sounds hung in the still
air. Good dude, said Sergeant Lover. Shame about him.
He came in here like a peach among cactus. There was just
something real serious and fresh about him. You know all
the others we get in here can fit into any of about a dozen
types. Back at Fort Benning we used to get real good at telling who was going to turn out to be what. The psychos. The
mamas' boys. The jerk-offs. You get to tell them quick. But
Kalman didn't look like the rest of the grunts. There was
something classy about him. But nice. No bullshit airs to
him. He'd do the shitwork with the rest of them. But somehow he didn't belong here. He belonged in some headquarters. Doing brainwork.

One day when he was over here he came to me and said
he wanted to go out on patrol. We'd had most of our patrols
shot up at the time. It was bad. You'd send off a squad and
know that by next morning most of them would be dead.
One time we sent patrols out around Ben Cat every night
for four nights. One man came back. When Kalman asked
me, he looked like a man who'd spent too much energy convincing himself that he should be sent out on patrol. He was

desperate to go out. You see some guys who get horny for a shoot-up. It's how they get their rocks off. So I thought okay we'll send him out. Maybe he was that kind. His patrol was unusual that week. Only half of them got killed. But those who came back swore they'd never go out with him again. He froze. Just seized up and then went to pieces out in the field. But he wasn't like Bannon. He didn't freak and get people killed trying to save his own hide. He just got so scared that he couldn't move. He finally told the others to go ahead. Just leave him behind. He was terrified he was going to disgrace himself even more. And that's when the shooting started.

Two weeks later he came to me asking to go out again. He didn't really ask, he pleaded. I said no and he broke down like the pieces of him had come unglued. He went on about how he needed to show he was not a coward. I told him to get lost. But about a week later we had an easy little patrol, nothing serious, along some roads near Bien Hoa. I liked him. So I told him he could come along. It was like a reprieve for him. I went out on it too just to see what would happen. Our easy little patrol wasn't so easy. We walked into a shitstorm. Roads mined. Gooks behind every blade of grass. Ambush. Mortars. You name it. Kalman was useless. Worse than useless. Fear had just grabbed him by the throat. First he froze. Then he ran the wrong way. Then he dropped his gun. Guys dying all around him and somehow he survives. After it was over it was like he was in a trance.

The funny thing was that nobody really hated him for what happened. Most guys like that become lepers. Nobody wants them around. In his case people just felt sorry for him. He was trying so hard to prove he was brave. But it just wasn't in him. He was a coward and there was nothing he could do about it. The only person who thought something could be done about it was Isaacs. He hated the idea of a coward in his unit. So he called in Kalman and chewed him out so loud the shouting could be heard all over the base. Then he assigned him to the most dangerous sentry jobs on the base. It was like putting a cat in a cage surrounded by dogs. Within a month he was a nervous wreck. He became skinny. And old. No more California beach boy. It went beyond the point of any useful purpose. Isaacs kept him out there night after night dangling in the wind. I went to talk to Isaacs about it but he wouldn't listen. No one's a coward in my brigade was all he would say.

Kalman almost stopped talking to people during those days. But he would write. He spent hours writing letters to his wife. One day when the tent flaps were up I saw him alone, writing. I went in and tried to talk to him. Cool him out. He just looked at me as if I wasn't there and said he was writing to tell his wife the truth. That he was a coward. I told him to think it over. No, he said, I'm going to tell her that she married a coward. I waited until he had finished writing this letter. Then I watched him mail it over at the PX. A friend of mine was managing the PX at the time. After it closed for the night he and I pried open the mailbox, got Kalman's letter and burned it. I figured he'd be back to normal in a little while and the letter would have only embarrassed him.

But I was wrong. He never got back to normal.

A few hours before the end he came up to me and apologized, saying that he was sorry for all the trouble he had caused. I told him to forget it but he just said how sorry he was. That night was when it happened. It was real quiet out there. The nights when the rustle of grass is like a waterfall. Spooky. We heard firing from the south perimeter. A lot of it. We went down there and found no sentry. Kalman had disappeared. The firing came from somewhere out in the trees. I went out there with three or four other guys but we got pinned down before we took three steps. We could hear Kalman yelling. Cursing at them as he fired. He seemed to be all over the place. It was incredible. We yelled to him to get back but listening to us was the last thing he wanted. We crawled back to the sentry post and began pumping .50 cal into the darkness. But it was no use. We couldn't tell where he was and where they were. It went on for a long time and then the firing from his side stopped. There was just this spooky evil silence.

We sent up a flare. All we could see were a lot of zapped bodies getting stiff on the ground. No sign of Kalman. We had to wait until morning. When we went out there, we found half a platoon of their guys all bleeding into their black pajamas. But no Kalman. He had wiped them out. By noon we began getting reports back that some crazy Lone Ranger was out harvesting assholes. It was Kalman. Still painted in his night-black, dressed in not much more than ammo belts. He was walking out toward the heavy jungle, opening fire on anyone who looked remotely like the enemy. We sent patrols after him. The funny thing was that even Isaacs got into the act. The whole episode thrilled Isaacs. It was everything he believed in coming true. A coward becoming a hero. He was like a doctor who'd just made a cripple walk. Suddenly Kalman was Isaacs' favorite son. Daylight shone out of his ass. Isaacs sent half the goddam brigade out with us to find Kalman. And then Isaacs even dropped what he was doing and came out with us to find him. We scoured the boondocks all day following the corpses of dead Vietcong. Kalman had the whole province terrified. He was like some night-fighting angel taking a dump on them. As the hours passed, Isaacs became more obsessed with finding Kalman. He was mentally awarding the poor bastard a truckload of medals.

We found him. We found him all right. And the terrible

thing was he was still alive when we got to him. They had nailed him to a tree. Literally nailed the poor fucker up. And then they had taken their knives to him and done their own form of plastic surgery. From toes to nose and anything in between that stuck out was carved off. He was still alive and raving when we got to him. The fear and pain had made him a total lunatic. I sent all the other men away. Isaacs and I stood there in front of him. I took out a pistol and looked at Isaacs, who just nodded. I shot him.

Isaacs and I never talked about it. Not one single word. But the episode really shook Isaacs. I know him. I cleaned out Kalman's locker after he got killed. It's a weird experience man. Just by touching some dead guy's stuff, it's like snooping. But in Kalman's case I snooped and didn't think much about it. I wanted to know why the hell he did it. Inside his locker was a letter that was half written. It was dated about a month earlier. It was to his wife. And in it he apologized for being a coward. For letting her down. It was one sad piece of work. And all his wife's letters were in there too. I read 'em all. Every one of them. Not one of them ever mentioned anything about him feeling he was a coward. So I figure she never knew what was really going on.

She didn't, said Barney. Sergeant Lover looked at Barney out of the side of his eyes. You got something going with her? he asked. Barney nodded. I kinda figured as much, said Sergeant Lover. Even before Bannon started blabbing about it the other night. Does Isaacs know any of this? Barney shook his head and said he didn't think so. Good thing, muttered Sergeant Lover. Good thing.

The light began to fade. They sat in the bunker, each with his own images. The sequined blur of a woman flashing across the stage, the sureness of her eyes, her command of all around her. And the haunting uncertain looks in the same eyes of the girl who talked of her husband and his bravery. Yeah, said Barney vacantly, my problem is that I'm in love with her. So is the brigade, grinned Sergeant Lover.

From outside the bunker came another voice. A voice over a loudspeaker. They scrambled outside into the twilight. The clouds were thick and heavy and seemed to swirl through the contours of the valley. The wind was strong enough to make them lean into it when they stood in the open. When it whipped through crevasses in the bunkers the wind whistled in an eerie voice. Tent sidings flapped violently. At the far end of the camp, Isaacs stood on a sandbag wall. He was speaking through a megaphone that carried his words in a powerful metallic voice. He was calling for order. Across the camp, men became still. The howitzers ceased. The loading of sandbags stopped. Ammunition cases were left for the moment. Total stillness.

Isaacs let the silence settle. And then he began the speech he had known for as long as he had been a soldier that he would one day make. I want you all to understand why you are here, boomed his voice, carried by the wind and swallowed into the distance of the jungles behind them. You are not here simply to engage in battle. You are here to make history! Isaacs walked across the sandbag wall, never missing a step. There was an awesome certainty to his every motion. His every gesture. This is not simply a camp! he said, the words gaining power as they left the megaphone. And this is not simply jungle. *This* is the very edge of civilization as we know it. We are here with all that we have toiled for over the centuries. All that we have perfected. But we have become weak. We have lost our will to fight as we must fight if history is not to cast us aside. We have been pushed back. Too far back by those who should be honoring us. Our achievements. Our powers. Our civilization. But this is as far back as we go. Do you understand? This is the edge—the *end* of civilization.

Oh dear god, muttered Sergeant Lover. This is it. On the sandbag wall Isaacs was pacing back and forth. The force of his words, how they were spoken, blasting forth, had galvanized the stillness across the camp. It was as if Isaacs alone shored up individual wills which were faltering.

Isaacs motioned toward the jungles that disappeared into the racing clouds. From those hills will emerge the forces of darkness. Of superstition. The very forces that we have allowed to push us back. And so at this moment we are at the Rubicon. We are Poitiers. We are Borodino. We are Normandy. There is no return. History demands victory! Or submission! And we shall never submit! Gentlemen, civilization is in your hands. Fight for it. Fight to the very end. You are the chosen. May God bless us all.

Barney stared at Isaacs.   The Lord is my *tummler*.
I shall not *darf*
He maketh me to *kvell*
in green pastures,

he murmured to himself.

TWENTY-THREE

Darkness descended. Barney felt his blood drain away into parts of him that could only respond like anchors. Fear had settled in. It had tightened around his reactions and those of the men near him. Someone had turned on a tape cassette. From it came the curling, seductive strains of *White Rabbit*.

. . . and the white knight's talking backwards
And the red queen's off her head
Remember what the dormouse said
Feed your head
Feed your head.

But this, an anthem of the stoned soldiers of the war and the peace now evoked only angry, tense, murmurs from the darkness, threatening to shoot the cassette. Or its owner, or both. Angry grumbling in reply and then a click. Then the roar of the silence that sucked up breath. Sergeant Lover crawled over beside Barney and placed an M-16 nearby. People keep offering me guns, whispered Barney. Just be thankful they do, said Sergeant Lover. They were crouched behind a sandbag wall. If I was you I'd keep it damn close, like a third arm. Barney shrugged. Isaacs told me he was going to turn me into a killer. Something within Barney made him want to laugh at what he was saying. But

Sergeant Lover froze the laughter with a look that returned laughter to its perch of fear. Barney realized that Sergeant Lover, who looked so calm, so in control, was terrified. Well boy, Sergeant Lover drawled, I'd say that right now he's holding all the cards. Besides, it's better than being a corpse.

They waited. Across the camp men crouched or paced in small arcs in the night. Sleep was a mist that had been burned off by fear. Barney stared at the M-16. A piece of steel that gave him the power to extract life from living being he had never seen before. He wondered if the fear showed. The pounding in his chest. The dryness that went all the way through him. The fear showed in some of the others, who unconsciously rocked back and forth, or shivered in the warm night. No one had ever actually stated that the attack would come on this night. Yet by some communion with the enemy, by some common perception of destiny, it *was* to be this night. The only unrefined element was the exact moment. In the darkness it seemed to Barney that the secondhands had synchronized with every heartbeat to create a mental pounding that was deafening in the silence.

When the endless moments had stretched together into an hour or more some of the soldiers could stand the silence no longer. Whispers could be heard. Talking of other sieges. Of Khe Sanh. Of Dong Ha and all the other meaningless little outposts that had suddenly become the horror movies of the war. The whispers were fragments of thought. Wondering what had gone wrong in those places. And how it would be different here. *If* it would be different.

It began with a single tiny sound. From somewhere near the headquarters tent a standby order was quietly given. The order shot through the camp without another word being spoken. It was a human electrical impulse that sped through emotional wiring strung tight to the point of snapping. Rifles waved into the night. Eyes stared, unblinking, into nothing. Breath came in segments. And then the night exploded. It was as if the earth had blown up behind them. The shelling from the hills overshot the camp. With a roar, geysers of earth were sucked into the skies, one after another, as if the earth were coming unstitched and its pain was causing the howl that came from above, below and all around. The hillside blackness blistered with mortar fire and then the howitzers replied with a barrage that turned the night into a whirlpool of noise. The hillside erupted. It caught fire for moments. All around Barney men fell over one another in the darkness pressing closer to the sandbags as the earth erupted behind them. The range had been found by the distant attackers. A tent blew up behind them. Curses and prayers and combinations of both were hurled into the roar. There was nowhere to go. The shells behind and the enemy in front. A soldier beside Barney stood up in an instant of indecision. He began to crawl over the edge of the sandbags at the moment a flame blossomed behind him. A perfect silhouette. He was hurled back with most of his chest gone, pinwheeling blood as he fell. *Lights! For christsakes. Lights!* The screams shot down the row of men pressed into the wall and from somewhere a switch was tripped and the night was peeled away by the powerful lights hidden beyond the perimeter. Oh sweet jesus, said Sergeant Lover as he peered out. The horizon between the blackness and the light was moving! Like a mirage. It shifted and crawled.

There were hundreds, maybe thousands, of *them!* Rustling, crawling, sliding across the ground. Faster and faster. The enemy was moving toward them. Ripples building into a wave. This was the only moment that counted. All else was paper work and every mind went parched with the terror of that sight. Barney clutched the M-16 and stared into the writhing nearby horizon. One of the lights was shot out. It was the signal. From one end of the camp to the other, the Americans poured automatic weapon fire into the night. Like a ricochet it came back ripping into the defenses. Howitzers, mortars and .50-caliber machine fire were poured into the crawling horizon from which tiny spasms would indicate a hit—a man being jerked off his feet and flung backward. Yet still they came.

From somewhere off to the side of the camp enemy snipers suddenly opened up. They had waited until enough of the defending Americans were standing and firing over the top of the wall for a few seconds at the time. It was like a scythe sweeping across the top of the wall. Men were cut down, some wordlessly, falling to the ground dead before they hit, while others cried out in terrible shrieking sounds that lodged like shrapnel in the minds of those who still desperately fired into the night. Behind Barney two men writhed on the ground. He crawled back toward the nearest man. The ground beneath him felt soft and pulpy and he found himself praying it was not blood that had soaked into the earth. Other men were scrambling to remove the wounded, who lay in matchstick rows. Cries and orders were screamed into the din. Other hands stretched out from the half light and motioned him away from the wounded man, who writhed nearby and held his hand to his head as blood spurted from it. The man would not live. He was kicking the final pains of life out of himself. Barney crouched mutely as someone yelled at him with words that were barely heard over the shelling. He had never before watched anyone die. He wanted to say something to the man, something that the man might take with him in his last moments. Some comfort. Some hope. Or words to let him know that he was loved. That it had all been worth it. In a clamoring rush to escape, thoughts of the man's family, or a wife? or a child? split the darkness and the chaos and Barney began yelling into the roar telling the man that he was loved. People love you! he screamed, aware but not caring of the absurdity of it all as the shelling smashed his words and the incoherent ebbing replies of the man before him who had lost most of what he was trying to hold in with his hand. Flames lit up the night as another tent exploded. Barney crouched staring at the man until an angry impatient hand tugged at him and without a will or direction of his own he was suddenly helping to carry another casualty, a soldier so young that Barney felt paternal in his presence. The boy had been shot in the stomach. He said nothing nor showed any pain. It was as if he were in a trance. They carried him back to a medical tent that had become a writhing, racing, frantic mass of men stemming death or succumbing to it. Barney turned around to look at the silhouettes in front of him. *This is the edge?—the end of civilization?* . . . . .

. . . . . says the old voice in his mind. And he sees Sam Senior give his best comic shrug. *So what's the problem?*

A chain reaction of explosions erupted from somewhere beyond the perimeter. It was the land mines that had been planted weeks earlier. They detonated in staggered rows that snapped the momentum of the enemy advance in its own form of bloody chaos. Suddenly the enemy wave had crested. Confusion burst. Barney could see enemy soldiers, masses of them, writhing across the ground, some crawling into other land mines that set off new explosions. The Americans poured fire into the attackers and suddenly an exultation shot across their ranks. The barrage swept the faltering enemy back.

The firing lessened. A euphoric murmur rose. But Sergeant Lover knelt behind the wall and stared at the ground so hard he seemed to be visually drilling a hole in it. Barney watched him. Then suddenly he snapped his head up and said, We've been tricked! His eyes were like polished coals glowing with a secret fear. Sergeant Lover picked up an M-16 and jammed it at Barney. Don't you ever put this down! he yelled. Not unless you're dead. You hear? The words were spat out. Then he raced along the line yelling that they had been tricked. No one understood what he was saying but in the storm of noise and smoke his voice was just one of many incoherent cries. But Sergeant Lover screamed into the din until his voice carried over all else. He ordered them back. Back to the opposite perimeter from which no attack had come. No one moved until he grabbed one man and threw him back, shoving him in the direction of the opposite perimeter. Others followed, not knowing why they were moving or if it was a retreat or just plain madness. They stumbled and crawled through the tangled night of cries and explosions, with only a company of men holding the wall they had just left. Barney groped his way beside Sergeant Lover, who yelled again that it was a trick. A diversion. The *real* attack was yet to come! His words poured out like body blows.

Another explosion lit up the night and in the midst of the marathon of racing men Sergeant Lover stopped. Barney had also stopped running. He too had seen the fleeing figure dart into the bunker in the center of the base. It was Bannon. If the flames had not shot up at that instant Bannon would never have been seen. Sergeant Lover raced into the bunker and before the light had ebbed Bannon was flung out like a small animal from the jaws of a dog. He slithered and skidded along the ground jabbering his own form of terror as Sergeant Lover hurtled after him, kicking him toward the perimeter wall. Bannon babbled for mercy, pleading to be left alone, sobbing that he was afraid. His sobs were the sparks in the tinder of Sergeant Lover's memory. He slammed the butt of his rifle into Bannon's head, screaming at him to get up and fight the way he had not fought on the night in the jungle when his wailing had brought death to an entire platoon. Bannon's face was a death's head of fear contorting in the shadows. Again and again he was kicked toward the perimeter by the relentless fury of Sergeant Lover. Bannon's moaning suddenly turned with the unheard click and the glint of a switchblade knife that flashed in a whirring arc.

A neat, horizontal incision was suddenly visible across Sergeant Lover's combat shirt. Before he was aware of it, or of the blood that instantly oozed from the khaki tatters, Sergeant Lover had kicked the knife from Bannon's hands and battered him backward. All reason seized solid as Sergeant Lover screamed into Bannon's dying terrified face while he slowly drove the bayonet down between the ribs.

It was Barney who dislodged himself from his own frozen terror and cross-checked Sergeant Lover with the length of the rifle he was holding. Sergeant Lover was knocked backward but the bayonet remained, clutched by the flapping hands of Bannon as he shrieked and kicked upon the ground to which he was fastened. Sergeant Lover seemed suddenly emptied of fury. Oh dear jesus, he muttered, looking down at Bannon. It was as if he were seeing what had happened for the first time. Barney took a step toward the bayonet but Sergeant Lover stopped him. Let him die first, he said, talking as if Bannon were not present or was merely a spectator to the event. There ain't no way he can live now. When you pull those things out they just make a fountain of blood. Bannon's terror exploded in a flailing, frothing howl. His eyes bulged out as he looked down and clawed at the blade upon which he was impaled.

Then there was a choking sound and Bannon heaved against the blade and fell back, his lips working furiously, bubbling words up through his rotted teeth. Bannon was dead. Barney stood looking at Sergeant Lover, who returned his stare with a coldness that came from somewhere dark and lifeless within him. I got a dozen dead friends who're gonna sleep now, he said.

At the wall of the opposite perimeter, Isaacs was already there. From the moment of the first attack he too had suspected a trick. It was an intuition that came from the marrow of his years in combat. The attack had been all wrong. It was too small. Too noisy. Too easily repelled. It had to be a deception. Isaacs stared at Sergeant Lover when he arrived bleeding from a strange knife wound. In all their years together they had never communicated so perfectly, with such clarity, as they did at that moment. Of all the men in the remote base in the jungle, only they could *feel* what was to come. Words, plans, strategies, tactics—they all withered in the winds of unleashed memories that had wrung a native cunning from sieges of their past. Neither spoke to the other yet they worked as a team. Sergeant Lover swept aside young captains and lieutenants, whose orders would sometimes emerge like bubbles drifting into the air. He drilled staccato commands at the tense uncertain men, who still had no idea why they had been moved across the camp. He raced the length of one wall shouting position orders. And he bled slowly across the neat cut in his shirt.

Isaacs had unholstered the pistol that he always wore. Behind him was an M-16 rifle and the megaphone. And behind those was the radio tent, his only link to the gold-braided clerks in Saigon who already were flashing the messages he had left unanswered. *Immediate clarification requested. . . .* Isaacs paced quickly behind the lines, staring out into the darkness, knowing that history was gathering in a way that none of them back at MACV could ever understand. *Urgent: Advise deployment of following battalions: . . .* He felt an almost mystical exhilaration. It was as he had hoped. He had placed the heaviest of his artillery, the most massive of the walls, the most carefully positioned land mines, here at this the unlikeliest and most difficult perimeter to attack. In every defensive measure, there had been an offensive purpose. He wanted to draw the enemy in. To let the enemy charge as close to him as he dared. And then to seize them, to lock as one in the most mortal of combat. *Request location of 4th Battalion 503rd Infantry. Urgent.* There was something about the moment of battle that the theoreticians, the military intellectuals, never understood. It was something that could never be divined from the cooled-out rooms where all the blood and shelling and chaos were distilled and purified into bits of plastic gliding across illuminated maps before lunch while their human counterparts were clawing across distant pieces of earth.

The attack on the opposite perimeter was still continuing when Isaacs nodded to a lieutenant and flares were shot into the air. The night went green. When the light burst it was like lifting a rock on moist ground. The night festered. The enemy! Thousands of them! They were already so close that the shades of green had caught them in silent flight. The silence was instantly swept away by a howling charge. There was no time for panic. Emotions jumped the lines from simple fear to a piercing hopped-up terror turning at speeds that could vent only in a ceaseless hail of fire that piled up the corpses in front of them. Closer and closer. The night was disgorging thousands of *them* and in the bellowing maelstrom of the American lines mental projectors kicked into synch with the deepest suburban fears of the ultimate horror movie where *they* came right out of the screen into the screaming shrieking audience . . . which was now pouring fire out across the perimeter wall.

For Isaacs it was a precise and expected moment. It was the focus of a lifetime. All the years had converged in that one awesome sight. Their sheer numbers shot fear and exhilaration through him. It was to be big, far bigger than he had dared hope.

In front of Barney, a part of the sandbag wall blew up with a muffled concussion that threw him back. The chaos of the battle suddenly went shortwave. The yelling and the barrage drifting in and out of his ears as some mental tuner scanned for reception. The cries of men calling out in the pale-green light rang with a strange frantic remoteness. Barney crawled across the ground not knowing why he was moving back toward the perimeter wall. Someone lurched from the shadows, stumbling over him, and men clutching at themselves slithered past, some shrieking for help and others as silent as ghosts, as if they had already slipped over the line. Another part of the wall blew up, not far from the first explosion but this time a dozen men had been huddled behind it and the night spun with something warm and moist and gritty. Barney felt a stinging spray across his face over and over again.

Across the perimeter, other direct hits shattered the wall. The length of the American line suddenly became jagged. Through the smoldering hole in the wall Barney looked out beyond the perimeter and within him a trip-hammer suddenly went berserk pounding at his heart as *they* raced out of a green night. It was grenade distance, no more. The land mines were triggered. A rotor of earth spun like a chain reaction across the attack. For a moment the attack faltered and involuntary cheers were wrenched from the American lines. It would be like the first attack on the other perimeter. It had to be.

But it was not. *They* kept coming and the ground zero panic exploded in cries to fall back, retreat, and already parts of the line were seized in the ultimate grappling nightmare. The base was being overrun. Men were running backward and sideways firing, trying not to stumble in the chaos. Barney groped his way back past the tent, where a radio operator was screaming over the roar that they were being wiped out. A silhouette became Sergeant Lover lurching into the light, his shirt drenched dark red. My arm don't work! he screamed jamming his rifle at Barney. His left arm hung limply at his side. Load it! Barney clawed at the magazine, changing it in the moment that Sergeant Lover seemed to shudder and then without a word sink to the ground with a neat red hole on his forehead.

In the instant it took Barney to realize that Sergeant Lover was dead the green of the flares was swept back as part of the darkness caught fire. The ammunition dump had been hit. A fireball swept into the sky, sucking up all around it, billowing across a part of the perimeter abandoned to the North Vietnamese. Some of the enemy were caught in the middle of it, suddenly curling stiffly like dried leaves while others raced from it trailing flames that spread around them, slowing them down and finally stopping them as if the flames had great weight. The explosion did what the land mines and the M-16s could not. It halted the momentum of the attack. And in the sudden light of the fireball all ambiguities were cast aside. There were no longer shadows. *They* could be clearly seen. Faces, eyes, arms, hands. All distinct and individual instead of the anonymous masses thrashing through the night. In the starkness of that light all fate and decision was rendered exquisitely simple. Barney stood still for the merest of instants while men he had never seen before came toward him for the sole reason of killing him.

And at that moment, Isaacs was right.

Civilization was suddenly whoever survived. Reason was whatever could be thought. And laughter was the defense that must come to those who could still reason when it was over.

Barney raised the rifle and fired.

TWENTY-FOUR

There was no way to measure the number of men Barney killed. He crouched low against the ground and fired at them until each magazine was empty. Then he would reload and fire again, each time scurrying back through the night that blistered with explosions and screams for help from men who could never be helped. When his rifle overheated he flung it away and grabbed another from the ground. The camp was littered with bodies and rifles and men who crawled across the earth, tearing at it as if they were sliding down a sheer rock face. Barney ran back, firing as he went, until he had backed up against other men who were firing in the opposite direction. The camp was being overrun from both sides. In scattered groups the North Vietnamese still poured across the shattered perimeter, weaving through the flames of the ammunition dump.

It was Isaacs who strode forth from the American lines, holding only a pistol and bellowing orders through a cordite mist that sprayed from the rifles. There was an antidotal madness in his every step. Walking forward, when all others were in retreat. Overpowering the chaos with his will. Bellowing curses at the enemy, walking farther and farther away from his own men. Others followed, rising from the ragged herd-drawn circle. None of Isaacs' words could be made out, yet even fragments of sound cinched in the desperation. In front of Isaacs an enemy soldier appeared and was instantly felled by a shot from his pistol, fired without a break in stride. Isaacs stalked forward in angry defiance of the dead hand of probability. Others followed, walking and then running in short bursts toward an enemy that had suddenly ceased all forward momentum. Isaacs, in the ultimate taunt, turned his back on the enemy and in that instant he stood hurling orders to his own men, who were slow in following him into the chaos. His face was an exuberant mask, shifting from shadows to light in both exultation and fury. Fear had long passed through and what remained was only a fervor.

Isaacs saw Barney. They stood facing one another, two figures solitary in their momentary stillness. The mask of Isaacs' face began to break into a smile and then laughter as Barney stood before him holding the M-16 that he had just used to kill. Around them other men stumbled and shouted into an onslaught clawing back across ground they had already yielded. The explosions and gunfire sustained as one deafening roar pierced only by Isaacs' laughter. It was the sole human sound that could be heard.

They were not more than a dozen yards apart. Behind Isaacs was the instant of locked physical combat, of enemies gripped hand to hand in the ultimate reduction of the funnel of technology. For now knives and the strength of a man were the only tactical requisites. But all this was background and in front stood Isaacs, his laughter ringing out, telling Barney he had killed, he had taken lives and now *he* was not laughing. Barney raised the rifle, following some inner dictates from depths and voices that had never seen light. The laughter was framed in the sights of the rifle. Yet still Isaacs laughed in the fraction of a moment that stretched into hours within Barney's mind. The blurring savagery behind Isaacs, the motion of death, and the fierce taunting laughter in the gunsight raced through the moment that Barney stood, perfectly still, his legs apart in the classic firing position.

Barney waited. And then he fired a single shot.

TWENTY-FIVE

He killed in the name of reason, of civilization, of impulses he would never want to comprehend. Behind Isaacs one of the enemy had risen up from the wounded. In the periphery of the gunsights Barney saw him. He too was poised to kill and in the instant trinity, Barney had only to wait, to remain staring through the gunsights into the laughter, and Isaacs would be dead, cut down by the lurching figure behind him.

When Barney fired, Isaacs never once flinched. The single bullet caught the enemy soldier in the chest. The man jerked back and then folded at the knees, sinking slowly onto the ground beside Isaacs, who looked down at him. Then Isaacs looked at Barney with a smile that spoke calmly of victory, of conquest . . . . .

. . . . . and then it is dawn. The earth steams. It is covered with the dead. Some lie in sickening grotesque poses while others lie in heaps like a firewood pile that has collapsed. Not a structure stands intact. Canvas flies softly from the ruins of tents like tattered flags of war. The living stand in shattered little groups across the wreckage of the camp. They communicate. But each man reacts with heavy numbness. Mental doors have slammed shut, and personal defense perimeters have been hastily erected against the on-slaught of memories and of what they see around them. They search for the wounded, ragpickers of humanity foraging through the slaughter. Empty sentences spoken to no one in particular are news bulletins of death. *Christ here's Forsyth . . . Goulding took it . . . Oh jesusdeargod Sal got wasted.* The wounded enemy soldiers lie silently no matter how bad their wounds for they do not require sensitivity to pick the heavy wash of murder out of air beginning to reek from the smell of the survivors' dead friends. The enemy wounded and dead somehow look scrawny, pathetic. They seem almost the size of children, too small to kill. The daylight has burned away their mythology. And from somewhere under or among the dead the tape cassette plays. Again it is *White Rabbit* that curls into the cries of the wounded and the silence of the living, the song that will soon be denounced by a Vice-President of the United States as having dope-drenched lyrics unfit for decent human consumption. But through the haze somewhere behind the eyes of young soldiers now infinitely old, picking through their dead it all makes sense that

> . . . if you go chasing rabbits
> And you know you're going to fall
> Tell 'em a hookah-smoking caterpillar
> Has given you the call . . . . .

. . . . . it makes far more sense than the long way to Tipperary. And it makes more sense than the Nightingales singing in Berkeley Square and all those other decent, humane, melodies of noble souls which send tears upon yesterday's medals. It makes far more sense to the young soldiers who look out across the dead and learn to their eternal amazement . . . . .

. . . . . that it is a victory! For Isaacs has surveyed the carnage and informs them that they have won. He is the sole figure of motion. He alone strides across the shattered camp and sees what the others cannot see. He sees history. He sees the price attached to destiny.

Near the medical tents the first of the helicopters sets down. At first their crews just stand and stare. None of them has ever seen anything like it. From one of the tents, Barney emerges. He is bent with fatigue and exhaustion. He has carried the wounded and the dying until the blood across his clothes has dried in layers. Nearby, one of the wounded rises from his stretcher and tries to scream mutiny across the camp but the words clot in his throat and he falls back in a coughing fit that makes something burst. At the far perimeter, Isaacs walks through the slaughter. To those who watch him, he seems almost serene. There is grace to his movements. And a calmness that the others cannot understand . . . . .

. . . . . except Barney, who picked up a discarded megaphone, and suddenly his voice is shot across the remnants of the base. Into the distance, men stopped and looked, some slowly and almost dazed. Others turned sharply, drawn in amazement to the voice that rang out as an echo of what they had heard before. *You are here to make history! You are not here simply to engage in battle. And this is not just jungle! This is the edge of civilization!* Barney walked among the wounded, the megaphone pressed to his mouth. But it was not his voice that emerged. *We are here with all that we have created over the centuries. All that we have perfected.* A kind of stillness had settled over the camp. Only the wounded cried out or moved. Barney walked among the stretchers and the dead. He walked through the destruction and the pile of bloody helmets and the shattered equipment. He walked to the center of the carnage, the words still pouring out. *Do you understand? I want you to know why you are here! . . .*

And across the base, the survivors hear Isaacs' voice come from Barney's mouth. As Barney puts the megaphone down, there is a silence louder than all the applause he has ever heard. All around him there is a stillness. But Barney is aware only of Isaacs, who faces him across the wreckage. Because now it is all different. It is not at all like the times when Isaacs would remain motionless amid the waves of laughter.

It is a small silent laugh, scarcely more than a smile. But Barney understands what the laughter is all about, for at that moment across the gulf of the dying and the shattered, he and Isaacs understand each other with a perfect clarity. For in that one instant they have reached a mutual ground zero: *Todlachen!—Laugh till it kills you!*

They have arrived from opposite ends. One from the laughter. And the other from the killing.

TWENTY-SIX

The battle at Xuan Loc caused hastily convened meetings at MACV in Saigon. As details came in from the camp they were carefully molded to fit the official version. The battle was declared a victory. Terms were carefully chosen to explain the more contentious elements of the victory. The fact that they had been overrun was described as a *full tactical engagement*. The official displeasure with Isaacs for disobeying orders was temporarily suspended from public view. Because of this there was no choice but to award him further medals.

Barney waited all day. When the last of the wounded had been evacuated, he flew out on a helicopter. It rose in its lurching fashion up from the camp, which had just been reinforced by fresh troops. From two thousand feet the wreckage of the battle became harmless blotches of color. Almost pretty in an abstract way. It was almost dark when the helicopter descended at Bien Hoa. Stretchers and ambulance trucks were scattered across the landing zone. Parked nearby was a battered old Citroën with a case of Canadian beer in the back. Most of the beer was already gone. Woody had consumed part of it while waiting for Barney. And he shared the rest with one of the stretcher bearers, who wanted to get terminally drunk. When Barney drew closer in the twilight, Woody stared at the blood caked across his clothing. Woody was momentarily without words. I know what they mean when they talk about a bloodbath, he said finally. I take it you didn't have much time for jokes. Barney shrugged and said that it was all a joke. Woody thrust a beer at him. Dr. Woody's tonic, he said. To be taken in copious amounts.

They found fresh clothing for Barney and then went to the club. Barney was hoping Donna might be there. But it was almost empty, as he had known it would be. There were none of the regular entertainers. Only a soldier playing the piano was on the stage. He was a captain with a face of infinite sadness. Barney recognized him as one of the survivors of the previous night. The captain seemed to be in a world of his own. There was no audience, just scattered groups of men standing around at the back drinking and talking somberly. Above a makeshift bar was a sign in Vietnamese and English that said *Happy New Year*. Someone told them that the next day was the Vietnamese New Year. *Tet*, it was called. Tomorrow there would be celebrations. At the American embassy in Saigon there was to be a party. And Isaacs' baseball team was to be shown off.

Outside, the baseball team was again practicing under the lights that had been installed for them. Barney watched them from the bench beside the Club. The baseball team seemed totally out of place. After the terror and the fighting of the night before, it was like watching a fantasy. A harmless, irrelevant fantasy.

The Vietnamese boys were practicing on their own. On this, their final practice before the game at the embassy, Tan, the tall first baseman, had taken charge on the field. He was hitting line drives to Kanh, who was still finding new acrobatics to stop the ball. The others, Kien the pitcher, Minh the chubby second baseman and the rest of the team, all showed a peculiar tension.

In the night sky behind the team, a tiny cluster of lights appeared. The lights grew larger and with them came the roar of helicopter rotors. It was Isaacs. He was returning from Xuan Loc. His helicopter set down in a clearing behind the baseball field. Isaacs emerged with aides and junior officers, who swarmed around him. It was a moment of triumph carefully created by the aides and the photographers who had been summoned by the press relations men. But Isaacs quickly waved them aside. Alone, he walked out onto the baseball field and stood with somber pride surveying his creation.

Later there would be the official inquiries. The hearings in Saigon. The paper war with the clerks. But at that moment Isaacs cared for none of it. He cared only for the instrument of athletic precision that he had fashioned from the fumbling exuberance of nine little Vietnamese boys.

Barney thought there was something peculiar about what was happening on the field. It was as if each of the boys was a machined part that was not meshing properly with the others. There was a stiffness. It was possibly nerves. Or perhaps it was just the presence of Isaacs. Woody joined Barney and from the shadows they watched. As Isaacs again walked over to Kien, the team seemed to stiffen as a unit. They looked over to Tan, who stood very still. Then from somewhere outside the base came the sound of a huge explosion and the lower part of the sky turned orange. One of the ammunition dumps had been blown up. Isaacs stopped in mid-step. The boys on the team turned to look at it also and then one by one they turned back to Tan, who walked over to Isaacs. From the distance it seemed as if Tan reached out to Isaacs. But the motion of his arm was somehow too swift. And there was a glint from something in his hand.

On the field, the knife in Tan's hand sank swiftly. It was aimed for Isaacs' throat. But some instinct had told Isaacs to shift his weight backward at the critical instant and the blade instead went into his shoulder. Isaacs clutched at the knife and a kind of roar came up from somewhere beneath the wound. His eyes went wide in fury and pain. He lurched at Tan and grabbed at his shirt, tearing at it. He hammered Tan with a blow that almost knocked the boy senseless.

The others began pounding at Isaacs with their fists but the bellowing grip could not be freed until Kanh pulled at Tan, who still clung to the knife. The wound widened. Kien bit and scratched Isaacs' encircling arm. Tan was lurched free as they swarmed over Isaacs. Tan fell backward, his shirt ripped off. Across his body were massive disfiguring scars that had never properly healed. They were napalm scars. From bombs dropped anonymously by some American plane years ago.

Tan bounced to his feet, his eyes never leaving Isaacs for an instant. From somewhere in the webbing of his first baseman's glove he withdrew another thin round knife. It was the same knife that had finally finished off the sentry from Georgia. But Isaacs was not the sentry. Nor the printout clerk who had died before he hit the ground. Nor the third-base coach who just stared at the team in disbelief as the knife formed the sluice along which his life flowed out and onto the ground.

Isaacs cuffed Kien senseless. Kanh was knocked to the ground. The others were regrouping fearfully around Tan. But the shouting had brought others running toward the field. As Tan circled Isaacs a sentry took aim with his M-16 and in the part of a second that it took to empty the weapon on automatic, the boy died. Tan was spun around, pin-wheeling blood from his chest.

Isaacs remained upright for a few steps. Then he slowly sank to one knee, tugging uselessly at the knife in his shoulder. Other rifles were pointed at the baseball team. Not one of the boys on the team showed any fear. They stared silently at Isaacs, who knelt in front of them breathing heavily. From somewhere beyond the perimeter came another explosion. Smoke began billowing into the air. It was a massive attack of some kind . . . . .

. . . . . but Isaacs is oblivious to it all. He cannot take his eyes off his baseball team. It is the team that is to play tomorrow at the embassy. It is the team of young boys with ancient eyes who stand around the body of the best first baseman Isaacs ever coached. Isaacs can only shake his head and mutter words that are lost in the explosions that redouble somewhere outside the perimeter. And then he sees Barney standing beside the coach from Texas. Isaacs rises to his feet with difficulty, his gaze locked onto Barney. He waits for the explosions to subside but they do not: Victory! says Barney quietly. Isaacs turns numbly to his aides. Get those little bastards out on the field, he orders.

And so with the prodding of automatic rifles the team is sent out onto the practice field. Even before the knife is removed from his shoulder by the medic, Isaacs has regained enough of the fury that has always made his teams the best. He drives them relentlessly, and while the shouting of orders is somehow too desperate the symmetry of the team is not right without their first baseman. The medic stops beside the body of Tan and looks at the terrible scars across his body. The medic decides that it was at least five years ago that the boy had been caught in an Air Force bombing raid. He decides that the boy must have lived in pain for months.

On the field Isaacs paces and yells. The practice field is surrounded by the soldiers with their rifles turned inward toward the team but at their backs the sky is billowing orange with explosions. The soldiers grow nervous. It is a major attack. Mortars begin to overshoot the field. Sirens are heard through the gunfire. But Isaacs hears none of it, and sees only the eight members of his team to whom he yells angry orders of Victory! And as the mortars fall nearer, the soldiers begin to break ranks and move back to cover. Fires rise across the base but still Isaacs walks through the chaos. His team is fleeing. They fall back racing toward the bushes and the tall grass at the edge of the field.

Isaacs stands in the smoke and the explosions yelling after them, cursing them. Shouting that they would never win. . . . . .

The attack was the beginning of what was called the Tet Offensive. It was an event that was to change history. It, and not the battle at Xuan Loc, became the turning point of the war. History would forget Xuan Loc and its dead. And its commander. The Tet Offensive was a massive attack against American installations and territory. Entire cities were captured by the enemy. Large parts of Saigon fell under enemy control. The grounds of the American embassy, where Isaacs' baseball team was to have been presented, were invaded. It was the event that was supposed to have been impossible. It was the event that clinched the decision of the American President to step down from office.

For almost a week Barney was forced to remain at Bien Hoa. The roads to Saigon were too dangerous. During the week he asked several helicopter pilots who were flying into

Saigon to take messages to be forwarded to the Catinat Hotel. He had no way of knowing if any of the messages ever reached Donna. And there was no reply. In the messages he told her simply that he was alive, well and anxious to see her again. He signed them with love. When they were finally able to return to Saigon Barney went directly to the Catinat, walking through the courtyard to her room. He knocked softly on the door and after a brief interval it was opened by a small man with precise features. He spoke in a British accent. The room had been vacated just over a week ago he said. He had moved in at that time. He was a journalist working on a story and was busy at the moment.

Barney returned to his own room somehow hoping that when he opened the door he would find her there. His room was exactly as it always was when he returned. All his possessions arranged neatly by the maids. An emptiness that almost swallowed him. On the bed was a note. It was from Donna. In it she told him that she loved him. That she had to leave Vietnam. It had suddenly become more than she could cope with. She said that she wanted desperately to see him again, and please would he meet her back home. She left an address of a place that Barney knew was a coastal town in California. And she asked his forgiveness for leaving.

Barney sat on the bed reading the letter over and over again. Outside the open door, Sheldon stopped and peered in. Jesus kid, he said, you've been away so long I thought the enemy had signed you to a contract. Hey how's the money out there? Barney shrugged and said it was okay. Jesus, muttered Sheldon, I heard it was a shitkicker though. You ain't going back there are you? Barney said nothing for a moment. Probably, he said finally.

Well if you do, said Sheldon, practice on your timing. It's everything kid.